Love in Lindfield

ALSO BY DAVID SMITH…

Searching for Amber

Death in Leamington

Love in Lindfield

David Smith

Copyright © 2016 David Smith

The moral right of the author has been asserted.

Apart from any fair dealing for the purposes of research or private study, or criticism or review, as permitted under the Copyright, Designs and Patents Act 1988, this publication may only be reproduced, stored or transmitted, in any form or by any means, with the prior permission in writing of the publishers, or in the case of reprographic reproduction in accordance with the terms of licences issued by the Copyright Licensing Agency. Enquiries concerning reproduction outside those terms should be sent to the publishers.

This is a work of fiction. Names, characters, businesses, places, events and incidents are either the products of the author's imagination or used in a fictitious manner. Any resemblance to actual persons, living or dead, or actual events is purely coincidental.

Matador
9 Priory Business Park
Kibworth Beauchamp
Leicestershire LE8 0RX, UK
Tel: (+44) 116 279 2299
Fax: (+44) 116 279 2277
Email: books@troubador.co.uk
Web: www.troubador.co.uk/matador

ISBN (Paperback) 978 1785892 257
(Hardback) 978 1785892 264

British Library Cataloguing in Publication Data.
A catalogue record for this book is available from the British Library.

Printed and bound in the UK by TJ International, Padstow, Cornwall
Typeset in 11pt Aldine401 BT by Troubador Publishing Ltd, Leicester, UK

Matador is an imprint of Troubador Publishing Ltd

In memory of Charles Eamer Kempe and his many admirers

CONTENTS

Prologue	xi
Chapter One The Village Belles	1
Chapter Two The Web She Seeks to Weave	10
Chapter Three Love Ever Living Strives	27
Chapter Four Monday's Child	55
Chapter Five Old Place	69
Chapter Six The Gardener	96
Chapter Seven The Envoys	106
Chapter Eight Photographic Memories	126
Chapter Nine Imago Amoris – Filia	154
Chapter Ten Imago Amoris – Storge	173
Chapter Eleven Imago Amoris – Eros	178
Chapter Twelve Imago Amoris – Agape	189
Chapter Thirteen Village Day	203
Chapter Fourteen Love's Labour's Won	217
Chapter Fifteen Love's Labour's Lost	234

She approached their meeting point in the old churchyard in moonlight. It was late, there wasn't another soul around. The hooting owl made her nervous. Why had he suggested meeting here of all places? She checked her watch. The time was right but her suitor was late. Jumping at shadows she took shelter in the porch and then heard a noise inside, like a small bell, calling her. Gingerly she turned the old iron latch and pushed the heavy door ajar. There were tea candles lit along the floor in a little path. She followed them, calling out his name but getting no response. 'It's dark, this is scary,' she whispered. But there was still no response. She stopped at the end of the candles in a little space at the back of the church and waited for what seemed to her to be an age. Suddenly two hands descended from behind her, covering her eyes. She jumped and then felt a tall shape against her back. 'God, you scared me,' she said relaxing a bit at his familiar form. 'This place is creepy enough!' 'Heaven or hell?' asked the voice, deep but strangely unfeeling. 'What?' she asked. 'Soar or burn?' it asked again. 'Soar I guess?' she replied, expecting him at any moment to lift her in his arms and kiss her. But instead she felt a dark felt mask being lowered and tied over her head and those two muscular arms gripping her tightly. Then her hands were bound. She felt hot breath on her neck. She could hardly breathe. She knew he had exotic tastes but this...? Her hair was pulled aside and she felt a kiss, deep and passionate. She felt a tingle of excitement in her body, but still she was scared. 'Come on, this ain't a joke no more,' she said. 'What are you doing, let me go?' But there was no answer, instead she was pushed roughly forward and her foot jarred against the first tread of a staircase. 'Heh,' she said, you hurt me.' 'Up,' said the voice. Doubtfully she began to climb. Where was he taking her? They climbed the circular staircase to a little platform. Then she remembered, the bell tower, she knew that, she'd been there once before. She felt a larger rope being attached to her bound hands. 'What are you doing?' she asked. 'You said heaven?' said the voice. 'But I didn't mean...' 'Then soar!' came the reply before she could finish and let off her first muffled scream; because she was already flying through the air...

PROLOGUE

A good friend of mine, who for the moment must remain nameless, was recently helping out with the clearance of Old Place in Lindfield, West Sussex, when she came across a set of very interesting documents relating to the history of the parish. They included the introduction to unpublished material collated by the designer John William Lisle about one of Lindfield's most famous residents: the stained glass master Charles Eamer Kempe. That discovery provided her with the germ of an idea. She has been working hard to pull the material into a new book on Kempe's life. This tome will accompany the forthcoming BBC production of Henry James's novel *The Spoils of Poynton*, presently being filmed at Old Place. From the first drafts I've seen, I'm sure it will be a fine volume, one that I personally hope will increase the awareness of that underappreciated master's work. My friend has asked me to acknowledge her great debt to John Lisle's late daughter Margaret, whose earlier book *Master of Glass* has provided her with many of the details of Charles Kempe's life story.

The little tale that follows, therefore, may prove something of a curate's egg; in the majority, it's pure fiction, but there are some genuine facts inexpertly woven within. Oh, I should probably thank Henry James for 'allowing' me to expropriate the plot of his novel – one that has provided both the catalyst for my meetings with the main protagonists (whose real names, of course, I have kept carefully hidden) and the secrets of a few of love's 'spoils' hidden within!

The Author,
Lindfield, West Sussex

Charles Eamer Kempe was born three score and ten years ago on June 29th, 1837 at Ovingdean House in Sussex. He was always a most gifted, kind and enthusiastic man; a friend and mentor to me and many others. He believed strongly that man's highest endeavour should be to praise and glorify God. True to that vision, he used his wonderful talent solely to that very end. During his lifetime he became a master of stained glass design and manufacture and probably the pre-eminent church decorator of the last forty years. History, I'm sure, will judge him kindly.

The studios where we worked together in London and Sussex have produced almost four thousand windows over the years as well as a myriad of designs for altars, church furnishings and memorials. Sadly, he passed away on April 29th last at Nottingham Place, London. His funeral was held at Ovingdean shortly afterwards and was attended by hundreds of mourners. Now that he has departed from us, we realise through his loss of course that he's left behind not only a flourishing business, but also a great legacy of work. But none of that can take away the great hole he has also left in our lives. Unfortunately he has no direct heir; for as is well known, he never chose to marry. All the same, I as chief designer and draughtsman, Alfred Tombleson the manager of his glass works, and Walter Tower, his cousin and now Managing Director of the firm, are all dedicated to keeping his great work and reputation going for as long as we can.

Mr Kempe was born and brought up at Ovingdean, a peaceful hamlet just east of Brighton. It nestles in the cosseting folds of the Downs; between the High Weald and the chalky-rind of The Channel. He was the youngest of five boys and had two beloved elder sisters, Louisa and Augusta. There's no doubting that he was the darling of an affectionate and cultivated family. Unfortunately he outlived all his siblings.

The Kemp family's prosperity was derived from the wool-trade, and more latterly coal. With the growing demand for that black gold, the Kemps became wealthy landowners and extremely well-connected in Sussex society. Mr Kempe's father Nathaniel, a Justice of the Peace, was a succesful man but childless from his first marriage. Following the untimely death of his first wife Martha, he remarried in 1823, still desirous of a family.

His second wife and Mr Kempe's mother, Augusta Caroline Eamer, was the daughter of the illustrious Sir John Eamer, former Lord Mayor of London. She was only twenty-eight when she married Nathaniel, nearly forty years her senior; she was forty-two when Mr Kempe was born, her seventh child. It appears she conveyed on him all that motherly love can bestow; he was her little lamb and his early years were full of blissful and happy memories.

Nathaniel Kemp died in 1843, aged eighty-four. But by then the family's rural idyll was already under threat. To the east, the genteel resorts of Eastbourne and Hastings were expanding rapidly; to the west, Brighton was on the verge of becoming the London-on-Sea we know today. Around the same time, Nathaniel's nephew Thomas Read Kemp died a broken man in Paris. He'd lost everything in the speculative development of the impressive crescents and squares of Kemp Town on Brighton's eastern side; earlier he'd sold his Brighton farmhouse to the Prince of Wales – a parcel of land that became the site of the famous Brighton Pavilion.

Charles Kempe was still only six years old when those two tragic events occurred. But still he often recalled to me memories of his father, a kindly man who'd 'stroked his hair and walked about in church'. He had a clear recollection of the grandeur of the funeral that so exactly presaged his own in the same church sixty-three years later.

As I said, Mr Kempe never married; but it's a commonplace that every man has at least one great mortal love in his life. I believe he also had such a love, but I will keep my counsel as to who I think that person was. He revealed hints of that knowledge only to a very few.

On the other hand, the substantial images of his greatest and immortal love are there for everybody to see in the legacy of his windows: his lifelong dedication to the love of Christ. But even then, if you look more closely at that great body of work, there are fragments of deeper passions revealed within; some that I believe reflect his own earthly longings: his 'Imago Amoris'. Maybe you too will detect in one of those images clues to that mortal love.

In any case, he had many male and female admirers alike who loved him dearly. This little collection of letters and recollections is our devotion to that love and our combined memories of him; contributed and compiled by those he knew best over his glorious seventy years.

John William Lisle,
June 1907

CHAPTER ONE

THE VILLAGE BELLES

Here is the golden close of love,
All my wooing is done.

Alfred, Lord Tennyson, *Marriage Morning*

The Tyger Inn, Lindfield, Sussex, March 21st, 2015

It was a fine day for a wedding. All Saints Church was decorated beautifully for the occasion and the whole congregation, it seemed, had been involved in the extensive preparations. It was truly a village celebration. The recently arrived young curate was to marry the lovely Maggie Swift, a popular and charming local girl, who helped out part-time in the village school, sang in the choir and occasionally even rang the church bells. It had been a whirlwind romance over a period of less than eight months, but everybody agreed they were made for each other. The ancient church was full to overflowing that morning and the service was carried off by the Rector pretty well perfectly. It was one of those village occasions that everybody wanted to be a part of, one which would be talked about for years to come, the conclusion of a shy but public romance that had kept everyone on tenterhooks in anticipation of a happy announcement. The bride looked absolutely stunning in tulle and antique lace as the bells rang out and she emerged with her joyful groom into the spring glory of the dappled churchyard. If she still had doubts about whether she was yet ready for marriage, they were nowhere to be seen.

After the main ceremony and photographs were over and the congregation had dispersed, a smaller group of invited guests gathered in The Tyger Inn next door for the wedding breakfast. Maggie's elder sister Ellie was the chief bridesmaid. She was busily occupied, efficiently and purposefully putting the last touches to the arrangements, the girls' dear mother being unfortunately no longer alive. Joe Swift, their father, although usually reluctant to socialise, had made a great effort to look the part in his borrowed morning suit and tails and after downing a glass of local cider for courage, was entertaining their guests merrily.

The Tyger was the oldest pub in the village, run by a tall, blonde and interestingly festooned woman called Monica Malling, the daughter of an old Lindfield family, but from a slightly superior and more moneyed social circle than the poorer Swifts. Even in a small community like Lindfield, subtle gradations of belonging and acceptance exist, however long you've lived in the village and however wealthy you are; it's something that is hard to put your finger on. The Swifts were still regarded as relative newcomers in that respect, even though Joe had first moved there forty years ago and the girls were universally admired and viewed as delightful. The Mallings, on the other hand, had been there for ever and were everywhere. They were not landed aristocracy but they certainly had money, even though no one was quite sure where it had come from, some said illicit brewing, others land speculation. The truth was probably mercantile and much less exciting and they had certainly achieved a position of respectability in local society despite their dubious forebears.

But Monica Malling was different somehow; she didn't quite fit and was something of a reversion to that past, the black sheep of the family. She'd started amiably enough; she'd attended the same junior school as the Swift sisters, and then gone on to attend a local private school for a few years. But although she enjoyed all the advantages of wealth, she'd gradually rebelled. Her behaviour had become increasingly erratic and eventually she was expelled over some misdemeanour with one of the teaching staff. Ironically, she'd ended up back in the same class as the Swifts at the local comprehensive. However, although the Swift girls had resumed their acquaintance with Monica, it was never as close as their childhood friendship and they hadn't really mixed. In fact it was worse than that. There was no doubt she bore them a grudge and by then she had acquired some very exotic and unsavoury friends. Then there was some unfortunate rivalry over boys. The Swifts began to avoid her and then lost touch completely when the girls left school. Without the grades for university, Monica had taken a catering course at the local college and to everybody's surprise had knuckled down and had progressed well in that career. She was eventually appointed as manager of the Tyger; and later, with a little monetary help from her family, she'd bought the property and was now owner in her own right. Despite her continued strange tastes and odd sense of dress, she was acknowledged to be making a pretty good go of it and the restaurant was usually booked up well in advance.

Her present partner, Ryan Ross, who'd also attended the same junior school but had gone on to an even more prestigious local private school, was assisting her serving the guests at the wedding breakfast and very smart he looked, too, in his white tux. He was commonly viewed as the handsomest and most desirable bachelor in the village, and had left many a heart fluttering over the years. He certainly wasn't shy when it came to women; by reputation he had little sense of commitment and even less sense of propriety. Nobody could quite work out exactly what he saw in the vampish Monica, but she certainly seemed to have established some deep hold over him recently.

Ryan's wealthy grandmother was there too, but as a guest of honour: Mrs Serena Ross, the owner of Old Place, the large house behind the church. Serena did not usually attend such humdrum village functions but had been persuaded to do so this time, as she'd known Joe Swift from way back, when he worked there as a gardener. Some said they'd once had an affair before he married the girl's mother, but there was no evidence of that. It was probably all just village gossip.

In any case, she was in her usual feisty mood that morning and had left no one in any doubt about her distaste for the changes Monica had made to the pub, replacing many of its historical details and artefacts with a 'great deal of modern tat'. She was obviously not keen at all on her grandson's present choice of partner. But even so, she was doing her best not to spoil things for the bride and groom and had given them a beautiful and tasteful antique tea service as a wedding present. Still she was a calculating soul. The second reason why she'd accepted the invitation was that she thought the wedding would be a good place to look out for a more suitable future partner for her grandson than Monica. She was therefore searching eagerly around the room, weighing up each young woman in turn with the well-practised eyes of an aficionado of feminine nubile charms.

Indeed, it was not long before Serena's observant eyes

alighted on Ellie. In her view, she was definitely the 'most likely', a seemingly delightful girl who had no visible airs or pretensions and was now efficiently in charge of the arrangements for the luncheon. Serena had noticed how she'd earlier looked almost embarrassed to catch the bridal bouquet. Although she considered that Ellie did not present herself particularly well – slim, pale, her strawberry blonde hair not quite correctly styled, her flurried bundle of petticoats rather quirky for a bridesmaid – she did see in her someone with potential, someone who understood fine things; more importantly, someone who might be shaped. She admired the way she was dealing with the guests and trying to make them feel welcome, even if she was clearly unpolished and unpractised in such arts. Most importantly she'd noticed the stares of rival hostility Ellie had received every so often from Monica.

After the speeches were over and impatient to progress her plan, Mrs Ross beckoned Ellie over with a discreet hand signal and whispered to her behind the protection of her menu card.

'Are you safe, can I utter it?' she asked. Ellie looked at her perplexed.

'I'm sorry?'

'Isn't it too dreadful?'

'You don't like the food?'

'No, no dear. The décor; it's horrible, horrible. What a dreadful mess she's made of this place.'

Ellie laughed, at least relieved that her complaint was nothing to do with the wedding feast, which she thought was actually going down rather well.

'Well, yes, I suppose it's an acquired taste!'

'And my grandson wants to marry that girl, too. It's such a shame, terrible really.'

Ellie was surprised but intrigued by her words. She'd found it hard to avoid noticing Ryan, because, of course, they had a distant romantic history stretching right back to schooldays. But she hadn't seen him for some years, as, unlike her sister, she was now living away from Lindfield in Ovingdean with her father. Ryan had certainly grown up, and moved on from the cocky tousled youth she remembered into a very handsome young man, although she hesitated to concede he'd matured. Along with half the rest of the village, she'd had a bit of a crush on him when she was younger. Okay, so he was never the brightest lad, but he was cheekily good-looking, pleasantly artless and usually quite well behaved with her when they met at dances and such (unlike the adventurous rumours spread about him by some of the other girls).

She knew Monica too, of course, and was also somewhat surprised to see how grown up and businesslike she looked, and even more surprised that she and Ryan were now a couple. She remembered Monica's distinctly chequered past. They used to call her 'psycho' at school – she was into every extreme lifestyle and fad that came along, eventually fashioning herself as a grungy Amy Winehouse-type. But there was no doubt they were now a couple. Earlier, there'd been an awkward moment when Ellie had walked in on them snogging ravenously in the kitchens. Well, awkward for her. Ryan seemed embarrassed, too, but Monica didn't seem to mind the discovery of their intimacy at all; in fact, it'd appeared to Ellie that she'd played it up for her benefit. In any case, that was their concern; she had a wedding to organise. And she was distinctly off men at that moment anyway...

Later, as they were getting ready for the bride and groom to leave for their honeymoon, she overheard Mrs Ross ask

Monica if she'd 'take a breath of air in my garden with me' as it was 'quite stuffy' in the 'winter garden'. She assumed that was a little dig at the overheated glass conservatory Monica had installed during the autumn. Ellie watched them carefully as they left. Strangely, Mrs Ross suddenly seemed quite affable towards Monica, in contrast to the views she'd expressed privately in their earlier conversation. It was as if she was ritually respecting someone who had rival influence over her precious grandson. But Ellie could tell her true intention was false. She also noticed with a kind of snobbish amusement that Monica walked with difficulty in her Jimmy Choos through the turf, so that when one heel got caught and she had to pull it out, she dropped her Gucci bag in the process. *Sophistication never was her thing,* Ellie thought, somewhat cattily even for her.

Needing some air herself, she followed the two women at a distance up towards the church and soon realised that Ryan was walking alongside her, quite a way behind the others. Although it was a bright day, there was still a chill in the air and she wrapped her pashmina closely around her shoulders. For a moment they matched strides but did not speak and she smiled inwardly to herself; it was amusing for Ellie to wonder, given Ryan's reputation and their prior history, whether this encounter had been pre-planned on his part. She was intrigued by that possibility, even though he represented by reputation such a lot she hated about men, but still he was certainly good-looking… It was he who broke the silence, asking quite politely how she was getting on and where she was living.

She answered vaguely and quite cautiously, not wishing to seem in any way too keen but feeling a little flutter of excitement in her stomach as she did so. She sneaked a glance at him and thought again how good he looked in his tux; in fact, he was absolutely beautiful with his tanned golden face, curly hair and muscular frame, but still she was wary of his intentions. She asked him what he was doing. He said something about landscape gardening but was not particularly coherent or forthcoming. In fact, he seemed rather ashamed about that and nervous of her. During that short conversation she realised that despite all his fine education, he was probably still wonderfully dense. That confirmed her earlier suspicion that Ryan, at any rate, was certainly not the clever one of the couple, that honour clearly belonged to the still strange but now entrepreneurial Monica. It made her think that if she were ever to marry or anything, she'd also need to be the one to contribute the cleverness; things were certainly better that way round. They continued to walk in silence. She found herself flirting already in her facial expression and hand movements.

She certainly hadn't expected Ryan to pull her aside and kiss her behind the yew tree, but the champagne had left her light-headed and somewhat open to his approach. It was both thrilling and delicious. She found herself responding enthusiastically, regrettably disturbed at last by a call from one of the departing guests. And it was indeed from that flushed and huddled moment in the churchyard that Ellie subsequently became aware of a quickening of her previously subliminal marital ambitions.

Of course, neither had she expected to be the one to catch the bridal bouquet earlier, but having done so, she felt inside that maybe there was at last room in her life for a more substantial relationship. After all, her biological clock was ticking, as they say. But she wasn't going to be rushed, either. Any potential suitor would have to meet some pretty high standards. But she had to admit to herself that she had rather enjoyed that late-afternoon smooch. And he was certainly viewed as a catch in the village.

As she returned to Brighton on the train through the rural fields that evening, she began to imagine for herself a future full of things she particularly loved. Some of which might even include a romance with Ryan Ross, despite the fact she knew they were in so many ways poles apart. Especially if his grandmother was soon going to fix it for Monica to be off the scene.

CHAPTER TWO

THE WEB SHE SEEKS TO WEAVE

'Now do you know how I feel?' Mrs Gereth asked when in the wondrous hall, three minutes after their arrival, her pretty associate dropped on a seat with a soft gasp and a roll of dilated eyes.

Henry James, *The Spoils of Poynton*

Two months later – Ovingdean Hall, near Brighton, Saturday, May 23rd, 2015

By May, Ellie had been working for over a month assisting Serena Ross on the inventory of Old Place. Her newly married sister Maggie was also helping her out in her spare time. The work was interesting and it had also given her the opportunity to reacquaint herself with village life and brought closer the prospect of a renewed relationship with Ryan.

When they were small girls, Ellie had always been the princess and Maggie the tomboy, but somewhere in their teens they'd kind of swapped roles. Ellie had gone on to become a political and idealistic animal, not always the most easy-going characteristics, while Maggie became much more homely, practical and good-natured, taking baby-care classes and then joining the Red Cross. So it was no real surprise that Maggie had married first. However, even so she knew Maggie still had some doubts about marriage, it had all happened so quickly and Maggie had confided in her that she felt ill-prepared. Nonetheless, Ellie was in no doubt that there would be a baby along for the couple soon. Even after a couple of months, as far as she could tell they were still at it every minute they could find for themselves!

As she got older, Ellie's idealism had developed into strong and deeply held principles, whether it was CND, socialism or later the green agenda. Unlike Maggie, for most of her teens Ellie had avoided both sport and boys (apart from that brief dalliance with Ryan Ross) and worked diligently at her studies. She'd developed quite a creative side too: she was talented and had a natural ability. She'd been encouraged to draw and paint and then to act in various school plays; but she never got the pretty parts, always the smart villains. Her sweet younger sister mostly did the pretty parts.

After school, Ellie had started on a theatre course, but a riding accident had cut short that plan. Undaunted, after recovery, she'd found a less physically demanding course studying fine art at a college in South London. They said she showed great promise. After a while she'd started to specialise in jewellery design and engraving. In fact, she'd even been selected to help with restoration work for private clients and museums in London including pieces for the Wallace Collection. However, fate struck again. A one-night stand with a married lecturer, the unfortunate result of her inexperience with men and a spiked drink at a party, had brought a sudden end to that ambition. She got pregnant. Initially, the guy in question had taken no responsibility for the situation beyond fine words, fearing the break-up of his marriage. But under threat from her father, he'd eventually promised a financial arrangement if she kept things quiet. She'd returned to Sussex to have the child that was the unhappy product of that fling. Tragically, she lost the baby.

So the putative father had never even had to come good on his meanest promise.

After a brief period of understandable grieving, she'd sorted herself out with counselling and restarted her jewellery studies at a different college. About then, she'd also found a new passion for painting in acrylics. Again, she had natural flair. She began to sell her somewhat unique interpretations of local landscapes to a few galleries in Brighton. By chance, an article on one exhibit attracted the attention of a well-known local collector. After buying some of her work, he mentioned a position going as an artist-in-residence at the local arts centre. He was on the Board. She applied without much hope and was therefore surprised to be offered the job. It was only later she found out he'd put in 'a good word' for her that had swung it her way. That was her first official connection with the old boys' network. It filled her with distaste but also a guilty exhilaration.

Soon came the predictable expectation from him of a social meeting. She realised she was potentially heading for trouble again. After a bad experience with one married man, she knew she needed to be more careful the second time round. Her friends warned her that affairs with married men never went well. But she ignored them. After several further invitations, she felt herself slowly weakening, even falling, for him. She consented to drinks in a Brighton pub but it was businesslike and she thought nothing more of it at first. He was well known as a financial supporter of the greens as well as the arts. But although he was attractive, good company and clearly influential; Ellie was determined not to allow a second relationship to become physical. But soon, at the drunken suggestion of a friend, another scenario began to occur to her. The more she thought about it, the more daring she became.

She found herself beginning to weave an age-old trap. Why shouldn't she use her smarts to her own end this time, to ensnare her generous but likely amoral pursuer? Her agreements to see him steadily became more calculating, as his own intentions became more obvious. This eventually involved a hastily arranged hotel room where they'd finally done the deed. She'd cried after he left, staring out defiantly at the accusing sea, both thrilled and angry with herself. But she was more than ever determined. She'd realised he'd be a fantastically useful source of contacts in the arts world; he seemed to know just about everyone. Why shouldn't she use her own feminine attractions and his shimmering access for her own benefit, for once? But she did force herself to read several learned tones on third-world protest movements in penance that weekend.

However, it wasn't long before she found out she wasn't his only dalliance with a twenty-something ingénue that summer. She quickly noticed he had a roving eye, and, of course, the more spiteful of his friends told her stories of other girls and the presents he'd given them. He had previous. But she bumped into his attractive photographer wife at an exhibition in Ditchling. As it turned out, this lady was no stay-at-home frump; in fact she was more than gorgeous. What she saw in him therefore, Ellie initially had no idea.

They got chatting. Ellie was seduced by her flamboyant and unconventional personality. She was quietly shocked that this 'wife' seemed to know about and even condone his flirtatious behaviour, but at the same time, intrigued too. He was the one with the money and contacts. She clearly had the talent. From the subject of her photographs, her appetite appeared very broad too. She invited Ellie to her studio and it was soon apparent from her propositions that the couple enjoyed what was known euphemistically as an open marriage. That meant she could see pretty well whoever she pleased. The studio was her hunting ground. It was all very Bloomsbury and flattering. But, by then Ellie had begun to understand her own power; she continued to play along with him (and her) for a while, getting into even more ludicrous liaisons in the process.

Through association with their contacts, however, she'd also begun to develop a new and lucrative side-line. She discovered she had a good nose for sniffing out the more talented up-and-coming artists. Soon she got one or two requests from his wealthier friends to select art work to adorn their sea-view penthouses at the posher end of Kemptown. Within a few months, that initially ad-hoc trade had developed into a business: she was soon buying, in a small way, for the contemporary collections of many wealthy local clients. She wasn't sure it quite fit in with her conscientious instincts or even socialist principles, but she was confident she could usefully distinguish between wealth and values. The government had taken so much out of arts funding through its austerity measures that someone had to replace it, and why not be part of that social contract? By the beginning of spring, she was able to count several 'retired' rock artists, a DJ, a film actress and even a well-known reality TV star amongst her clients. The next development, however, was a surprise even to her.

Ellie's second meeting with Serena Ross had taken place at Easter, shortly after the wedding. Of course after that brief snog in the churchyard, she'd daydreamed about the chances of a renewed relationship with Serena's grandson. But nothing much had happened and she was too busy to wait for his occasional hurried phone calls. She wasn't short of social offers in Brighton, given her growing reputation. She'd even been invited to speak at a couple of conferences as well as supporting the local greens in their campaigning.

Serena Ross had been widowed for two years after twenty-six years of marriage. She'd always led a very independent and somewhat patrician life. However the empty and staid friendships of that old life were now boring her. She wanted to be free to travel, to meet new people. Serena had also come to realise that the time had come to downsize from her empty mansion. The big house on the hill was far more than she needed, however it would be a huge task to sort through its eclectic contents. By chance, Ellie was independently recommended to her by an old Brighton friend as someone who could help her sort through Old Place before its impending sale. Mrs Ross was intrigued: she remembered warmly the girl she'd met at the wedding and was therefore immediately aware of the double opportunity such a project might also present: for her to get her wayward grandson Ryan back on track.

When first approached by the intermediary, Ellie had felt unsure. Serena Ross clearly didn't fall into the typical profile of her clients, she was well above her normal social circle and she had a radical's antipathy to old money. However, a meeting had been arranged and Ellie had been suitably charmed and charming. When Serena told her she saw in her something of the determination and discrimination of herself as a younger woman, Ellie was hooked. On the spot, Serena had made her an offer she couldn't refuse financially. Ellie was both flattered by her words and also totally fascinated by the project. Of course, she already had an inkling she might be letting herself get drawn into a somewhat complex family situation too, but was sure she could handle that. One comment in particular had betrayed what was surely in Serena's mind when she'd referred to Ryan:

'If only that dreadful woman was off the scene, I could get him married off to someone decent.'

Serena Ross's grandfather, a succesful Oxford lawyer named John Wynter, had bought Old Place from Charles Eamer Kempe's cousin Walter Tower in the 1920s. Three generations of Wynters had grown up in the house and gradually added to its eclectic collection of furniture and furnishings. Serena was the only child of that third generation and had known the house since she was a little girl. After her parents were killed in a car accident, she'd been brought up by her grandfather at Old Place itself. In 1987, on her betrothal to the banker Augustus Ross, her grandfather had entrusted the house to her on his death as part of her marriage settlement, but only for as long as she continued to live there; after that it was to pass to her next lineal descendent. She'd lived there ever since.

Her two-year-deceased husband had been an amiable old-school type who'd made a fortune and accumulated quite a collection of modernist objets d'art in his own right. On their marriage, he'd blended these incongruously with the more traditional spoils the Wynter family had accumulated. Away from the main rooms, the house was therefore furnished in a haphazard jumble of styles, with attics stuffed with decades of unwanted overspill. It was the story of a life, in fact of two lives, in fact of a dynasty. One in which she had fully paid her part as collector-in-chief, arbiter of taste and centre of a wide and influential social circle.

But since her husband's death, Serena had begun to tire of all those false friends and hangers-on, and tried to integrate herself more with village-life. Recently she'd reached the landmark age of sixty. Although she didn't necessarily feel this was old, she still felt the time had come to move on. There were places she wanted to see, things she wanted to do. After a brief negotiation, she'd agreed with her grandson Ryan to remove herself to a charming, but slightly squeezed, Queen Anne property called Poynting's at the other end of Lindfield High Street. Ryan was thrilled with her decision, and started to harbour plans to sell or develop parts of Old Place himself. Initially, therefore, he was happy to say that she could take whatever she needed with her. Given the contents of Augustus Ross's will, he was not expecting her to hang on to the whole property or its remaining contents after she'd vacated it.

Although she'd had no real formal education, Serena was a woman of catholic convictions and very particular tastes. She'd agonised for ages over which choice pieces from her lifetime collection she'd take with her to Poynting's: furniture, porcelain, clocks, fabrics, embroidery. However, she was even more daunted by the prospect of clearing Old Place of the rest of its contents. That held far too many difficult memories, which was precisely where Ellie would come in. Although an unusual request, Ellie was fascinated by the opportunity. Eventually she'd need to bring in a professional auctioneer, of course; however, Serena had promised her she could keep her first choice of whatever she wanted from the collection. That was the deciding factor (apart from maybe the opportunity to see Ryan away from the ever watchful eyes of Monica). There was a lot to do though, which is why she'd dragged Maggie in to help her with the inventory. Her sister was good at that stuff, computers and everything, and Ellie had seen that she needed something to keep her mind occupied outside school hours while her husband was busy around the parish.

At first, Ryan was quite taken with the idea of Ellie helping his grandmother out. 'It's awfully kind of you to help my gran with this. We really need to get the place cleared,' he'd told her.

But soon after, things had changed radically. Monica and her mother, Mrs Malling, had visited Old Place to view its fine furniture, cases of enamels and Venetian velvets. However, that visit had not gone at all well: to Ryan's consternation, they were both highly disparaging about Serena's lifetime work. Mrs Malling in particular had described 'the spoils' as being 'most striking but rather old-fashioned and probably reproduction'. Ryan had watched with horror the telling and very visible effect of that shocking remark on his grandmother's face.

Of course, Serena had remained calm at the time, but that'd been the decisive point when she'd made up her mind to take ALL the best pieces with her to Poynting's, rather than risk leaving any to 'those philistines'. So when Monica and her mother had subsequently visited Serena in her new house and realised exactly what had happened, there'd been an almighty row.

Newly arrived from Brighton that afternoon, Ellie had been cleaning some valuable porcelain in an upstairs room, while calmly evaluating yet again the merits of a potential liaison with Ryan. A noise outside had caught her attention and she'd watched with dismay as Ryan and Monica, her mother and Mrs Ross started debating angrily on the terrace. She distinctly heard Ryan at one point tell Serena that he intended to marry Monica come what may and that he required all the 'things' to be returned to Old Place immediately.

After half an hour, when the noise had died down and she'd thought it was safe, she ventured downstairs to speak to Mrs Ross and soon realised that she'd come down prematurely. She was at once confronted by Serena's embarrassing departing words to Monica in front of the other guests.

'We still haven't had the talk we should have had, have we Monica?' she said to Monica dismissively, and then turned very deliberately to the already red-faced Ellie as she addressed the room.

'…but here's Ellie – yes, with you, I believe I might at least rest in my grave!'

Ellie flushed and stared angrily at Mrs Ross. As soon as the guests had left, she turned to her and said, 'How could you?' Mrs Ross just smiled at her and shrugged as if to say: 'Try harder dear'.

Ellie took her leave and rushed back as quickly as she could to Old Place, where Maggie was fortunately there to give her comfort and calm her down. She recounted bitterly the events at Poynting's, but soon they were both giggling about it all.

'God I hate the Ross's. Why did I ever agree to get mixed up with all this?'

'Calm down Ell, you're nearly done now, another week and it will be ready for the auctioneers.'

'Another week, I'm not sure if I can bear the stress!'

'Yes you can. Have you decided yet?'

'I don't know, I quite like some of the enamel miniatures, but then there's that pretty picture of Valetta, too.'

'No, not the artwork, you dope, I meant Ryan. Any joy?' her sister teased.

'God knows. You can guess exactly what he wants out of a 'relationship' but Monica's still got him well under her thumb as far as I can see,' Ellie replied sulking. She was acutely conscious that in accepting Mrs Ross's offer, she was walking a fine line between her aesthetic ideals, ethical scruples and her own unsatisfied desires. She could see that Maggie knew so too.

'Well that's a good thing if you ask me. He's not good news.'

'You're probably right, but have you seen his eyes and those muscles? Land sakes what I'd like to do with that body if I got the chance.' They both laughed.

'Anyway sis, changing the subject, do you have any plans for tonight?'

'Just some concert that Sal wants me to go to at the Festival.'

'Anyone I've heard of?'

'I doubt it. She told me, but I haven't a clue who the band is!'

'Well, you never know, you just might meet Prince Charming. It'll take your mind off 'Flash', at least!'

'No 'Flash' is just honest lust,' Ellie laughed. 'Anyway, are there any Prince Charmings left in Brighton? I doubt it somehow. I'm sure I'd rather be having a nice night in like you cuddled up on the sofa with your brand new hubbie,' she continued, and winked at her sister, who reddened.

'Hey, I forgot to mention, you know that little sandalwood box you found yesterday without a key?'

'Yes?'

'Well I managed to get it open with a clothes pin and pliers.'

'You devil, you. What did you find?'

'Some lovely handwritten letters.'

'What, to Mr Kempe?'

'No, they seem to be a collection made by a guy called John Lisle, Kempe's chief designer. Tributes he collected after Kempe's death for some sort of memorial that never got published.' She showed her the first letter from John Lisle.

'Wow, that's wonderful. Let's see the rest?'

'This one, for instance appears to be from a childhood friend: a Mr Jack Beard, a gentleman farmer in Ovingdean. A lot of it's in dialect.'

'Beard – yes they were landowners in the area until quite recently.' She read the first couple of paragraphs. 'Oh Maggie, isn't this amazing stuff! You're a real star!'

Dear Mr Lisle,

Thank you for your letter. It was very good to make your acquaintance at the funeral. With regards to your request, I am not generally a writing man but the following is a memory I still treasure of Charlie Kemp from our childhood. I am sorry about the indelicacy of the subject matter, but I always found it a most amusing story and Charlie and I have chuckled about it on many occasions since. I have told it as faithfully as I might do in my own words in the circumstances.

It was a spring day and as I remember, we'd been wading in the pool fed by the gubbery little spring that runs along Hog field. I was carrying a homemade net and rod, our jars were already full o' nymphs and beetles and all sorts, including a crested newt, the poor thing thrashing about dimly in the cloudy water.

'Cum 'ere Charlie, luk at dis,' I said. 'Wot's dat, Jack?' Charlie replied. He must have only been about five or six in those days. His brownish hair was smeared with sweat and chalk slurry from the bank; his clothes a real mess too, as were mine. We crouched down on our bellies and stared into the little pool left by a field post discarded into the water. A pair of dragonflies was scurrying amongst the reeds.

'Mousearnickles,' I replied. I was a year or so older than him. My Pa was the local farmer in Ovingdean back then.

'No not dem, dat in de water,' he said. He pointed to where three small dark greeny-brown shapes were darting from shadow to shadow, flitting from weed to weed. Every so often, their bony backs glinting in the sun as they scurried through open water into the greeny mass, our eyes drawn by their colouring and scuttling.

'Sticklebacks,' I replied. We tried to fish 'em out, but there were too much algae to use the nets proper. So instead I clasped my hands together to form a sort of cup. I scooped at one of 'em shapes in the water as it passed, then pulled my fists up into the sunlight to see what I'd bagged. I remember shrieking with the pain.

'Ow, jigger,' I said. 'It's git spines sharp us nails, deys dug rite inta ma finger, mortal surelye.'

Charlie stared at the creature next to the little blob of pink-red blood that was oozing from my finger. The fish was a squirming silver-grey shape, twisting in the creases of my hands. It had bright kingfisher-blue eyes and delicate pale-scarlet gills.

'Quick de abbler jar,' I shrieked, and we popped the little minnow safely in the largest jar to join the gasping newt. We watched in awe as the creatures danced round and round, the one dabbing the glass with its snout the other gulping for air in the thick stug-stained water.

'Ah dat's a monstus gud un,' I said. 'Wot a haul we got now!'

Charlie took the jar back from me and held it up to the light to see the little gobby eyes of the fish. They were beautiful and clear as if stained with colour. There were faint striped markings along its back and three raised spines. 'It's mighty purdy,' he said.

'Tis indeed, yung 'un. Cum on Charlie, let's see wot else der is,' I said, wiping the blood off my finger with my sleeve. We crept further along the bank till we found a second, stagnant pool. That one was teaming with life, full of little black wiggling creatures, some swimming free, some still attached to their egg sacs.

'Wot's dat?' asked Charlie. I guessed he'd never seen that particular miracle of nature before.

'Frogspawn,' I said, 'un dem's taddies, liddle frogs.' I scooped up a handful of the jelly and plonked it dripping into the second jar. 'Ya can kep um till dem's grown tails un legs 'n all, an' den watch 'em goo off in de grass. Dursn't tell ya ma though, I knows ur don't like sich things in ur house.'

'Taddies,' said Charlie. 'Dat's a queer name.'

'Ya cud be a taddie yaself, chuckle-head, with dat gurt big 'ed an globby har,' I laughed. Cum on Charlie, we best be gittin ya home and cleaned up.'

Charlie nodded back. He loved being out in the fields with me. We climbed up out of the ditch onto the droving path that led along the lane called Greenways back through Grange Farm. That's where I lived with my ma and pa. Further down the lane was the big house where Charlie lived with his family. It was getting late and the shadows showed how long we'd been out in the fields. We both knew he'd probably be in for a beating from his pa if it was dark by the time he got back. In the distance we could already hear the fox-hounds in my pa's kennels howling for their evening feed. We began to jog along the road, past the Old Smithy, but as we passed the pile of old logs by its side wall, Charlie started.

'Summut moved, Jack!' he shouted. We went closer to the logs to see what it was. Indeed as I inspected the pile it seemed as if the whole pile of wood was moving.

'Rats,' I said, dropping the stick I'd started poking the pile with. 'Ugh, I hate dem fiends. Quick, run strate past 'em Charlie.'

But before we'd gone a couple more steps, two of the beasties were already amongst our feet. In fright, Charlie shrieked and dropped the jar. It smashed on the ground and the chalky-grey liquid flowed out leaving the poor animals squirming together in the dusty pool of water. I knelt down and tried to scoop them up into the second jar with the frogspawn. But in Charlie's fright, he'd already started running towards the stables that were next to the Smithy's yard. Laughing, I called after him to stop.

'Cum back, ya chavee, stop being afeared an' maak'n sich a fuss, dey won't hurt ya.' But I figure Charlie wasn't so sure and just kept running.

He told me later that once inside the stables he began to feel safer at first. He could smell the warm hay and straw and horse dung. But there were two working punches inside, a load of old machinery and the dog cart that my pa used to get up to town. The two huge beasts were stomping noisily in their stalls. Charlie could see their great red-stained eyes staring back at him in the gloom and could hear their haunches pushing against the stall doors. He was afeared again. He hadn't been in the stables before without me or one of the farm hands. He scrambled away from the horses across to where the fresh straw was kept and then up the steps into the hay loft.

Once upstairs, he found that something else was moving. His heart was beating fast and he wished dearly that I'd come. *Maybe there were rats up there too*, he thought. Below him the two great shires had settled down a little and the place was quieter. He thought about going back down, but he could hear a new noise, a rustling. He lifted his head up further into the loft so that he could see what it was. 'Oh Lord,' he thought, 'I hope it ain't more rats.'

The last rays of the evening sun were streaming by then through a broken slat, the blinding beams dancing around the hay dust. He could see a shape moving and then heard a low-groaning noise; up and down, up and down, casting humped yella shadows on the wooden planks of the loft. As his eyes adjusted he saw the shape had drifts of golden straw-like hair attached to it, like a glowing scarecrow. He heard panting and groaning. He was really scared but curious all the same. He bit his lip and moved closer. Outside, I was still calling for him to come out but he ignored me.

The movement in the hay stopped and there was a low moan as if someone had been hit in the belly. The upper shape rose and he saw a face and glinting blue eyes and the white cotton of a girl's blouse open to her waist, two sweet round love-apples hanging freely from within. He said as they weren't like his ma's, but smooth and soft and rose-tinted, heaving up and down with the girl's panting breaths. He heard two voices.

'Sam, sshh, what was that?'

'I think ya knows dat goistering well anuf, yun missie!'

'No you thick oaf, there was a shout, quick there must be someone outside.'

The girl's voice was fine but anxious. She clasped her dress to her upper body and pulled her petticoat and skirt back down from where they'd been hitched up around her hips. Charlie knew that voice of course. He'd known it all his life. It was the sweetest voice on all the face of the earth. It was a voice that had sung him to sleep so often in his nursery…

'Lulu,' he whispered. Cos it was his sister, see.

As I said Mr Lisle, I must apologise for the indelicate subject, but we did laugh again and again over that incident. I dare say some wouldn't ever recover from the shock of that, with girls and all I mean. But I reckon as it did him no harm when it came to meet 'em later. He was never that afeared of 'em after that, he joked.

>Jack Beard,
>Gentleman farmer,
>Grange Farm, Ovingdean

CHAPTER THREE

LOVE EVER LIVING STRIVES

*Our Love can never rise to an Excess
Within no Bounds can ever acquiesce;
Love to Perfection ever strives to Soar.*

Thomas Ken, *Hymnotheo or the Penitent*

Ovingdean Hall, Sunday, May 24th, 2015 (the next day)

Harry Jamieson mouthed the last line of the poem he'd so carefully committed to memory that morning. He'd picked out the quote to impress her, but now it just seemed clichéd. At the last moment he'd lost his nerve and bottled. As planned, however, he bowed when she appeared; taking off his cap in a sweeping motion as the in-his-mind wholly glorious object of his desire emerged from the door of the college. She stood there, stony-faced, keys in hand. She was dressed for action in jodhpurs, oversized hacking jacket and muddy walking gear. Kitted out for a date she certainly was not. He noticed moreover that she hadn't bothered at all with make-up and there were faint lines and freckles around her face. He shrugged it off; it didn't really matter. To his eyes, she was a babe in any wrapper.

'You're late!' she bridled.

'You look gorgeous!' he countered rapidly, again under his breath. She heard him though, and cringed inside at his fawning; she certainly wasn't going to be bought that easily by some posh boy. She already thought she knew his type; she'd experienced and dealt with his flatmate's inappropriate exploratory charms outside Sticky Mike's the night before. Her friend Sal had dragged her along to a gig there and then Tom and Harry had latched on to them. Ellie wasn't looking for romance, but clearly from his demeanour all night, he was.

'Ta, but this gal weren't born yesterday,' she slurred in an improvised Sussex drawl. She calculated that her put-down would probably send him off balance, allowing her to get the upper hand in this all-important little opening tussle. She was yet to decide whether she fancied him or not.

'I can see,' he muttered. He was wounded, but he knew he had more. He hoped her words were spoken out of curiosity not malice. He'd already realised she was going to be hard work. But he'd decided the previous evening that she'd be worth it. His enthusiasm was undimmed. Beneath that stern exterior was... well what?

'You have to be joking!' she said, letting out an involuntary guffaw. *God, is she reading my thoughts*, he wondered? Potentially lustful thoughts, he had to admit, *but to have them interrupted so cruelly before they'd even begun?* It was a while since he'd felt this way about any girl.

However, from the direction of her gaze, he realised her laughter was triggered not by anything he'd said, but by the accurate identification of his car. It was a brand-new roadster, very red and very Japanese – desirable but somewhat out of place in a staff car park full of quirky Citroens and beat-up Fords. It also wasn't actually his.

A typical rich boy's toy, she thought. *Why aren't I surprised?* She bit her lip and was silent for a second, waiting her moment, pacing her attack. She had, of course, clocked his linen jacket, garish red cords and green wellies. *What a clown, perfect for a breezy walk*, she thought; he was an even sorrier case than she'd imagined. If nothing else, this was going to be fun, although, at least, unlike Ryan, she might get a decent conversation out of him. What's more, unusually for her, he was unattached apparently. If by some miracle she was wrong about him that was.

She'd only agreed to their little rendezvous under pressure from her girlfriend, Sal. It'd certainly been against her better judgement. Their 'appointment' (aka 'date' in his mind) was the unwelcome suggestion of her friend following a hastily contrived foursome the previous evening. Harry's flatmate Tom, the target of Sal's amatory interest, was the one with the wandering hands. She'd dealt with him easily enough, but when he'd hit on Sal, she'd had fewer misgivings. Now, as a result, she was stuck with his flatmate for the afternoon, while Sal got up to God knows what. Of course, there'd been that feeble tale about his interest in looking round the Hall. But she wasn't fooled by that; she pretty well knew his game already: an hour of unguent schmooze, a brace of effervescent drinks in the pub he'd mentioned, and then the obligatory walk-by-the-sea, probably a grappling attempt at a snog, etc. etc. She was sure his lizard act worked gloriously on the fragrant roses of the totty class, but it certainly wasn't going to work with her. College had been full of similar upper-class morons, whose whole idea of life was a mile removed from hers, full of brainless banter, over-indulgence and conspicuous coupling. And the guy standing before her didn't even have Ryan's physical attributes; in fact she thought he looked a bit of a wimp.

'Standard issue for a BBC researcher, I suppose, or is it

mummy's?' she commented (about the car, of course, not his body).

That's a bit harsh, he thought, but he liked her spirit. It was kind of edgy but provoking. He didn't have that much experience with women. For most of his teenage years and during college, he'd had just the one sweetheart. They'd been affectionate but agreed mutually (well at least she had) that it wouldn't go further than that. After college he was just too busy getting started in his career. Even when he met girls they were either unsuitable (code for after one thing really and not too bothered with whom it was performed) or too wrapped up in their own complexes. Of course, he knew he and Ellie were misfits as well. He couldn't exactly miss her leftie credentials: the badges, the strangely-styled part-razored hair. Her political persuasion had become obvious during their snatched conversation in the pub, a strident, rambling rant against Tories, hunting and posh schools. Yes, she was right, he'd attended one of them too (a minor one at least). But he said he wasn't interested in politics (or hunting); actually, on the whole he found those subjects a bore. He'd therefore been more than a little irritated by the way she'd pigeonholed him from the start.

Later, after she'd caved in to their meeting, he'd worried about 'wheels'. If she was as green as she claimed she'd probably expect him to turn up by bike or on the bus or something. But that wouldn't do. So he'd borrowed the roadster that morning from Tom as the price of leaving the coast clear at the flat. He wasn't sure yet whether he'd set out to impress her or just wind her up, but he could already see he'd certainly done the latter, and hit a raw nerve too. In any case, his rusting crate was in the garage and the bus didn't do it for him, whatever she thought.

'F-f-fancy a spin later?' he replied half-heartedly,

anticipating a further negative reaction. He was already losing courage with this one and his stammer was making an awkward return. He knew the worst thing he could do was to allow himself to be bossed around. She scowled and the empty pit in his stomach deepened.

She was tempted to say something cutting and rude about upper-class deviants, but decided against it; she'd noticed the stammer too. Maybe that would be a bit under the belt, unless he was aiming for the sympathy vote. In any case, it'd be more fun to play him along. No doubt he was harmless. She rationalised that she was doing Sal a favour by getting him out of the flat so she could pursue her nefarious plans. She'd get a decent lunch out of him at least and then send him packing. Maybe have a bit more fun at his expense. Okay, she'd better cut him some slack.

'No, we're walking. Haven't you brought your walking boots like I told you, or did you forget?' she asked mock-sternly. Of course she was quite sure he'd forgotten. He'd regret the wellies later if he tried walking in them too far, but she could fix that.

Ellie's father Joe was the janitor at the language school at the Hall and they both lived in a rented house in the village. In that brief rash moment the previous evening, she'd agreed to show this privileged clown around the buildings. He'd expressed some interest or other in visiting the Hall to Sal, who'd then been on her case all evening. That bit wouldn't take too long though, as there wasn't that much to see, but the pub he'd mentioned visiting was over a mile away.

But why drive when they could walk? At least it would be fresh air on what was turning out to be a bright if cool day. She was sure a good stiff pace would dampen his enthusiasm and then she'd be able to get back home in plenty of time. She reckoned on half an hour showing him round, a brisk stroll over the Downs to lunch and then a further brisk walk back. That should be enough. Not too much damage. She'd be back home by four at the latest, plenty of time to get other stuff done. If he kept up okay, she might even make a mug of tea at the Hall before he left. Annoyingly she had to concede he was kind of cute (in a foppish sort of way); it wouldn't do her frosty reputation any harm around the village to have him in tow for a few hours.

They made a whistle-stop tour of the Hall. As she'd warned, there really wasn't that much to see: a few period details, a couple of grimy paintings and bits of broken furniture. Most of the good stuff had been sold off years ago and various phases of institutional use had altered the interior plan beyond recognition. There was no sign of the Kemp family left – no memorial to Charles Kempe, the most famous scion or his notorious cousin Thomas Read Kemp. Harry took a few photos to justify his original inquiry and then she suggested they head off over Beacon Hill to the pub in Rottingdean. Out of misplaced sympathy, she'd found him some proper boots in the tack room. His jacket, also, was so thin that she lent him an old one of her father's.

They walked down the long drive past the candled horse chestnuts and mayflower. Wood pigeons simmered, the grass was brimming with gaudy dandelions and bossy magpies; it was a nice day, still and bright. She was happier now they were in the open air and quickened her pace to test his mettle. They walked up the suburban road that led past a string of tired thirties villas. One or two of them were newly burnished with zinc and plastic cladding, churlishly possessive of their narrow glimpses of sea. A rider trotted past, a girl that Ellie knew. The rider nodded at her and then glanced appreciatively at her companion. *Good, that would get the tongues wagging,* Ellie thought. They stopped at the pillar box at the top of the road and she pointed out where you could just see the chimneys of the posh girls' school across the Downs. The sky was deep and broad and split by sharp vapour trails. There was a light breeze on the heath; they could see the traffic moving carelessly along the coast road towards Brighton and the lazy cloud-shadowed sea beyond.

She decided to take the eastern slope in the lee of the wind, rather than go past the old hooded windmill. As they walked through nodding banks of cowslips past the dew pond, the bright blazing chill of the Sussex sky burnt their cheeks. She loved this precious stretch of heathland overlooking the bay, the last exhausted fold of the Downs before you reached the sea. A painter had once told her that it was like a green, panting mistress reclining on her long chalk bed waiting for her lover's touch; she liked that simile. As they reached the brow above Rottingdean, she sensed he was tiring and they rested for a moment while she began to mine him for information. She could hear a distant skylark. A woman was struggling to control a pair of Irish wolf hounds.

'Okay, come clean, what do you really do for a living Mr Japanese sports car owner?'

'Like I said, I'm a location scout for the BBC.'

'Bull you are, I wasn't fooled by that,' she laughed. 'No, I reckon you're a developer or an estate agent or something incredibly evil like that. I wasn't born yesterday.'

'Really, I'm not,' he replied, somewhat aggrieved but still catching his breath.

'Okay, then what are you working on at the moment?' she challenged.

'Well, as I said earlier, it's a sort of period drama.'

'That's not exactly informative, is it?'

She was about to send in the next verbal missile but at

that moment they were interrupted by the dogs looking for rabbits amongst the gorse. Harry seemed nervous of them so she led him hurriedly down a muddy shortcut past the tidy flint-walled allotments. The air was spiced with salt and screeching gulls, but as they descended, the more urban smell of mowed lawns took over. They rounded into Hogflat Lane towards the village green. He was much happier now; they were getting back on to level ground and normal roads. He really, really liked this girl despite, or maybe because, of her seeming antipathy to him.

When they got to The Green, she seemed to relax a bit and cheerfully pointed out Kipling's house and then on the other side of the road, the three buildings Edward Burne-Jones and his wife had combined into their country home. She liked this little community; it had an unexpected heritage beyond its sleepy setting, still largely unknown to the wider world. Georgiana Burne-Jones was also a bit of a feminist heroine of hers. She'd been one of the first elected women councillors in Britain and had defied the village mob after the fall of Mafeking, hanging a poster from her window declaring: 'We have killed and also taken possession'.

Obligingly, sensing her enthusiasm, Harry took some photos of the house with the blue plaque and the view over to The Green. While he was doing this, a fey-bearded old timer with a Sunday paper stopped them and they started chatting. Ellie had met him more than once at that spot, although she didn't know his name and he never seemed to remember meeting her. As usual, he was keen to impart his limited but privileged gems of knowledge – exactly the same ones she'd heard each time they'd met, the things she guessed he told all the sightseers who took an interest in the house. His main tale was about a bricked-up vertical slot in the main wall 'where they used to take old Ned's canvases out from his studio'. Ellie had never been convinced by that yarn. *Why would they have needed to do that when there were perfectly decent doors?* she reasoned. But it was a good story, one for him to engage the punters with, one polished with the telling.

At the old man's suggestion, they walked across the green to St Margaret's Church to see the stained-glass windows. Outside the church, the sign on the lychgate challenged: 'Blessed are they that hear the word of God and keep it'. Ellie had been inside several times before to meditate on the windows. The glass was bright and attractive but in a naïve style, the East windows depicting the archangels Gabriel, Michael and Raphael, made up by William Morris's firm from Burne-Jones's designs. There were two more stunning portrayals of the Virgin Mary and St Margaret in the chancel. You could recognise a Burne-Jones immediately; they were unmistakeable and she was secretly pleased with Harry's obvious appreciation for his work. The verger, whom she knew and who'd been arranging the church for the next service, thanked them for their thoughtfulness in removing their muddy boots and then showed them round the rest of the interior. Outside in the churchyard, she pointed out the plain stone memorials to Sir Edward and Georgiana in the south-west wall.

There was plenty more to see but she was getting hungry and slightly anxious about the time. Subtly, she tugged Harry away from his engrossed conversation with the verger. They made their polite excuses and wandered down the neat High Street towards the vinegar-stained sea.

The pub that Harry had mentioned was near the centre of the village, by the old Whipping Post. On their way, they passed a little museum on the left-hand side of the road. She pointed mischievously to a poster carrying the well-known image of *King Cophetua and the Beggar Maid* in the window.

'There's a good Burne-Jones question for you; who do you think the beggar maid is?' she asked.

'I don't know, some model, I suppose?'

'No, it's Georgie.'

'Georgie?'

'Yes, Georgie, his wife.'

'Wow, that's kind of weird. Not exactly a flattering image to paint of your wife?'

'Sexy though, all that leather, don't you think?' she teased.

'Not sure it would do much for me.'

'Oh, I don't know,' she laughed. 'Fifty shades an' all?' He laughed back, unsure of her meaning.

'Come on let's get some lunch,' she said. *Well at least Miss Stoneface was opening up*, he thought.

Unfortunately, the pub he'd planned to take her to was closed for a private function, so they decided instead to buy lunch at Snow's, the flouncy deli on the corner of the High Street and the coast road. He wasn't sure about it at first, eclectic was the word; the interior was overwrought, full of out-of-season decorations. She'd been there several times before, however, and assured him the food was pretty good. More importantly, she knew they'd get served quickly too.

In fact, unusually for a Sunday, it was almost empty. She ordered tuna crunch and elderflower pressé. He chose (rather weedily she thought) smoked salmon and cream cheese and a chocolate-striped cappuccino. The music they were playing that day was cheerful and pure fifties – *Johnny B. Goode, My One and Only, Tutti Frutti* and she found herself relaxing a bit. After giving their order, they settled down in a little booth and he took his turn to drill her for information. She remained coy though, and revealed little apart from the basics of home life, schooling and college. She explained she wasn't really local; she came originally from a village further north in Sussex but now she lived with her father near the Hall. She didn't care to mention that her mother was dead and he didn't ask. But she was flattered at least that he was taking a genuine interest in her, unusual in most men in her experience. As she studied him, she reflected he did have a very friendly face and nice easy conversational style and there was a certain old-fashioned charm in the way he spoke. *Maybe he was growing on her*, she thought; she'd have to be on her guard against that. She really didn't need any more male complications at that time. She'd also wondered earlier if he was gay but had decided not.

Her love life was sort of a mess. She'd been single for a while after that complicated relationship with the married guy (the art collector) and his wife. That'd foundered when she'd found out he was three-timing her (the rat). She'd like to have considered that episode closed, but she'd been guilty of allowing irregular, usually drunken, re-ignitions. She'd met a few single guys since at clubs and pubs in Brighton, but no one special, and she wasn't especially looking. Then there was Ryan of course, the teenage crush she'd met again at her sister's wedding. She kind of liked the idea of going out with him and had imagined that scenario developing further than it had. A diamond in the rough in contrast to the weedy aesthetes of the Brighton art scene, but he was still practically engaged to the evil Monica.

After that snog away from the gaze of other guests, he'd called her a couple of times. He'd suggested drinks in a local country pub, away from the prying eyes of the village, but no doubt with further furtive manoeuvrings in mind. She'd refused (he could at least buy her dinner she reasoned). So that was pretty well all that had happened. Any assignation while they were together in Lindfield was pretty well out of the question. Although she'd come near on a couple of occasions when he was working around the house. In any case, she still hadn't made up her mind about the likelihood of him leaving Monica. Her head told her he was pretty well a lost cause. Well, until recently that was, and the new opportunities that Mrs Ross's little assignment had presented. Anyway, she wasn't that bothered. There were plenty of other things to do in Brighton with her girlfriends without the messy complications of men.

As they chatted quietly, she realised she was slowly warming up to Harry, although she was still unsure where his real interest in her lay. Well, apart maybe from the obvious (assuming he really wasn't gay). The more she talked with him, the more she felt he didn't seem the typical hetero type either. He was really quite shy and considerate, almost courteous. However, she still didn't really believe the whole BBC filming hustle; and she just wasn't sure he was really her type; he was thoughtful but a bit wet behind the ears. So maybe he was gay? She guessed he must have plenty of posh girlfriends in Kemptown where, according to Sal, he shared a very smart flat in Lewes Crescent with the fabulous Tom, overlooking the sea. But she found herself staring at him a bit more freely than she expected, there was a curious chemistry that she couldn't quite fathom. He didn't even seem floored by her attempts to wind him up, even when she went on a rant about the misogynists at her father's college. No, he was just relentlessly charming. He had sparkly eyes and a cute little turned-up nose. Intrigued, she decided she was going to play this one long.

After they'd been there for twenty minutes or so, the

place began to fill up. Outside it had clouded over and she could smell the rain sighing in the air. A group of day-trippers came in for take-away coffee. Soon the condensation forming on the windows began to make her feel uncomfortable and claustrophobic. The weather was definitely closing in. She hurried him up with his sandwiches. She was eager to get back out on to the blasted hill and start the walk home, but suddenly he seemed reluctant to go. She soon realised why.

'Was it cream tea you wanted, sir?' asked the pretty waitress to the elderly couple at the table next to them. She watched Harry's eyes as she bent over to clear a table.

'Stop staring at that poor girl,' she snapped in disbelief, more than irritated with him.

'I wasn't!'

'Yes you were!' she replied. 'You were checking her out.'

'No really, I was just thinking she'd make a great Rose.'

'Rose?'

'*Brighton Rock.*'

'Good grief!' she replied. 'That's certainly a new one!'

She was, however, thrown into some confusion by that answer. She hadn't expected it; it was kind of cool really. However, not only was it unlikely, but it betrayed to her the probability he was just like all the others of his breed. The problem was she now kind of liked him. And yet he was apparently already on to the next attraction. *Bloody hell, just another posh boy,* she thought in irritation. *I mustn't let him get under my skin, however cute.*

'It's just my job,' he said.

'And me just a little ol' country girl an' all,' she replied, fluttering her eyelashes and pouting her lips suggestively to show just how unimpressed she was. But he didn't rise to it; he just smiled and found it funny. He was sly, *just where was he coming from?* He seemed far too pliable and nice and…!

'You're funny!' he replied, but laughed unnervingly. He stared at her while she gathered her things. She had a strong face, one of those where the skin is pulled tightly over the jawline and thinly over the brow; strong but somehow fragile, like porcelain. He loved the freckles too, and the ginger highlights in her hair.

They paid and left the café and walked down to the shingle beach. The dark rain cloud had blown away. Down the coast you could see right past Brighton pier as far as the industrial cranes at Shoreham. It wasn't the Riviera, but it had grit and soul. He climbed up on to a pile of scrap-metal and signalled for her to follow. The temptation to hold his hand when he offered was great, but she resisted and clambered up awkwardly herself. She was still annoyed with his wandering eyes and there was no sense in encouraging unintended consequences. She was still very conscious of the social gap between them and he seemed to her to be rather inexperienced with women. It wasn't hard for her to play hard to get, as a lot of men already knew.

'I'm the king of the world,' he said, spreading out his arms.

'You're a prize dork,' she replied, pulling him down, but she couldn't help laughing to herself. Now she'd touched him voluntarily, and he knew it. That was a stupid mistake. She knew she'd opened the door.

As they climbed down, he either inadvertently or deliberately attempted to wrap his arms around her waist, but she was too quick. Okay so he wasn't gay. She dodged him and jumped off the platform. *But he'll have to be faster than that,* she thought.

'Come on then!' she said and ran off back towards the car park by the White Horse. She was enjoying this. He began to chase after her but then thought better of it. Even he knew she was playing him. He sauntered slowly off the shingle, ambled straight past her, but then turned and grabbed her waist again. She screamed as he tickled her, trying to kick him away, but then smiled and looked at him earnestly. Another time and she might have even given him a hug at that point. *Come on girl, you're a dyed-in-the-wool socialist,* she thought, *more willpower needed with this son of privilege immediately.*

'Come on you idiot, I've got to be getting back,' she said. She hated to admit she was now quite enjoying his company, but she also had a ton of work to do later. *God what an unexpected outcome this had been?*

It was getting blustery. Rather than walk back over Beacon Hill, she suggested they head along the wind-protected coast path towards Ovingdean Gap. They talked about this and that, dodging walkers and cyclists and yet more dogs, divebombed by angry herring gulls. She noticed how he'd gained confidence all of a sudden and played the fool continuously; jumping on and off the sea wall, throwing skimmers into the sea, laughing and cracking jokes. She genuinely hadn't met anyone as easy to get along with for a while. His innocent enthusiasm was infectious. She loved hearing him talk about his work. Above them, layered cliffs of flint and chalk nodules formed an undulating protective curtain against the wind; below them, vanilla waves beat threateningly against the Undercliff. The air was cool and breathless and rotten. *This is kind of fun,* she thought. She looked at his reddish curly hair blowing in the wind as he walked. He did have cute eyes and a great sense of humour, even if his body was a bit out of shape, although maybe not totally beyond redemption. *Damn,* she thought, *get a grip on yourself, Ellie.*

When they reached the Gap, they picked their way carefully through the stranded shelves of shingle washed up on to the path by a recent storm. A family had brought fish and chips down to the beach. She envied their easy joviality and felt that ovarian stirring in her belly again. Next to the remains of the old pier she pointed out traces of Magnus Volk's Daddy Long Legs railway, the *'Sea Voyage on Wheels'*, whose rails had once run along under the surging water. A December storm had done it near fatal damage, finally closing down in 1901.

'That's cool,' he said, looking at the blurb on the information board. 'I'd have loved to see that in operation.' She thought she would have done as well. *Where is this going?* she wondered.

They climbed the peeling green-painted staircase back up to the coast road, near the blind veterans' home. At the top of the steps Harry stopped and asked if he could take a selfie of them against the sea. Contrary to her normal rules of engagement she reluctantly agreed.

'As long as you don't post it on Facebook later,' she said. He shrugged innocently, but she knew he certainly would and if she accepted his friend request he'd probably try to tag her too. But she was okay with that: her settings meant she could decide later if she wanted to repost it, which she definitely wouldn't.

The wind was getting quite strong, blowing the loose curls of her razored hair self-consciously in seductive ribbons across her face. She tried to brush them away but one got stuck in her mouth. Harry had already decided he really, really liked her. He liked the streaks of colour in her hair, he liked her sparky personality and he liked the tiny group of moles by the side of her upper lip. The more they talked the stronger the conviction had become. Normally with girls he was painfully shy, but with Ellie, her initial antipathy had spurred him on. But he knew before they got to the village he needed to make a move. He still had no idea if she'd be open to that; his limited inexperience with women always made him reticent of rejection. But she'd touched him, hadn't she, and not just by accident?

Tentatively, he reached towards her and lifted the disobedient curls back over her ears. She felt kind of excited by his proximity, looked at him, but didn't flinch. He in turn tried to resist the temptation to brush his wrist against her lips. Her eyes were wide open and gorgeous, glassy pools of glassy blue. *Jane Birkin eyes,* he thought. His were shining in the sunlight too, *like penetrating deep ochre spheres,* she thought. To tell the truth, Orlando Bloom was in her mind. They were only fifteen minutes from the Hall. Was the next move his or hers? He wasn't sure he dared. She wasn't sure if she wanted to encourage him. *No it was much too quick.* She felt her phone buzz in her pocket and fished it out, interrupting the moment. It was a message from Sal asking how they were getting on. She typed in three confused faces and then noticed it was already nearly three o'clock.

'God, is that the time. Sorry, Harry, time's up, I need to get back. I've got a ton of work to do tonight.'

'Had we but world enough, and time,' he ventured out of the blue. He'd memorised that one a long time ago but it was the first time he'd used old Andrew Marvell in anger; it was a sure thing, wasn't it? He watched nervously for her reaction.

God, she thought, *is this guy for real?* She had to be impressed that he even knew the line. She crinkled her nose at him, trying to think of a suitably acerbic response, but then realised he was intent on finishing the couplet with its lesser known sequel. She let him continue as he fumbled over the words.

'We would sit down and ...think which way to walk and ... pass our long love's day,' he recited.

'A bloody poet?' she exclaimed. 'Where did you steal that from, the cutting room floor?' He was relieved at least that she hadn't been more wounding.

'It's Jacobean,' he added.

'Um, Elizabethan I think.'

'Well close enough. Anyway, my Henry James's script's set in a Jacobean manor. The novel's called *The Spoils of Poynton*. That's why I thought of Ovingdean Hall.

'The spoils of what…? Never heard of it, but anyway you're a century too late. The Hall was built in the 1790s. I told you that already.'

'Yeah, but I figured we could always do a make-over job. Anyway, where am I going to find somewhere Jacobean that hasn't been used a hundred times before?' he added.

They were just passing the first neat flint-built Victorian cottages of the hamlet. She'd had her eyes on one of those for a while. For a second, a vision of her and Harry and kids running around the garden in the sun infested her mind. She put it aside straight away. Another hundred yards or so and they'd be back at the Hall and his time really would be up. He'd either have to find a reason to extend their outing or persuade her to see him again. Fortunately, she provided a temporary solution. His question had intrigued her. A Jacobean setting; she had just the thing.

'Well if you're looking for Jacobean, what about Old Place in Lindfield?' she blurted out. 'It used to belong to Charles Kempe. I'm doing some work there at the moment for the woman who owns the place.' Immediately she said it, she wondered why she had. Now there'd be no escaping a second meeting.

'I've never heard of him.'

'Yes you have, the Victorian stained-glass guy I told you about this morning.'

'Oh yeah, sorry. Okay, but Victorian's even worse?'

'No stupid, his house was Jacobean; at least the oldest part. I told you Kempe was born in the Hall. Mind you, now he's over there mouldering in the churchyard with the rest of his family.'

Harry's eyes lit up. Was that a gimme? Okay, it was another church and he wasn't that religious, but had she just given him exactly the excuse he needed? They continued on down the zigzag lane towards the flint building. He felt the first sweet spots of rain from the storm that had threatened all afternoon. Instead of continuing on to the Hall, he suggested they take shelter inside the church. Ellie considered this for a second. Although they were now getting very wet, it was also getting late. However, she reckoned she probably did owe him a short detour. Anyhow, she loved the interior of the church and it wouldn't take long. Ten minutes should be enough, hopefully that would allow time for the rain to blow over and her own mind to clear of her confused emotions. They turned up past the old rectory and rushed through the lychgate into the neat churchyard.

The burial ground was sheltered snuggly from the wind and rain, lying between the flint-built church and the eastern slope of the Downs. They squeezed through the tombstones past a great yew tree to the porch situated on the south side of the church. Now out of the main force of the rain, she pointed out Kempe's name on the family grave opposite. There was nobody else around to disturb them. Teasingly, but almost without thinking, she laid her hand on his arm while she asked the next question, watching his reaction closely. He blushed pleasingly. She felt the thrill of her feminine power within her. She had no idea however why she'd done that.

'Let's go in, it's quite a gem inside,' she said. He didn't

respond, seemingly unsure what to do about her hand, so she let it drop. It'd been enough to test his reaction. As they passed into the quiet conspiracy of the flint-walled building, she could hear the anxious squawking of watchful crows above the path. If she'd listened closer she might have heard the accelerated beating of his heart.

'A murder,' she shouted exuberantly.

'A what?' he replied shocked. 'Where?'

'No stupid, that's what they call a collection of crows.'

'Got it!' he replied awkwardly and laughed. She tugged his arm again and dragged him into the main body of the church. They stood in the middle of the small but brightly coloured nave.

'This is a memorial to his father, Nathaniel Kemp,' she said, pointing to a stone bust and inscription above the entrance. 'And these are the memorials to the Eamers, his mother's family.' Harry stared at the inscriptions.

'I thought his name was spelled Kempe, with an 'e' like on that grave?' asked Harry.

'Yeah, but the family name was just Kemp without an 'e'. He added the 'e' to make it sound medieval. A bit pretentious really. Despite his privileged start, being the seventh child wasn't always an easy ride. But there were lots of Kemps; it's an old Sussex family that came good with new money. Coal mostly, like many of the nouveaux riches, they got wealthy by blackening and blighting the countryside. His cousin, Thomas Read Kemp, built Kemptown, where your amazing pad is located apparently.'

'You've heard about that,' he said, reddening. 'Well, I'll gladly show you around,' he added hopefully.

Dream on, she thought, although she could definitely be open to persuasion. She could give her girlfriend Sal a run for her money on ownership rights over the residents of that fabled pad.

They looked up at the amazing painted ceiling and she showed him several windows of Kempe glass, inset in each corner with his trademark 'Wheatsheaf' symbol.

'He did these windows quite early in his career,' she said. 'Before he was well known; a memorial to his father. Over there's some later glass his firm installed as a memorial after his own funeral.'

'You seem to know a lot about him?'

'Yes, well coming from Lindfield originally he's always kind of fascinated me. Don't think I'm normally into rotten-at-the core Victorian capitalists, but he was different, a creative aesthete and self-made man. Not that there's that much to know about him. He was a bit of a dark horse really, even though he was probably the most successful of all the late-Victorian church decorators. I'm thinking I might write a book about him with the material we've found after I've finished this project.'

'Really, you should go on *Mastermind*.'

'Listen and learn,' she replied.

'So did he know the Burne-Joneses then, if they lived in the next village?'

She was genuinely fazed by that question, as she actually didn't know the answer. It was sensible enough; it's just it had never occurred to her before.

'I don't know. He didn't really get on with the Pre-Raphaelites,' she said, 'but it's a great question. Although he wasn't living in Ovingdean, he certainly maintained the local connection. Now that you ask, I think he and Georgie would have gotten on really well. Now you're going to make me look that up, aren't you?' she joked.

'Maybe they were even secret lovers! You know moonlit rendezvous at the Old Windmill!'

'A bit far-fetched, although it's said she had her

moments. Her husband Ned was the philanderer, but there was some sort of thing going on between her and William Morris at one stage. You know, one of the oddest things about Kempe was that he actually never married, despite his fame and fortune. They say he had a terrible stammer and was shy with women,' she added, staring at him. He looked intrigued. 'But I'm not sure I believe that; he had lots of admirers.'

'Interesting,' he said. He thought he might have guessed her drift. 'You mean he was gay?'

'Not at all. At least I don't think so. There was supposedly one woman he liked and tried to propose to. Unfortunately the story goes she misunderstood his declaration of love, finishing his sentence for him with another meaning completely! He never had the nerve to try to ask her again. Sad isn't it? I've always wondered who she was. She must have been a bit of a dragon not to let him get a word in edgeways like that!'

'I think I know the type though!' he replied ironically. She frowned, and then stared at him inquisitively. She could tell something was about to happen; it had been approaching them slowly all afternoon like that oncoming storm. What would she do if he tried to kiss her? She wasn't sure if that was what she wanted, but it might not be unpleasant either.

Okay, so things are moving on, he thought. *What next? Was she dropping hints?* He knew he needed to do something. He swallowed hard; his throat was dry. Suddenly he felt more nervous than he'd been in a long time. He knew what he wanted to do but here, in a church? Did he dare? It was totally quiet; you could hear a pin drop. He'd just caught something sweet in the air. Was it her perfume or incense? She was looking up at the colours streaming through the glass on to the whitewashed walls, almost like she was waiting for him. In that light, she was so pretty, the profile of her nose neatly turned up, lashes flittering against her glassy pale-blue eyes, a healthy red blush like a ripe apple on her cheeks. Did he dare? Yes he had to. He wrapped his arms around her and went to kiss her but she turned away at the last second and shook her head.

'Heh, buster, it's a church for heaven's sake!'

'Sorry, I'm not very religious.'

'Well *I am,*' she replied, exaggerating a bit.

God, had he blown it? For a second that seemed like an eternity he looked for a further reaction; any reaction. She stared back at him. He couldn't hold her gaze. He had to dig deep for the next line, one he'd read in one of those top-ten lists that always work with women.

'Well then, I think God did a good thing when he made you,' he said meekly.

Bloody hell! She thought. *What a line?* She relented and smiled at him. It was corny as hell, but she was touched by the sentiment. *Okay, so maybe all was not lost*, he thought; those words just might have let him off the hook. He looked at her an d she looked back at him. He felt a tingle in every limb of his body. She kind of felt the same but didn't want to admit it. She made herself think of Ryan and then looked at Harry to compare. She was unable to stifle a giggle. But she didn't need to say a word. The look was enough for him to know there was a connection.

Outside, the rain had stopped and there was a rainbow forming where the sun was shining through a cloud. On their way out of the church he walked alongside her in a trance. He was taken by surprise, therefore, when they turned the corner and came across another person, a dark-cloaked young girl sitting on a bench in the churchyard. As they approached her she smiled and got up and knelt to leave a small hand-picked bunch of heartsease by the side of Kempe's grave. Ellie recognised her immediately as the waitress from Snow's and nudged Harry suggestively. When the girl had gone they snuck down to read the note she'd left on the grave:

'*Love ever living strives,*' she read.

'How beautiful!' he replied.

She almost gave him a peck on the cheek for good behaviour then and there.

On the way back to the Hall, they walked together wordlessly down the pretty lane. The storm was threatening pretty hard with masses of dark cloud and occasional bursts of rain. Harry wondered still if he might have blown it. When they approached the Hall, however, Ellie did suggest that if he wanted she could arrange to show him round the Kempe property in Lindfield. She said she'd have to check with the owner, but the old woman had already moved into a smaller property. Ecstatic with how the afternoon had developed, Harry readily agreed that would be an excellent plan. He tried for the second time to sneak a kiss, this time on the lips, which she diverted on to her cheek. She looked slightly surprised. *Wow that was forward.* Anyone else and she would have slapped them but she felt a little sorry for him. Visions of Ryan in the churchyard were in her mind.

'No Harry. It's kind of complicated?' He was immediately crestfallen and she felt another pang of guilt. She touched him on the arm again to soften the blow a bit.

'But you can't blame me for trying,' he replied, looking into her eyes for a sense of encouragement.

'You're a nice guy,' she said. 'But I can't.' She squeezed his arm again and then held out her hand looking down at his boots. He was confused at first but then understood her meaning. Reluctantly, he handed back his boots to her and she retrieved his wellies. But having done that she just as quickly darted into the doorway and closed the door, mouthing and signalling 'Phone me', before waving goodbye.

He looked on open-mouthed. He was disappointed but at the same time exhilarated as he got back into the car. His 'date' had gone much better than he'd expected: a new potential film location and a second 'appointment'. He could really get into Ellie. And that last scene certainly wasn't an outright rejection. In fact he was feeling mildly encouraged by her last words: *'can't* not *won't'*.

She felt bad about teasing him like that, but at the same time she was feeling a lot more positive about him. As soon as he was gone, Ellie took out her phone and typed in, 'result?'. Now she really would be in for an inquisition. The reply, 'You or me?' came back rather too quickly.

She made herself a mug of tea and when she was sure he was gone went outside to walk home. The light outside was still good, so before heading back, she decided to walk up the lane away from the sea to see if he could find the pond referred to in the farmer Jack Beard's letter. As she walked through the ruts and puddles, trying to identify the landmarks, she passed an old stable block and a modern farm shed and then heard a shout.

A schoolgirl from the posh girl's school over the hill was sitting in running kit by the side of the road weeping. Ellie saw immediately that she'd got her running shoe stuck deep in the mud by the side of the old dew pond. She was trying to pull it out with a long stick but without success. Ellie took the stick from her and waded in with her boots to try it with her longer reach. Soon, it was moving. After she'd dragged it free and returned the shoe to her she asked: 'What's your name?'

'They call me 'Tadpole',' she said shyly.

'That's funny,' said Ellie. 'I've been reading about someone with that nickname too!' She took out a faded letter from her pocket book and read it to the little girl to cheer her up, explaining to her first who it was about.

'That's brilliant Miss,' the little girl said. 'I like the bit at the end about how he liked some of the girls but was too shy to talk to them. I know the feeling!'

'You don't have a boyfriend then?' asked Ellie.

'I wish,' she said, and then laughed. 'Do you miss?'

'I'm not sure,' Ellie replied and laughed with her. Maybe that afternoon that wish had come a whole lot closer to being fulfilled. She was going to sleep on that thought and see what the morning brought. 'Come on Tadpole, we'd better get you back to the school. Come and get cleaned up and I'll give you a lift back if you want.'

I first met that fine fellow, Charlie Kemp or 'Tadpole' as we called him, on the coach from Oxford to Dunchurch. We were both new boys at Rugby and shared a study in the Lower-Fourth. It was 1851, he'd just come up from Twyford, I'd been boarding at Mr Slatter's in Iffley. That old saint, Dr Arnold, 'The Doctor', had been gone a decade by then and Archie Tait (yes, the old Archbishop) had shuffled off to be Dean at Carlisle, so we were left with ghoulish Goulburn as headmaster. He was alright though, but strict. He influenced Charlie greatly with all his Resurrection beliefs and teachings and such.

Although the Doctor's reforms had made the school famous, we still hung on to many of the old traditions. We even had our own version of 'Flashman'; and there was still plenty of 'fagging' going on. Lewis Carroll was there a couple of years before us (Charlie knew his brothers at Twyford). From his writing he wasn't so keen on the school at all: 'I cannot say that any earthly considerations would induce me to go through my three years again.'

Poor old Charlie had quite a monstrous stammer back then; although he seemed to weather it better than most. Bill Darwin, for instance, (the scientist's son) was bullied mercilessly, although luckily for him there were no monkey caricatures around at that time, or it would've been a whole lot worse!

The three of us, Charlie, 'Swiper' Hawkins and I, were a sort of band of brothers; young Ishmaelites, getting into all sorts of scrapes: tree-climbing, bird-nesting, fishing for chub and jack in the Avon. Tom Wills was our star football player and captain of cricket. He was a real dodger, blue eyes and wavy hair, full of slimy tricks. He could speak Aboriginal lingo and became a legend when he returned down under. Our housemaster was Evan Evans. He later became Charlie's tutor at Pembroke (where he was Master). Under his influence, Charlie was always a bit inclined to the academic, preferring Virgil and Homer to the scrummage and Hare and Hounds. He got his nickname because with his great black head and thin legs, bearing a passing resemblance to a 'Tadpole' just like the boy in Tom Brown's Schooldays.

This is a quote from that fine novel: 'However they struggle after him, sobbing and plunging along, Tom and East pretty close, and Tadpole, whose big head begins to pull him down, some thirty yards behind. Now comes a brook, with stiff clay banks, from which they can hardly drag their legs, and they hear faint cries for help from the wretched Tadpole, who has fairly stuck fast. He had lost a shoe in the brook and been groping for it up to his elbows in the stiff wet clay, and a more miserable creature in the shape of boy seldom has been seen.'

Of course, there was still plenty of foul talk and bullying. I don't remember if Charlie got it particularly bad. Most of the fagging was menial rather than venial. But his stammer was a problem especially when it came to girls. Despite his handsome looks, it didn't matter much whether they were plain or pretty, his stammer meant he was never that confident with them (although he had a mighty fine imagination all the same!).

Of course, we had a steady supply of female relatives to admire. I remember he was quite enamoured of one of our friend's sisters. He confessed to me how she'd left him in a state of utter confusion with her 'pretty curtseys, ribands and divine countenances'. He thought he'd never seen anything so beautiful. I leave you all to guess how he slept that night, and what he dreamt of!

Then there were the delights of the town girls too. After the match, we would duck out of those celestial school fields with their noble elms and seek the earthier delights of old Sally Horrowell's tuck-shop. Her daughters were the most good natured and enduring of women, but a challenge too far for Charlie's love-tied tongue. I spent many hours with him, wallowing hot and ruddy in those wondrous kitchens in the chimney corner seats warming ourselves round the great fires. We'd partake of ginger beer and plates of 'murphies', smoking roast potatoes and sausages whilst less than discreetly ogling Sally's daughters.

'Put me down twopenn'orth, Sally…threepenn'orth between me and Kemp.'

Frederick Parker Morrell,
University Coroner,
Black Hall, Oxford

CHAPTER FOUR

MONDAY'S CHILD

One bonfire night a boy brought up two new faggots. Old Two-at-a-time looked at 'em and sed 'Bring 'em along, me boys, two at a time, two at a time, never mind where they cum from.'

Aylwin Guilmant, *Victorian and Edwardian Sussex*

The Tyger Pub, Lindfield, Sussex, Monday evening, May 25th

'Ryan just stop it, stop fooling around won't you?'

'Come on Mone,' he replied, rubbing his head amorously into her neck.

'No I'm too busy; I'm expecting a guest to arrive. I've got to get his room sorted.'

'Just a few minutes, then I'll be out of your hair,' he said somewhat desperately.

'Yeah that's about it with you, isn't it? No wonder they call you 'Flash' in the village, you oaf. And when're you going to get rid of all this stuff,' she said, pushing him away and kicking over a pile of cigarette cartons stacked up in the storeroom. 'You promised these fags'd be out of here by now. I'll lose my licence if the coppers find this gear.'

'I promise, just a couple of days more. Come on Mone, just let me…' He fumbled with the zip of her top, but there was the sound of a bell. Someone was at the reception desk.

'That must be him,' she said, but he continued to undo

her clothing and kiss her neck. 'No Ryan, leave off. And I want all this stuff out of here tonight, do you hear? Not a minute later. You can dump it in the river for all I care; I can't have it here. And when are you going to get things sorted out with your gran?' she added angrily. He was hard to resist when he was in that mood, but she had work to do. With that, she left him to stew and crossed quickly over to the pub where Harry was standing by the reception counter.

'Mr Jamieson?'

'Indeed, that's me,' Harry replied, marvelling at the fearsome creature that stood before him: tall, long-limbed, close-cropped bleached hair with eyes like blue beads. She was strangely festooned with tattoos and piercings and wore a very low cut black top and a pair of tight-fitting leather trousers. She thought he looked quite tasty, too.

The day following Harry's visit to Ovingdean was spring bank holiday. His car was still in the garage for repairs, so Harry had taken his bike with him on the train to Haywards Heath that afternoon, cycling the short distance from the station to the handsome village of Lindfield. He didn't know it well, but he'd ridden through it once before on the London-to-Brighton. He'd thought at the time it was a lovely place and would make a fine film set. It was strange how things worked out like that. It seemed to have it all: the requisite pretty church, a long sloping high street lined with period houses, a large village duck pond and a cricket pitch on the common. Rather neat and picture perfect and certainly very aspirational, quite different from the untidy multi-cultural mélange of his part of Brighton. He suspected neither place was particularly representative of normal Britain.

Haywards Heath station wasn't that welcoming to the casual visitor; the commuter town had sprawled out of the original railway stop that served Lindfield and its sister village Cuckfield. Its station and environs could certainly have done with a lick of paint. In fact it seemed run down and architecturally stuck in the seventies, as tired as the faces of the few commuters travelling that bank holiday.

Ellie had agreed to meet him at Old Place on the Tuesday morning. But he wanted to get the atmosphere of Lindfield first, which is why he'd booked a room in the local pub that evening. It was run by a certain Monica Malling. From first impressions, she seemed like quite a character in her own right, certainly worth mining for information.

Although he was the only guest, the restaurant was full so he had a quick, rather warmed-up bar meal and then strolled round the village. Being a bank holiday, there were still quite a few people wandering about. He got chatting to a couple of cyclists drinking outside one of the other pubs and learnt they had taken part in a 'fun run' earlier in the day; it sounded like it'd been more like a 'mud run' after a sharp shower of rain. There was a cricket match still in progress on the common. There were also a few people milling around the village hall where there was some sort of charity show going on that evening. He walked past all of these attractions and took the path around the Common towards the kids' playground. There he watched on with amusement while a couple of lads showed off their skate-boarding stunts to a crowd of giggling girls. He remembered the innocence of those days fondly. The place seemed to have some soul at least, even if it was a rather conservative, white middle-class sort of soul.

Harry decided to work off his dinner by jogging a few circuits of the common – out past the cricket pavilion, behind the tennis courts and back up the Lewes Road. After the morning rain it had been a beautiful afternoon but the evening had suddenly turned overcast and the wind was getting up. However, it was still fine. Despite the tranquillity that oozed from the scenery, he amused himself while he was running with the thought that Lindfield might be one of those places that was superficially calm but had hidden depths, dark secrets that no one talked about; a place where little happens until the crime squad arrive to investigate the latest murder mystery. It certainly had that surreal, superficially sinister feel about it in the evening light.

Once he'd done his four laps, he headed back up the High Street to find a shower and his bed. It was still light but he fancied an early night. However, when he saw Monica on duty behind the bar he changed his mind and decided to have a drink first to see what she could tell him about Lindfield. He showered and changed and then came back down to the saloon. He ordered a brandy. As there wasn't another soul in the place, they soon got chatting and she soon got to the point.

'So whattaya doing here?' she asked. 'There ain't many outlanders round here this time of year, and you don't look like no tourist or businessman to me?'

'No, well, I'm not really. I scout for film companies; you know locations for shoots and such. I'm working on something for the BBC. A friend recommended I check the village out.'

'Talent-spotting then?' she grinned, raising her eyebrows.

'In a sense! Is there any talent?'

'Oh, there's a fair few as thinks so,' she laughed and pouted her dark heavily glossed lips as if to prove it. 'But them's mostly into amateur stuff. Not pro-potential like me. There was a show tonight at King Edward's Hall, but you missed it I guess. Oh, and there's the church choir and such.

Come to Village Day next Saturday, you'll see all sorts. I'm on for a turn.'

'Really? So you have a talent, Monica?'

'Of course!'

'And?'

She leaned forward across the bar, in a way that intriguingly revealed more than he probably wanted to be aware of.

'I ain't sure as I should tell you just before bedtime,' she said in a rasping voice, tapping her nose and winking. 'You might get inappropriate ideas.'

'Go on, I'll cope.'

'You heard of burlesque?'

'I guess.'

'Well, I do that with a bit of pole-dancing thrown in.'

He laughed; he certainly hadn't expected that. 'And I assume you don't mean May-poles?'

She pulled out her i-Phone to show him some pictures. 'Look, me and the girls work out every Wednesday. It's a right laugh. You should come and give it a whirl! I'm sure the girls'd love to show you their moves,' she winked. 'Maybe try out a few yourself?' He looked at the pictures of the leather and fishnet-clad bodies contorted into impossible positions on the pole. Now he'd seen even more than he wanted to.

'I'm not sure I've quite got the right physique!' he laughed.

'Oh I don't know,' she said, checking him out. 'You could always tone up a bit.'

He blushed again. She was the kind of woman he'd always found it difficult to handle: the earthy direct type, with a blatant sexuality that he didn't know quite how to deal with. He suspected she was actually more than a 'handful', her bite probably worse than her bark. Monica, or Monday's child as the tattoo on her neck declared, was certainly fit as well as fair of face; in fact she was quite athletic judging from the shoulder muscles bulging from under her skimpy top. She was bleached blonde with dark roots, with a fake tan, piercings and come-to-bed-with-me baby blue eyes. But she wasn't perfect: he noticed her skin was quite pock-marked underneath her thickly-applied make-up. But he was sure that wouldn't bother her, as she clearly had more than enough personality to carry it off.

'So tell me, what else goes on in Lindfield?'

'Oh, all sorts.'

'And?'

'Well, we've got five pubs and the club, the footie and the Bonfire Society, of course.'

'What, Guy Fawkes?'

'Oh no, that's kids' stuff, much more pagan than that. Fawkes was Johnny-come-lately hereabouts. It's a big thing. We're a bunch of old firebugs in Sussex! Ain't you seen it on TV?'

'No, but I expect I ought to have done. Okay, so what do you firebugs get up to?'

'Every village does summat different. Here, we all dress up as smugglers.'

'Smugglers *and* arsonists? Wow you do have a few dark secrets.' She was beginning to confirm his previous speculation about this rather too-perfect village. 'I'd no idea this part of Sussex was so lawless. But we're a bit far from the sea, aren't we?'

'Oh no, it's historical. The smugglers used to come right up the river from Lewes; tea and gin and baccy and all sorts. Right up to Midwyn Bridge. There's even a smuggler's tunnel from the cellars here up to the church.'

'Real Enid Blyton stuff, then!'

'Oh worse than that, they say the tomb by the church porch was the exit. That's why it ain't got no inscription on it. They say as it was used to hide spirits from the Revenue. No doubt with a little present to the parson too. There was a Toll House further down the High Street, you know.'

'Yes, I saw the building earlier.'

'One of the last in the country,' she said proudly. 'But the villagers got fed up paying their sixpence and threw the gates on the bonfire outside the White Lion!' she laughed. 'It were never replaced!'

He laughed at the thought of that and then had an idea.

'A tunnel, really, so can you still get in?'

'No it's all blocked up, has been for years. Mind you I could take you downstairs for a looksee,' she winked.

He wasn't sure about exploring the pub's darkened cellars late at night with this alarming creature. He might not escape lightly, or even at all.

'Maybe another time. I think I can imagine it well enough for now,' he laughed. She grinned and winked, licking her lips seductively.

'Well don't leave it too long…'

He changed the subject.

'So how long've you lived in Lindfield.'

'Me? Born and bred.'

'Okay, then do you mind if I ask you about a house called Old Place,' he asked her. She looked surprised by his question.

'Don't get me started.'

'How do you mean?'

'My boyfriend's gran lived there till recent, like.'

'Mrs Ross you mean?'

'That's 'er. Right old witch.'

'Well, I've an appointment to visit it tomorrow with a lady called Ellie Swift. See about filming there.'

'Oh really?' she said curiously. 'So you know Ellie Swift, then. You two an item or summat?'

'Just friends,' he replied unconvincingly. 'We met at the Brighton Festival last weekend. She's a friend of a friend. Seems like a nice girl.'

'Yeah, she's a sharp one alright.'

'She certainly is,' he replied blushing, misunderstanding her meaning. For Monica that reddening of his cheek was enough confirmation of what she'd already suspected. *He'd known her for less than a week?* He must be a quick mover! That relationship could be useful though, as far as keeping Ryan in check was concerned that was.

'Well, it might be none of my business mind, but you'd better watch out with that one, she's pretty crafty,' she laughed.

'How d'ya mean?' He hadn't thought of Ellie as crafty in any way, but he was intrigued by the view Monica was now advancing.

'Caught her snogging my boy at her sister's wedding a couple of months back. She thinks I don't know but I made sure that wouldn't happen again. Weren't her fault though, stupid cow, I gave Ryan a right talking-to.'

So that's it, he thought. But it didn't seem in character at all. *So who is this lover-boy?* he wondered.

'Ryan?' he asked.

'Yep, my so-called boyfriend. You'll probably see him around. He usually stops round after closing. Then hangs around like a bad smell.' He could see the pent-up disappointment on her face. Obviously her 'boyfriend' was not quite the partner she thought she deserved. But he was now wondering if he was also part of the 'it's kind of complicated' line that Ellie had given him just before they parted on Sunday.

'So does he live in the old house?'

'Fat chance! His gran won't let him near it. *He can wait till I'm in my grave,*' she says.

'What does he do then?'

'Building work, landscape gardening, you know this and that, got a workshop in the grounds. Now she's moved out, by rights it should be his, according to her grandfather's will. But the situation's complicated, legal stuff an' all, arguing who owns the property by rights now it's vacant. Shameful really, arguing within a family. I told him he needs to get it sorted. He's not getting me to the altar till he gets *the spoils* back.'

'The spoils?'

'All the best furniture and ornaments and stuff.'

'They've gone?'

'Well, the best stuff 'as. She's taken it with 'er.'

'I see. Does Ryan plan to move in later then?'

'Not really, he wants the place sold for cash, though I could just fancy living there for a while. Lady Muck I'd be, Queen Bee. Get rid of all that old furniture and put some decent designer stuff in, you knows like on the telly. Fix a conservatory on the back, some decent wallpaper, a proper kitchen, a home-cinema room…'

'I get the picture! But I thought you said you wanted the old furniture back?'

'Principle, see.'

'Okay, but then nobody's living there now?'

'Well, that Ellie of yours is temporarily. I reckon as she and Serena are in cahoots. They want to stop Ryan getting his hands on the place. That's thieving in my book. Now if I were him…'

'Gosh,' he replied, looking at his watch. He hadn't realised there was such a backstory. This was all quite worrying information but also incredibly interesting. He wondered why Ellie hadn't hinted at any of this. It was also dawning on him that there were more than a few parallels to the novel he was working on for the BBC.

'Well look, I'm sorry to bail on you Monica, but I'm tired and I'm going to have to get to bed. It was great chatting, but I'm shattered. I think I'll turn in.'

'Okay, well breakfast's any time after seven, in the side room over there. Full English okay?'

'Perfect.'

'Can't tempt you with a night cap?' she asked softly.

'No, I think I've had enough.'

'Sure? I can bring you up a hot toddy if you'd like. Tuck you in an' all if you want!' she laughed. *God she's a real minx*, he thought. Now that she'd come out from behind the bar he'd also been unable to avoid noticing how tightly her leather trousers hugged her hips, and the band of taut tanned skin between them and her cropped top.

'It's a really kind offer, but no,' he laughed, swallowing before he choked on the last of his drink.

'All part of the service. Anyway serious-like, I'm just along the corridor if you need anything. Room five. Anything at all, just knock. I'm here all night. All on my lonesome…'

Is she serious? he wondered. In any case, at that moment a stocky muscle-bound guy with golden curls, an earring and a tanned slightly boyish face had just walked in. He was dragging a greyhound on a lead. Harry had already guessed he must be her unreliable boyfriend, Ryan. It was hard to see someone like Ellie letting this character make any sort of pass at her, though. He seemed like a somewhat rough piece of work. He made his final excuses and started up the stairs but noticed how her chirpy voice changed in tone as she addressed the newcomer.

'Where you been Ryan? I was looking for you earlier? I tried your mobile, no answer as usual.'

'That's cos I was clearing out the store, like you said. Who's that?' he asked, nodding his head towards Harry who was disappearing from view. Harry's interest had been piqued and he paused at the top of the landing so that he could listen in on the rest of their colourful conversation.

'That's Mr Jamieson, like I told you. He works for the BBC. A gent and a paying guest for once. You been drinking?' she replied, smelling his breath. 'Lord, you've been down that club again, haven't you? I don't know why I'm wasting my time here if you and your mates bunk off down the club for your boozing.'

'Well, angel, it's a damn sight cheaper than this place now you've jacked the prices up.'

'Don't angel me; they don't have my overheads.'

'Or charms,' he replied, stroking her cheek. He looked up the stairs to check the guest was gone. But Harry was still there: he'd secreted himself behind a chair at the corner of the landing.

'Come on then, give us a kiss,' he said and squeezed her backside. She slapped him playfully but he just continued and ran his hand up over her top. She pushed him away.

'No. I'm not in the mood, Ryan. I told you you've got to get things sorted with that old witch first,' she said, but involuntarily also looked in the direction of the stairs.

'Okay, I get it. You've already got your claws into fancy boy up there, then?'

'Get lost you dork! Of course not. Mind you, don't tempt me, he's lush. And he's got class too, something you'll never learn,' she replied indignantly.

Despite appearances and her better judgement, Monica really did have a thing for Ryan; but he could be a right pain in the neck when he was drunk, which was pretty well every night. She wasn't asking for much; she didn't need much, just someone attentive to take care of her. It didn't help that he was so cute and knew it. Of course the prospect of his inheritance helped. There were plenty in the village who thought he was still a potential catch: rough but good-looking, handsome in a chiselled way, and at some stage coming into decent money. But she'd been working on him for too long to give up that easily.

She'd known him vaguely at school but had met him again down the gym after her dance class one day. After she'd worked out his normal routine, she'd be there without fail at the end of his weights session in her skimpiest leotard, looking for help with the equipment. She was good and he hadn't resisted her allures for long. Since then, though, she'd had to fight off more than one competitor. In fact she'd had to sort out the last couple good and proper. They wouldn't be coming back for more anytime soon. A ducking in the pond for one and she'd certainly swung it all right with the last one. She fingered the diamond on her middle finger that her Nan had left her. She even had the ring ready, see. They'd been careful too, taken precautions. No worries there. But she'd never as yet had a hint of any sort of real commitment from him, just a load of broken promises. Of course, it didn't help that that witch, Serena Ross, was dead against her marrying her precious grandson, too.

The week before, Ryan had promised her 'on his mother's grave' that Serena would soon just have to do what he said. Under the terms of Serena's grandfather's will, the house was his as the next in line as soon as she was no longer living there. That sounded cut and dried to her, but he'd let the lawyers get involved and now who knew what would happen. So she could see that for now most of his words were just empty promises. At times she wondered if she was just wasting her time with him, especially after his various flirtations. She knew if Serena had her way, she'd soon have him hitched up with someone else in the village. Like Ellie Swift and her fancy ways. Yes, if Serena had her way, Ryan would have to get shot of her. But she intended to show that bitch. She'd up the ante. She was going to ride the crisis, digging in for a long fight, and she had plenty of assets at her disposal to ensure victory.

In fact, since Ryan's last dalliance, she'd hardened her line even more, tried to force things along, apply pressure. But he was weak like that. He didn't want to give her up, but he wouldn't face up to his gran either. Life was too easy for him; she was a source of booze and benefits. Maybe she was too obliging, you know, with the benefits (and the booze). She knew he was just a little boy with the usual cravings. And she was suspicious of Ellie, especially now she was working for his gran. It seemed like she was trying to muscle in on the action again, and she didn't trust her one bit, or her sweetie-pie do-good meddling little sister, Maggie. She'd told Ryan to blank Ellie of course, after she caught him out and confronted him, but somehow she'd guessed that he hadn't. Such a shame as well; she used to like Ellie till she'd seen them at that wedding. They were the dangerous kind, those that couldn't give a man up. She couldn't let that happen again, could she? She was keeping a close eye on her. She had a plan and Harry Jamieson could prove to be a godsend. She was intrigued by what might be going on between him and Ellie and could see how she might use that knowledge. But first she needed to get something on him that would stick.

No she was definitely not giving up on Ryan. Despite the fact that he wasn't the smartest lad in the village, he did have several redeeming qualities. He was mostly well intentioned, if stupid. Blue eyes, golden hair and a giant radiant smile that showed off his gold-capped gleaming teeth. When they'd first dated, he was really into her, a real lover boy. To spite Serena, they'd often sneak into the grounds of Old Place with her Goth friends and 'muck about' on the mound in the gardens. Drunken pranks and water fights, naked dancing in the moonlight; all pagan and ritualistic. Most of those friends had got married or moved away in the last year, but she was left behind and still no engagement. Lately she caught him out looking elsewhere again. And then there were his little contraband schemes... All in all, it had begun to drive her a little crazy, but she kept taking the pills for that too...

CHAPTER FIVE

OLD PLACE

*And you, Old Place, are still as young.
And warm in welcome, as of yore*

T. Herbert Warren, *To 'Old Place' Lindfield*

Lindfield, Tuesday, May 26th

Harry woke next morning around seven to the sound of cats fighting in the pub garden. He'd been dreaming about meeting up with Ellie and felt happy and somewhat stirred by those thoughts. But as always with such dreams, it'd been interrupted at the most important moment. He drew the curtains and looked out on to a dew-stained lawn bounded by two mighty Scotch pines. It was a still blue morning with wispy cotton clouds floating across the sky, a peaceful scene that augured well for an important day. He was excited about what that day would bring.

Rubbing his eyes, he inspected the surroundings more closely. Surrounding the pub grounds was a jumble of old cottages and gardens. Straining, he could just see across to the church and the dovecotes of Old Place. There were squirrels running playfully between the trees. On the roof of one of the pub outbuildings, he watched a robin with an insect in its mouth pause before darting into the eaves, and then a few seconds later heard the buzz of squabbling chicks.

It was all somewhat different from his normal morning view over the brisk confidence of urban Brighton. Down below, a pair of magpies was scrapping over some half-eaten rodent on the grass, probably abandoned by the cats. He realised all of a sudden that he too was hungry. The tempting aroma of frying bacon and sausage drifting from downstairs was aggravating the hole in his stomach. He sat back down heavily on the bed and began to gather his clothes from where he'd discarded them in a heap the night before.

The Tyger was one of the oldest buildings in the village, and therefore full of intriguing sounds and echoes. He'd certainly had a disturbed night. After saying goodnight to Monica, he'd phoned Ellie around ten-thirty to confirm their arrangement for the morning. He'd intended to pump her for the low-down on what was going on between Monica, Serena and Ryan. She'd seemed cheerful enough and had apparently used her day productively to get her chores done and prepare for the final stages of the house inventory. They chatted cheerfully for a few minutes until she asked him slyly if he'd found out anything that linked Kempe with Georgie Burne-Jones yet. He said no, but was somewhat irritated by her comment that 'maybe you need to work harder on your research then'. He changed the subject: 'Was he wasting his time with the Ross's,' he'd asked in a roundabout way?

She'd been a little coyer about that. When Harry pressed her she seemed torn and he noticed her tone had turned distinctly cooler. She said she was sure that Serena would be good with the filming and that Ryan would be fine as well if Harry spoke with him later in the week. But she was almost grudging when he asked her about Monica; she just said she'd had a troubled childhood but seemed better adjusted recently. He could hear the disdain in her voice. It didn't put his mind at rest, but reluctantly he'd let it go at that and said he was looking forward to seeing her again. She repeated that she'd enjoyed their walk and wished him a good night, amiably enough, but he continued turning over their conversation in his mind for a while, and of course got his search engine going again to look up Kempe and Burne-Jones. He drew a blank, surely there must be something?

He must have fallen asleep around eleven but had awoken at the creak of the landing floorboards an hour later. He assumed it was Monica passing his door on the way to her room. He was relieved there was no knock on his door. After that, he'd been unable to get back to sleep again. He'd still found nothing on any Pre-Raphaelite link apart from the fact that Kempe, Morris and Burne-Jones had worked on a number of projects at the same time. He read his notes for a while, teased by the hooting of the owls outside, researching as much as he could on his iPad about Old Place instead. It was certainly a good prospect for the location he needed. He was getting more and more excited about a positive outcome from his pending visit and, of course, the prospect of seeing Ellie again, but was also increasingly worried that the family were going to prove a problem. But making a good second impression on Ellie was his main concern.

At some stage he must have drifted off to sleep a second time, because during the early hours he awoke, iPad in hand, imagining he'd heard more noises on the landing and then fifteen minutes later heavy footsteps on the stairs? He sat listening in silence, half-expecting a tap on his door. But none had come. He concluded that Monica's boyfriend had probably sneaked up to her room to satisfy his nocturnal urges before going home. Whatever the truth, she was apparently up bright and early. He could hear her distinctive Sussex twang singing downstairs, chanting 'Love of My Life' alongside the indie artist on the radio. She sounded breezy enough.

Her comments about his (lack of) fitness the previous evening had hit a nerve. Maybe he should try to tone up a bit. He did some core exercises on the floor using the bed as an anchor and shadow-boxed the bathroom mirror, then showered, shaved and dressed in his smartest clothes. He wanted to look professional for Ellie. His plan was to do a recce of the house, ask her down to the village for lunch and then persuade her to explore the environs together during the afternoon. If the location was good for filming, he'd arrange to see Mrs Ross during the week, as he realised he'd need to ask her permission to do a more thorough survey. He didn't pack, having decided he'd stay over at least one more night. Around seven-thirty he went down the stairs to the little side room where Monica had told him she'd be serving breakfast. The cats were still going at it outside. Monica burst out of the noisy kitchen, looking stressed. He soon found out why.

Although he knew he was the only overnight guest, the little breakfast room was full to the brim with pensioners. One of the local old-timer clubs had a regular get-together each Tuesday, and they were happily munching through mountains of sausage, eggs and bacon. Monica looked run off her feet. He nodded to them cheerfully and was greeted like an old friend. They invited him to join them at their table. He looked questioningly at Monica, but she rolled her eyes as if to say: *Well, why not*. So he accepted the invitation readily and soon discovered them to be a mine of information. He quickly found himself on his second plate as he listened eagerly to their village stories, making mental notes on things to follow-up. He was especially taken with the story that Friar Tuck was once a parson in the village; he'd gathered a bandit gang around him that plagued the local countryside in the early fifteenth century. More of Lindfield's dark secrets to add to his growing collection!

Unfortunately, his appointment with Ellie at Old Place was not until ten, so after he'd eaten his fill, he drank another cup of coffee and went out on to the High Street. It was clouding over a bit. He bought papers from the corner shop and wandered down to the bench he'd spotted the night before by the village pond, hoping to read the day's news in peace, while he waited impatiently for ten o'clock to arrive.

The High Street was filling up with morning traffic but he realised it'd be a while before most of the other shops opened. By the time he arrived at the bench, a group of young children were being led, chattering, by their mothers up towards the school for their half-term club. Still, it was a lot more orderly and genteel than the chaotic morning rush in Brighton. He noticed that the barber's shop was about to open up across the road. *I could do with a haircut,* he thought. Maybe he'd call in later. He guessed it'd probably be a good place to gen up on local news as well. Further up the road, the postie was collecting letters from the pillar box outside the post office. There were one or two people walking their dogs. Ducks were squawking on the pond. He was enjoying his little break, soaking in the run-of-the-mill fabric of peaceful mid-Sussex village life.

Harry settled down on the bench to read the papers but soon tired of the grim national and instead opened up the local rag. It was the usual mix of village fêtes, petty crimes, small ads and planning applications. His eye was caught, however, by a spread on the upcoming Village Day in Lindfield. There was certainly a lot planned: a procession, a fun-fare, a tug-of-war. *All in all, Lindfield must certainly be an agreeable place to live,* he thought. He noticed the Britain-in-bloom award sign by the bench and the golden jubilee mosaic. He wondered whether the people there really appreciated how special it was. But then something jarred the peaceful picture he was building; he spotted an odd story on the inside pages about a series of strange, unexplained fires in the neighbourhood. He read it closely. There seemed to be more than a pattern at work. *Monica's fire-raisers again,* he thought. He'd have to ask Ellie what she knew about all that. Further on, there were also a couple of stories about unsolved attacks on local girls and an editorial about the dangers of youngsters being out alone late at night. This all jarred a bit with the rest of the idyllic image. He consulted his iPad to try and work out what was going on, had the village been hit with a crime wave? But there was little more information. Just a series of random events it seemed.

Every ten minutes or so he checked his watch, the time seemed to be moving terribly slowly. So a good fifteen minutes before his ten o'clock appointment, Harry finally folded the paper impatiently and marched slowly back up the High Street. He passed the unusual pollard lime trees that he'd read had originally given the village its name and proceeded towards All Saints Church at the top of the village. It had a pleasing appearance. The old church was built of thick, rather northern-looking ashlar. It was settled contentedly beneath a cedar-clad steeple, surrounded by a raised churchyard contained within thick stone walls. Harry walked through the churchyard along its neat brick path, admiring the motley assembly of worn monuments in the sparkling light. He noticed the tomb with no inscription that Monica had referred to. It was certainly strange, but he couldn't see any way of lifting the heavy slab that covered it! He wondered if she'd just been spinning him a line about that to get a rise out of him.

He was still going to be early so he spent a few minutes reading the notices in the church porch. But it was all pretty mundane and ultimately it wasn't the church he was interested in; he skirted round the south side of the church and crossed a gravel road towards the entrance to a sixteenth-century manor house, the oldest wing of Old Place. As he approached, he caught a glimpse of the full disc of the sun above an impressive avenue of trees that would have formed the old carriageway entrance. It was gated and locked, so he proceeded as previously instructed up a side road, through a gate and then into a large shingle courtyard. There he located the side porch and wooden entrance door, where he checked his watch again, pulled the bell and soon after heard bolts being slid on the other side in anticipation of its opening. He was shaking with anticipation, a jumble of words in his mind of what to say when she appeared.

'You're Harry then?' said a boyish pixie-like face poking through the gap in the door. He looked on surprised but then realised that this must be Ellie's sister Maggie. She removed the chain. He could see immediately the family resemblance in those eyes. *Another Jane Birkin*, he sighed, not too disappointed though.

'Yes,' he replied meekly.

'Well you're a bit early but you'd better come in,' she said somewhat sternly, opening the door wider. She looked at him somewhat inquisitorially but then laughed awkwardly seeing his dismay. 'Sorry, I don't bite, really.' He met her gaze and apologised instinctively before scraping the mud off his shoes. She beckoned and he stepped through the threshold into a small porch. It was hardly the most enthusiastic welcome he'd ever received. Such diffidence must run in the family, he thought. Fussily, she ushered him into an inner hall, then with difficulty shut the heavy oak door loudly behind them. The place was a bit of a mess, the quarry-tiled floor piled high with boxes and stacks of books. He could see an internal corridor that led off to further ground-floor rooms and a rickety back staircase up to the first floor. She didn't ask him to remove his shoes. The place was full of echoes now that a lot of the contents had been boxed up.

'Sorry about the mess,' she said genuinely, and looked him up and down seemingly approvingly. 'Come through to the kitchen. Ellie's upstairs, she'll be down in a few minutes.' There was the glimmer of a smile; she seemed to have warmed to him. He liked that and felt relieved. It wouldn't do to get the sister offside.

They walked down the inner corridor, past more stacked boxes, into a spacious kitchen. This room was in a similar state, with crates stacked with utensils and pans perched on the old-fashioned wooden worktops. Along the walls were a tired gas stove and a range of old appliances. It was all very dated.

'Tea?'

'Yes please,' he replied.

As she put the kettle on and prepared the teapot, he noticed that she seemed somewhat stressed. A phone was buzzing on the counter but she studiously ignored it. He tried to make out what was behind her frowning countenance. He remembered that Ellie had said she was recently married and that was confirmed by the gold band on her finger, but she hardly seemed full of the joy of a newly-wed. She was wearing a worn denim skirt and a large woollen top, both of which were rather unflattering. Her thin henna-dyed black hair was pulled back into a mass of knots, pinned in position on her head. In fact she looked quite tired and drawn and her skin was somewhat blotchy, although she'd made some attempt to apply the briefest swatches of make-up. It was clear that she must have been doing a lot of manual work to prepare the house for the packers. He wondered whether that was entirely willingly. She cleared a stool and indicated that he should sit down.

'Ginger nut?' she asked.

'Thanks,' he replied. She spilled the packet of biscuits unceremoniously into a saucer.

'Sorry, all the Bourbons have gone.'

'No problem. They tend to do that.' She laughed nervously again. She really did have a nice smile beyond that frown though. Okay, that was better. Maybe she was just sizing him up. But she really didn't look well either.

'So you'd like to look around?' she asked, as if he was some official or something.

'Yes, if it's convenient.'

'Ellie told me you're some sort of location guru for the BBC?'

'Yep, that's about it.'

'Well, we haven't told Mrs Ross about this, you understand.' He caught a hint of anxiety in her voice and understood. Okay, so maybe that was what her reticence was about.

'But it's very good of you all the same,' he replied reassuringly. At this she smiled again briefly and began to look at him more closely. The radio was playing some sort of R 'n' B to which he noticed her body was mildly grooving. There was obviously a further question on her mind. He could probably guess what that was.

'So, you two an item?' she asked seemingly innocently at last. It was the same question as Monica's the night before. He hadn't expected anything quite so direct.

'Er, no, we're just friends,' he stuttered.

'Hmm,' she said. She didn't seem completely convinced

by that answer. He wondered whether Ellie had said something different to her, whether her raised brow was a sign that Ellie had given her a firmer answer, positive or negative, as she surely would've been asked the same question. In any case, at that moment Ellie appeared. She too was dressed in work clothes, in her case dungarees with a striped French top. She had a smear of dirt across her face. She still looked great though, and he felt that thrill run through his heart again. But she only acknowledged him briefly and instead picked up her phone that was still buzzing on the counter.

Maggie poured them all tea and then excused herself as quickly as she could. He did catch a wink she gave to Ellie though and a little positive sign with her fingertips. He took a sip of the tea, which was far too strong for his liking, and then put his mug down. Ellie was still responding to a message on her phone. Having finished texting, she turned back towards him and put the phone firmly down on the worktop. He noticed the name on the message list before the light went off: 'Ryan' it said – *Okay, well that's interesting*, he thought.

'If you don't mind, we'll start upstairs,' Ellie said without any further greeting. 'I'm sorry the whole place is a bit of a mess, we're trying to clear out the dross ready for the first pack next Monday,' she continued matter-of-factly. He nodded. He was disappointed she wasn't more welcoming but could tell she too was stressed.

As she moved off, he noticed that she still had a touch of stage poise about her. All her movements seemed primed and deliberate. But her face was pasty, like she hadn't slept well and she'd made up her eyes too thickly so that she looked like a mannequin rather than the natural, fresh-faced girl that had attracted him at the weekend. She seemed smaller too; more delicate without all that riding gear, even childish in her dungarees and the way she had put up her hair. He wondered if the texts meant something had happened with Ryan that morning that had put her in a bad mood.

'Tuesday's child is full of grace,' he whispered to himself. Whether or not Ryan was a rival for her affections, he still really fancied her and wasn't about to give up.

'What did you say?' she asked absently. He smiled but didn't respond and got up off his stool to follow her.

She indicated to him to proceed back into the inner corridor. They emerged into a second, larger, hall, where a fine much more ornate oak staircase led to the upper floors. On the wall hung a rather tarnished painting of an eighteenth-century beauty who stared down at them inquisitively with love-lorn eyes. Above it, an old brass Florentine chandelier swung from the ceiling. It seemed strangely out of place amongst the heavily carved wood. They ascended to the first floor landing and then went directly into a large bedroom at the back of the house.

'This is the Dial room,' she said as if a tour-guide about to start her spiel, 'Mr Kempe's bedroom.' They were standing in the middle of a very large room with a highly ornate stalactite plaster ceiling and marble fireplace. He looked round in awe. It was certainly impressive and seemed to be very much of the right period. They walked over to the shuttered window from which Harry soon got his first elevated glance of the amazing gardens outside. *Well, it certainly has the wow factor*, he thought.

'Amazing,' he said. 'It's got exactly the right period feel. I really like these windows,' he added stroking the leaded glazing, while discretely admiring her features in profile against the leaded glass.

'Yep, but it's all fake,' she laughed as if she'd already scored a small victory. 'This wing was built in the 1890s.

In Kempe's time there were three sundials in this window, hence the name "Dial Room". He used to say he could tell the time at any time of night or day,' she added, trying to keep a straight face.

It took Harry a few moments to get the joke. She rolled her eyes and then he laughed supportively. Okay, so she did still have a sense of humour, then. Up to then he hadn't felt any sense of the chemistry he'd imagined at the end of their meeting on Sunday. In fact, up to that point, like her sister, she'd seemed very standoffish and formal, more like a curator than the free-thinking artist she'd made herself out to be. He'd hoped they were already on a better footing but seemed to be back to square one almost. They passed through an internal door into a second large room with a big bay window facing east. That room also had an ornate ceiling and fireplace and was probably even bigger. He wondered what she was thinking, she still seemed distracted.

'And this is the Oratory,' she said. 'Or prayer room.' He wanted to ask her a question, but at that point, Maggie walked in on them. She had a box full of ornaments but he could tell she was more interested in sussing him out again. She was looking at him quite intently, obviously trying to decide if the relationship with her sister was more than just transactional. Questioning glances passed between both girls again. *Was he under some sort of examination?*

'He was quite religious, wasn't he? Mr Kempe, I mean?' asked Harry, reasserting his presence with the question he'd wanted to ask. He thought that was a good line of enquiry given her comments at the weekend.

'Yes very, this room was designed as a chapel for himself and his staff. Of course it's a guest room now.'

'So is this where he was laid out before his funeral then?' he added mischievously. They both looked at him shocked, as if they'd just heard that story for the first time. Now he had them. The tables were turned.

'I'm not sure about that?' replied Ellie hesitatingly. Maggie looked at her shocked face then grinned and giggled. He'd scored.

'It's just something I read last night,' he said innocently. He'd noticed a suitcase lying on top of the chest of drawers. One of them had obviously slept there the previous night. He assumed it must have been Ellie. Learning that there'd been a cadaver laid out in the room possibly wasn't the most welcome news! He noticed she'd gone even paler, but she soon seemed to recover her poise.

'Whatever, I guess so,' she said, swallowing deeply. The room was cold and she shivered as if a ghost had brushed her. *He had an annoying habit of asking the wrong questions at the wrong time*, she thought. She hadn't slept well that night; she wasn't feeling too good, Ryan was being a pain and now this joker. 'There are enough stiffs associated with this place already, so what's one more, eh Maggs?' she quipped tensely. She wasn't sure she was in the mood for Harry's brand of infectious eagerness this morning.

'Speak for yourself!' Maggie replied, giggling again to herself. She was impressed with this guy. It wasn't often Ellie was lost for words.

He laughed, hoping he'd understood their sibling code; he'd already learnt Ellie had a very dry sense of humour. She shot Maggie a withering glance and then signalled for him to follow her. She was obviously eager to move their 'tour' on.

Without waiting she headed up the stairs to the second floor expecting him to follow. There were a number of smaller bedrooms and bathrooms strung along two corridors at right angles to each other. They were obviously servants' quarters. He noticed the decor was all very faded and old-fashioned, with huge iron radiators running along one side. She was quite dismissive about it, but it might still be useful for filming though, he thought. He asked her and Ellie confirmed that the floor would originally have been for Kempe's staff. Indeed at the end of one of the corridors, she showed him a large servants' parlour. He noticed the padlocked fire escape out on to the roofs and wondered how quickly you could get out in a fire. They returned back to the main staircase, but he could see a further flight of steps up to the left, presumably the back stairs he'd seen by the entrance. The layout was all a bit confusing. And Ellie still wasn't saying much. This wasn't a good sign.

'What's up there?' he asked trying to engage her in conversation again.

'Access to the belvedere; I never go up there,' she said warily. 'It's a bit scary.'

'May I?'

'If you must, do, but please be very careful what you touch.'

He climbed up the steps and unbolted the external door. Light flooded in. Outside there was a small moss-covered platform. He climbed out gingerly. It was damp and slippery. From the elevated position, he had a magnificent view onto the gardens and remaining roofs. The wind was blowing from the north-east and still quite chilly. He shivered and looked over towards a pavilion at the opposite side of the gardens. It had a fine set of gabled dovecotes, the same ones he'd seen from his bedroom at the pub. To the west was the church spire; in the distance he could see across the Weald as far as the South Downs. He breathed in the fresh air. Contentedly, he rested his hands on one of the worn grey rails, which almost immediately gave way under his weight.

Fortunately he managed to grab at a solid flag post before he lost his balance.

'Damn,' he said. Alarmed, he retreated immediately to the centre of the platform. It was a long way down and he felt dizzy.

'I told you to be careful out there,' shouted Ellie anxiously. She'd heard the crack of wood and had climbed quickly up the stairs to peer out, worried, but she hadn't ventured on to the platform. The last thing she needed was him injuring himself out there.

'Please don't do a Nigel Pargetter on me,' she added ironically under her breath.

He took a couple of photographs and then retreated quickly to the safety of the stairs.

'The wood's all rotten,' he said.

'Yep, I did warn you,' she replied sarcastically. He sensed the irritation in her voice.

'I guess you did,' he said, cursing under his breath. This one was always right, wasn't she?

They descended back to the main hall and then proceeded into the dining room, one of three large reception rooms on the ground floor.

'Damn, I think I forgot to bolt that door.'

'Don't worry, I'll fix it later if I remember,' she replied. Her phone was buzzing in her pocket again. Couldn't Ryan leave her alone even for half an hour? She hoped Harry didn't think her too rude but she needed to get away and talk to Ryan in private as soon as she could. They descended back down to the ground floor where she planned to briskly show him the main rooms before making her excuses.

The dining room was an impressive space with a large bay window looking out on to the garden. The room was completely wood-panelled and fitted with bookshelves and ornamental cabinets. There was also a large bust above one of the doors. Harry looked suitably captivated.

'Virgil,' said Ellie and read out the inscription: *'Audaces fortuna iuvat.'*

'Fortune favours the brave,' he replied, showing off his schoolboy Latin. She was impressed. There was no doubt at all he was well educated. In contrast, she doubted if Ryan even knew what Latin was despite his expensive education. She carefully opened up one of ten large and beautifully crafted shallow drawers.

'We think this is where Kempe kept the cartoons for his stained-glass projects,' she said. We found some very interesting letters hidden in here at the weekend. I'll get Maggie to show you them later.

Harry absorbed that information but was elsewhere in his thoughts. He was picturing scenes from the script. He felt at once the room would be just perfect for some of the most dramatic encounters between Mrs Gereth, her young companion Fleda Vetch, her hapless son Owen and his scheming fiancée Mona Brigstock. He could just imagine it. It was certainly a tick in the box and the light wasn't bad either. He was getting more excited by the minute. They passed through into an even larger room with an impressive collection of what he initially supposed was reproduction Jacobean furniture. But he was wrong.

'The library,' she said. 'Wonderful, isn't it? The furniture's all original but it's too big for Mrs Ross's new house.' The room had yet another high ornate ceiling and fireplace, covered with what looked to him like William De Morgan tiles. They walked across the oriental carpets towards a bay window looking out onto the garden. A further side door led into a small garden room, which held a collection of unusual cabinets, this time meant for botanical specimens. Ellie still seemed to be in a hurry. They proceeded quickly through this room into the drawing room, the third and last reception room and to Harry's eyes, the most impressive of them all. The walls were completely covered in beautiful oak-carved Jacobean motifs; it had more heavily plastered ceilings and a large carved stone fireplace. But it was the glass that drew his eye. The leaded panes in the two bay windows at either end of the room, were punctuated by individual roundels of gem-like stained glass. Kempe's work, he felt sure and asked her.

'Yes,' she said. 'Unfortunately, the best glass is at Wightwick Manor now, but these two windows are still pretty amazing. This first represents the story of *The Lay of the Last Minstrel* a poem by Sir Walter Scott.'

'*For love is heaven, and heaven is love,*' he said. Damn, he knew that quote would come in useful someday.

'Wow, well done,' replied Ellie. 'And these windows here are called the *Imago Amoris* or "aspects of love".'

'Lloyd-Webber rip-offs?'

'I hope not!' she chuckled. 'The first represents David and Jonathan. It celebrates the form of love the Greeks referred to as *filia* or friendship; the next is Hero and Leander and represents *eros* or passion; the third depicts Sir Galahad and his mother and represents *storge* or affection; and the last is *agape* or unconditional love and shows the Holy Family: Joseph, Mary, Jesus and his brother John.'

'They're all very beautiful,' he said genuinely. Indeed, the scenes were executed with amazing craftsmanship. He was quite taken aback by the various forms of affection depicted in the narrative of each of the images, each drawn with vivid rich colours and an impressive sense of movement.

'In fact, there's something of the Pre-Raphs about them,' commented Harry, thinking back to their Burne-Jones conversation in Rottingdean.

'Please don't say that.' she replied. 'He'd turn in his grave!' Harry noticed how Ellie's earlier cold and businesslike countenance had melted somewhat. She had a dreamy expression in her eyes as they inspected the glass. She was obviously very fond of these images. She was truly really pretty when she wasn't scowling. He loved the way the copper highlights in her hair were accentuated by the coloured light from the windows.

'By the way, did Maggie already show you that letter I left in the kitchen?'

'No, which letter?'

'The one from Georgie Burne-Jones?'

'She didn't, no.'

'Oh,' she said. 'I just thought with your research and all?'

He could see she was teasing him.

'Sorry, let me get it, then,' she grinned. Now it was her turn to be triumphant. When she returned she was holding a piece of thin vellum inscribed in beautifully crafted and distinctive pen and nib handwriting.

Dear Mr Lisle,

Thank you so much for your letter and kind thoughts. You asked if I had any recollections of Mr Kempe. Well I certainly do but it was quite a long time ago. The first time I met Mr Kempe was nearly fifty years ago in 1857, about the time he went up to Pembroke. He was a very handsome young man, artistically inclined although he'd gone up to study for the ministry. He was a few years older than me. Ned and Topsy had introduced him to me one day while they were painting murals at the Oxford Union and we dined together that evening.

When we were introduced, I remember he immediately

made a very good impression on me – he was both serious and shy; but as I later learned, had an ever-curious manner and an amusing and avuncular humour. I remember him telling me over dinner that his chosen course had been to go into the Church. It was his first love, he said. Indeed his only ambition had been to follow the ministry of Christ. But he'd found that his speech problems were a great impediment, preventing him from easily preaching in public. Fortunately, at Oxford he'd come across a whole series of new influences. An alternative course of action had begun to open up to him. Inspired by Ruskin's 'Seven Lamps', he'd started a detailed study of local ecclesiastical architecture.

'I made up my mind that if I was not permitted [because of my stammer] to minister in the Sanctuary, I would devote my talents to the adornment of the Sanctuary.' I remember him saying.

Of course by that time, Keble and Newman's Oxford Movement had already led to a great flourishing of artistic endeavour in the Church. The traditional firms were struggling to keep up with the growing needs of the masses fleeing the countryside. The likes of John Ruskin and the Pre-Raphaelite Brotherhood, with whom my fiancé and his closest friends were associated, soon turned their talents to the decoration of those new church buildings. They tapped into many historical and 'gothic' sources for their inspiration. In that vein, Mr Kempe described to me how he had also begun to develop more deliberately his nascent talent for drawing and design.

Mr Lisle, following your request, I've looked back over my own journals from the period and reconstructed here for you a little vignette for your project of some of my first memories of that most interesting weekend in October 1857 when we first met. It all started on a Saturday morning at my fiancé Ned Jones's lodgings in Red Lion Square.

'My dearest Topsy! How delightful to see you back home so soon. What news from Oxford, old fellow?' Ned asked Topsy (the nickname we used for Mr William Morris).

Our dear friend shrugged and sat down heavily on the high-backed settle we'd placed in the room for visitors. He'd just climbed up the steep flight of stairs and was breathing heavily. Despite Ned's bright greeting, Topsy didn't speak for a moment, wringing his hands as he tried to recover his breath. He nodded and smiled at me, at last acknowledging my presence. I smiled back. He was always my favourite amongst Ned's little group, with his frizzy black hair and sweet bashful demeanour.

By then Ned and I were both living (separately, of course) in London and engaged to be married. Topsy and Ned lodged together in those rooms in Red Lion Square and I was probably their most frequent visitor. I lived only about half an hour's walk away with my family in Beaumont Street. My father was at the time a Methodist minister and preached nearby at the Hinde Street Chapel. I'd known Ned since I was twelve; he'd gone to school with my brother Harry in Birmingham. It was if we were destined to be sweethearts from an early age.

I remember I was so happy and in love at that time, even though there was little early prospect of us marrying due to the poor state of Ned's finances. Would you believe that he had no more than twenty or twenty-five pounds to his name! Topsy on the other hand was a wealthy man but sadly unsuccessful in love. So our little threesome had become quite convenient and domesticated. I like to think I'd become the source of calm and efficiency amongst their collective turmoil, but at the same time, I was still very much in awe of Ned and Topsy's artistic associates.

'Topsy, I wish you'd said you'd be coming back today. I'd have ordered in some lunch for you,' I said.

'No matter,' he replied.

'So, are the new rooms ready yet?' Ned asked, changing the subject. Topsy nodded silently. Ned looked back at him sternly, stroking the beginnings of that long-limp beard that later made him look so much like a woodland dryad. He continued without waiting for an answer.

'You know what Topsy, I've been wandering these dull streets the last two days, getting gloomier and gloomier without you. If I'd have thought you were coming back today, I'd have been as merry as a sandboy,' he laughed.

[I should explain that during the previous summer Ned and Topsy had been part of the 'happy band of brothers' who'd gathered together to paint the murals on the walls of the Oxford Union debating room. Ruskin and Rossetti had organised the whole project. But unfortunately there'd been a forced pause in the proceedings while unexpected technical issues were resolved, so they'd temporarily returned to London. They were due to travel back to Oxford to start afresh the following week. To that end, Topsy had just returned from Oxford via Paddington where he'd been supervising the transfer of their belongings and furniture from their old digs at 87 High Street to the new rooms in George Street.]

Topsy coughed and spluttered heavily, recovered at last from his climb up the stairs. As usual, his waistcoat was straining against its buttons as he spoke.

'Is she here?' he asked. 'In London, I mean?'

'Who?'

'You know who!'

'Really I don't old man.'

'I mean that dream girl of Rossetti's, the one from the theatre?' Topsy panted; he seemed very excited and was quite red in the face. 'Is she here? I heard that Christina invited her down for the weekend?'

'Oh, yet another new stunner you mean,' I laughed disapprovingly. Topsy growled at me.

'No, I don't think so, old man. I certainly hadn't heard anything about that,' Ned added, shaking his head and looking at me quizzically. I nodded back. Topsy looked disappointed. 'Why do you ask?'

'I heard she's agreed to pose for him at last?'

'Well, yes, I believe she has. She's to be his Guinevere. But they're both in Oxford, aren't they? Didn't you see them there?' Topsy acknowledged but ignored the question and consulted his pocket book. Ned continued painting.

At that moment, we were interrupted by Mary, the Red Lion housekeeper, carrying a tea tray. Mary looked at me questioningly when she saw Topsy there. She hadn't been expecting him back that afternoon either, but she hid her surprise well. She was used to such things. My baby sister, Louie, ran in with her too and greeted 'Uncle Topsy' enthusiastically as usual with a hug before sitting back down at the table to resume her drawing. My engraving tools were lying in an open case on the other side of the large medieval-style table where I'd been working that morning. My folded-over copy of 'Barnaby Rudge' lay beside them. Topsy cleared a place for the tea tray, made admiring comments about Louie's picture and then picked up my book and inspected it, beginning to read aloud:

'When I talk of eyes, the stars come out. Whose eyes are they? If they are angels' eyes, why do they look down here and see good men hurt and only wink and sparkle all the night?' he read.

'Hmm. Well, what about the Sid, she doesn't mind this new girl sitting for him?' he asked after a while.

'She's not around; she's up north in Matlock or Sheffield or somewhere,' I said.

'While the cat's away, you know,' Ned winked. I scowled at him. Topsy didn't look impressed either. Rossetti's loose affections always appalled him even though they'd been good friends for quite some years.

'Look Ned, I must find her,' Topsy interrupted. *'I need her to model for Iseult. Ruskin says I've painted a grotesque. I've got to redo her. From Nature, he says.'*

'Well I'm hardly surprised, old man. I saw your little tragedy when I was down there last week!' Ned laughed. *'"The ogress Isolde",'* were Ruskin's words, *'"she's hardly human!"' he said.'* Topsy thought to object but passed.

'You see then, Ned, I need Janey!'

Two days later, we were all back in Oxford again. Ned and Topsy went to have breakfast together with Rossetti. They were eating together at Johnson's in George Street. Arthur Hughes the painter was there too, with Val Prinsep and the poet Coventry Patmore. Of course I wasn't invited to such an event! I was with my sisters, visiting our brother Harry who was studying at Corpus Christi. Harry was yet again 'involved', on that occasion with a local girl called Peggy. He was struggling to maintain focus on his studies. We'd gone to encourage him back to the true path, but by then, I think he'd all but lost interest in pursuing Papa's chosen course for him of the ministry.

From Ned's account, Val Prinsep, as usual, dominated the conversation. He was a complete giant of a man, six feet one, fifteen stone and well-built. I always thought his hair was like fine wire: short, curly and seamless.

'What fun we had! What jokes! What roars of laughter?' Val shouted.

Across from their party, sat at the next table, were a group of younger students. Ned knew one of them: Cormell Price from Birmingham. He was there with Skef and Wilf Dodgson and Charles Kempe, his new friend. They were guests of Bodley the architect, who by chance I believe was the son of the Kemp family's doctor in Brighton and at that time part of Gilbert Scott's firm. Ned told me later he'd been struck how they were all looking on at the bawdy display with a mixture of wide-eyed wonder and dismay. Prinsep continued to regale the whole dining room with his tales of soda-water fights and general bohemian mayhem, recounting practical jokes played in their old lodgings.

I can quite understand from my own experience how ill at ease Mr Kempe must have felt in such company. He was just up from Rugby, shy and ignorant of such jargon. What's more, I understand his stammer made him feel even more uncomfortable amongst such bonhomie. Rossetti, of course, was the peacock as always, dressed in a plum-coloured dress coat. His blond curls and Italianate colouring always gave him the appearance of a demi-god in contrast to our friends' pale English faces.

Later that morning, I was invited to join them as they resumed in the Union chamber to inspect the progress of the frescos. But I could see how the jovial gang soon began to feel quite dejected. Amongst the group that Rossetti had gathered, only he and Arthur Hughes had much experience in such projects. The need to work in distemper at height between large whitewashed windows meant that the chalk and size-tempered paint was already fading. They'd originally planned to have the job finished by the end of the Long Vacation, but it was October and still the murals were nowhere near done.

Corm Price, Ned's school acquaintance, had volunteered that morning to help out with painting the black lines for the patterns on the roof. He'd dragged his new friend Kempe along with him too. Ned introduced me to him and I was immediately favourably impressed.

But after a while I could tell that he was ill at ease. We were standing next to Topsy's nearly finished mural: '*How Sir Palomydes Loved La Belle Iseult*'. He looked somewhat disturbed by it, but pretended politely to admire the brushwork.

'It's most remarkable in form,' Kempe volunteered. Topsy frowned and Ned laughed. I could tell Topsy was annoyed.

'The young man's right Topsy, quite remarkable!'

'I believe it has some merits as to colour, young man, but I must confess I should feel much more comfortable if it had disappeared from the wall as I'm conscious of it being extremely ludicrous in many ways,' Topsy whispered between his teeth. He turned to look at Rossetti who was inspecting his own less complete work, 'Sir Launcelot's Vision of the Sanc Grael', on the other side of the room.

'How are you pleased with it, Gabriel?' he shouted.

'It's beginning to be unintelligible,' Rossetti replied, cursing. Indeed, the glare of the sunlight from a gap in the whitewashed windows made the detail almost impossible to see. Only the radiance of its variegated tints gave any great impression of its rendering. You could just discern the face of his new muse, painted in the form of Guinevere standing amongst the branches of an apple tree. She was staring down at the sleeping Launcelot with the Holy Grail by his side. There was no mistaking her dark, crinkly hair, her slightly tilted nose, enormous dark eyes and sublimely long neck.

'Where she standeth in the night, clasped about with a solemn light…' I heard Topsy mutter.

'What were they going to do with the Grail when they found it, Mr Rossetti?' asked Kempe innocently. He clearly hadn't read Mallory's work. He seemed totally in awe of Rossetti, and seeing his idol's cringing face, clearly immediately regretted his somewhat naïve question. Topsy smiled sympathetically at him and laughed a belly laugh; by then he was stomping backwards and forwards, as was his wont, muttering about heaven and a rose garden full of stunners.

'What sort of a question is that?' asked Rossetti, frowning somewhat disdainfully.

Ned cried loudly, 'Oh but Gabriel, he does have a point! Adultery and purity make such unhappy bedfellows don't they just?'

At that point, the model for the painting herself, the stableman's daughter Jane Burden, entered the room. She was dressed in a flowing medieval gown, her pale face glowing with stage rouge. Her neck, unusually long, supported her striking profile. She had large almond-shaped eyes. To me her looks were always quite unsettling, and were also not apparently at all to Mr Kempe's taste. I believe he had a far more homely conception of female beauty in his own mind.

With Corm's encouragement, Kempe suggested to Topsy that he might also like to help with the drawing of the ceiling design. Topsy readily agreed; he was only too glad to have such willing young helpers for the difficult task of painting from ladders and scaffolds. Kempe watched Rossetti and Janey curiously as he worked at his allotted tasks, observing their combined loveliness from afar. He seemed entirely innocent of such amorous relationships. The blatant freedom of romance signalled openly in their behaviour appeared a new and almost shocking experience for him.

As I said earlier, that night, Kempe and Crom dined with us. Kempe asked after dinner if he could sketch my portrait.

The face he drew was a face of devout fidelity; I was rather flattered and have kept the sketch ever since. I'm told you can see elements of that very image in his early Madonnas and virgins. On the back, Topsy later wrote these words for me in jest:

"They were the mark of the love and greatness of heart that wielded the strong will in her, which, in its turn, wrought on those firm lips of hers that serious brow which gave her the air of one who never made a mistake."

Lady Georgiana Burne-Jones
North-End House,
Rottingdean

CHAPTER SIX

THE GARDENER

It must be borne in mind that horticulture is still a comparatively new profession for women.

The Hon. Frances Wolseley, *Gardening for women*

'Wow Ellie, okay you win. This is amazing, real history and so atmospheric!' said Harry. But Ellie just smiled, sphinx-like.

While he read the letter, Maggie joined them again with a tea tray and biscuits and they sat down on the tapestry-covered sofas to drink. There was silence for a moment. Maggie was watching them closely, trying to detect the slightest romantic signals. If she was still at all doubtful about showing him around without Mrs Ross's explicit approval, her misgiving had been overcome by the realisation of what a nice guy he was. Maggie had been delighted when she'd heard Serena Ross had chosen Ellie for this difficult job. She'd always been the one with an appreciation of the arts but she was usually hopeless when it came to men. Maggie was now even more impressed with her discovery of Harry. He was certainly a big improvement on that idiot Ryan she was obsessing about.

To break the silence, Harry mentioned he was also keen to look around the gardens. He said he was particularly interested in the setting of the scene at 'Waterbath' at the beginning of the novel, the scene when Mrs Gereth first begins to plot how to get her son Owen to marry Flora Vetch instead of the philistine Mona Brigstock. As neither girl was familiar with the novel, this meant little to them. Ellie was worried about the time and looked out doubtfully at the weather; while they'd been touring round it had started to rain.

'It's a bit damp, though,' she said, 'and I've got to get some other stuff done. I've got another client to see in Brighton this afternoon.' That was the first he'd heard about that and his disappointment was easy to read on his face. There went his plans for lunch and an afternoon romantic walk.

'Stay inside if you'd prefer, I won't be long,' he said, finding it hard to hide his feelings.

'Sorry, Harry, I can't, one of us will have to go with you in case the neighbours are around. I don't want tales of strange men wandering the grounds getting back to Mrs Ross. It looks like the rain's easing, but I really don't think I've got time. Maggs, could you do the honours?'

Maggie looked at her quizzically. She knew the client meeting wasn't till much later. Was sis actually playing hard to get? How cool was that?

'Sure, whatever you want, Ell,' she replied obligingly, although she too had to get back pretty soon to prepare her husband's lunch.

'Ellie, before you go though, do you know anything about the history of the gardens?' asked Harry keen to get as much out of her as he could before she disappeared.

'Well, I'm no expert, but they were very important to Mr Kempe's overall vision,' she said. 'They extended over two hundred acres at one time.'

'The view from that belvedere was certainly impressive,' he said.

'Yes, although it's quite difficult to make out the original concept now. I think it was a mix of arts and crafts and more formal Jacobean shapes, the yew hedges and statuary dividing it up into more intimate areas.'

They looked out again. It did seem as though the rain was easing at last.

'Come on, it's only a bit of rain, it won't take long!' he said encouragingly. But Ellie shook her head again. Harry was perplexed. Was she avoiding him? Was this about Ryan? Maggie sensed the tension.

'Well, anyway I'm up for it,' she said breaking the awkward silence. She pulled out wellies and a mac from the garden room and offered a pair to Harry. Ellie made her apologies and promised she'd speak to Harry by phone later. Harry and Maggie went out through the garden room door and walked over the wet grass in the direction of the Pavilion.

'Cheer up,' said Maggie. 'Your face looks like the weather.'

'Sorry,' he said, 'I was hoping I could take her out for lunch.'

'Yes, she's in a funny mood, but she definitely likes you,' she said, squeezing his arm, and then began to explain how Kempe once used the Pavilion building as a workshop, but it was now a private house. Harry was somewhat reassured but was worrying about the text from Ryan still. He wanted to ask her about it but before he could she'd changed the subject.

'Have you ever heard of the gardening pioneer, Frances Wolseley?' she asked.

'No, I'm afraid not,' he replied.

'Well, by coincidence, our great-grandmother worked for Kempe as a maid in London,' she said. After Kempe died, she went to work for Frances Wolseley, who was one of his great friends. We've still got some of her letters describing her time there. Frances and her mother Lady Wolseley visited the house a lot in the 1890s. In fact they laid the foundation stone for this final wing. It was through Kempe that Frances got to know many of the important gardeners of the time, the likes of Gertrude Jekyll and William Robinson from Gravetye. Later she started a school for lady gardeners at Ragged Lands near Glynde.'

'Wolseley, come to think of it, perhaps I do know that name,' he replied. He looked at his notes. 'Yes, I was looking online last night to see whether Henry James had ever visited Old Place. It turned out he did. I found a letter of his from March 1897 to a Lady Louisa Wolseley where he described such a visit. It sounded like she'd been trying to persuade him to come for some time. The letter's very precise: he caught the 11.40 from Victoria arriving in Haywards Heath at 1.17 where he met up with Lady Wolseley coming from Brighton. The train was late!'

'Nothing's changed, then!' laughed Maggie. 'But yes that would be Frances Wolseley's mother, I'm sure.'

Harry went on to read from the notes he'd made on his iPad. 'James described Kempe as 'very amiable' and the house as a 'phoenix'.

'The man himself made the place more wonderful and the place the man. I was greatly affected by his courtesy and charm.'

'Fascinating. So could Old Place have been the actual setting for the book, do you think?' she asked.

'It's possible although the timeline doesn't quite work. *The Spoils* was published a year before his visit, but Lady Wolseley is often cited as a source for the main character of

Adela Gereth. She might well have described it to him in enough detail for him to use in his novel.'

Maggie seemed very pleased with the revelation. 'Thank you,' she said. 'I love that story. I'll use it with my class next term.'

They walked towards a large carriage entrance known as the Bishop's Gate. It had two magnificent stone piers adorned by Greek urns and statues; on each was hung a huge ornate iron gate.

'These are half-size replicas of the originals in St Pauls. They were built for Kempe especially. It's like they lead the eye naturally to that line of conifers over there,' said Maggie. Harry looked across to where she was pointing. His gaze then continued along a further line of pleached limes to the iron gates at the far western end of the garden, the same gates he'd found locked earlier that morning. Beyond them was a lovely view of the church tower from the east.

'It's all still very impressive.'

'Yes but unfortunately they lost a whole load of trees in that terrible hurricane in the eighties. There was originally a further line of oaks, called a *claire voie,* to the south, with a vista to the Wilderness.

'The Wilderness?'

'Yes, it's a lovely wild area. Unfortunately, if Ryan gets his way, they're going to build a load of posh houses on it now.'

'Will he get permission?'

'Well, Monica's uncle's on the planning committee,' she replied in a resigned voice.

Suddenly there was a bang in the distance followed by another a few seconds later. Even he knew they were gunshots; they appeared to be coming from the direction of a building sheltered by a group of trees at the far end of the garden.

'What the hell?'

'It's probably just Ryan out shooting rabbits, or murdering crows or something. He quite often does that when he's in a bad mood. His workshop's up there.'

'God, he's a bit close to the house, isn't he?'

'That's Ryan I'm afraid.'

'Well, we can't have that while we're filming…'

'Don't worry, I'll speak to him about it.' At that moment a pair of scared jet black crows flew straight passed them.

'Blimey!'

They turned back towards the house. Harry was still shaking a little from the shock of the gunshots. He could see up to the roof and the belvedere where he'd almost fallen half-an-hour earlier. God, it really was a long way down. He'd been dead lucky. It made him feel sick to think about it. *There are a few health and safety issues to think through here!* he thought. He hoped the risk assessments would sort all that out okay. But they couldn't have Ryan shooting whenever or wherever he wanted to!

They returned inside. Ellie had indeed left to see her client in Brighton, but Maggie, intrigued to find out more about Harry, offered to show him some photographs of Kempe. She explained she was a keen amateur photographer herself.

She fetched the album out of one of the packing boxes. Harry was fascinated by one group shot that showed Mr Kempe's friends dressed in historic Tudor clothing. There was a label with all the names on the back. One lady was identified as Harriette Morrell, the wife of Kempe's school friend Frederick. She was with her daughter Frederica. He'd read she was another of the candidates for the source of Mrs Gereth's character.

'He was a bit of a stud,' he joked.

'Yes' she laughed, 'although he never got hitched, he was certainly a hit with the ladies!'

'Lucky guy!' replied Harry.

'Oh I suspect you've had your moments too,' she said coyly. He flushed.

Before he left, Maggie had one last piece of advice for him.

'Keep trying with Ellie,' she said. 'She likes you really. It's just her way.'

'Is that a sisterly hint?'

'That's what we're here for. And I think the filming idea's really exciting; it'd be great for the village as well.'

'Yes, this would be a brilliant location. Of course, we'll need a survey, but it's got tons of promise. Thanks so much for showing me round this morning, Maggie.'

'Well, remember you've got to sweet-talk Mrs Ross first. Then there's Ryan…'

'Yeah, I might need your help there! Would you be able to do me a favour and ring Mrs Ross? See if I can see her in the next couple of days?'

'Of course,' she replied and then paused. She wasn't looking forward to that conversation. He saw that on her face.

'Look, if Ellie's not around, can I buy you a drink this evening? Discuss next steps etcetera?'

'I'm not sure what Ellie or indeed my husband would think about that!' she laughed. *'You're really not hitting on me I hope,'* she added to herself silently. He was a bit of a charmer.

'Sorry, yes of course, strictly business!' he replied rather too seriously she thought, it was only a joke. Now that she'd realised he was the sensitive type, she'd have to be careful how much she teased him.

'Well, Tuesday night's bell-ringing,' she said, 'you'd be welcome to come along if you want. I'll be there with my better half. We're both learning the ropes as they say at the moment. We can pop into the pub afterwards with the others. The bells have an interesting Kempe angle, too; I should tell you about that. Seven-thirty in the church?'

'Perfect,' he said.

'Oh yes, before you go, I've got something else to show you,' she said.

'Yeah?'

'It's a letter from Harriette Morrell to John Lisle. As I said earlier, she married Frederick Morrell, his school friend from Rugby, and later became his life-long friend and adviser, almost his châtelaine. It's interesting too because her maiden name was Wynter, suggesting she might also be a relative of Mrs Ross on her grandfather's side. Their son was Philip Morrell, a liberal MP, who married Ottoline Cavendish-Bentinck, the Lady Ottoline who became the famous society hostess at Garsington.

'I've read a lot about them for another project,' Harry said.

'Yes, and the period she describes in this letter was a particularly important one for Kempe. He'd linked up with George Bodley, the architect, and had just done his first solo commission – the Bishop Hooper window at Gloucester Cathedral. But it wasn't a universal success I'm afraid: somewhat embarrassingly he'd managed to dress a well-known protestant martyr in Roman Catholic robes!'

'Whoops!'

I first met Charles Kempe in the summer of 1865. Frederick and I had been invited to dine at the vice-chancellor's house in Oxford. My friend Loo Erskine was staying with me at the time, which is why Frederick hit on the idea of inviting Mr Kempe along to make up a foursome. I was doubtful at first; from what little I'd seen of him about town, he seemed quite reserved. We'd never spoken and Loo was anything but shy. But Frederick assured me that Mr Kempe's social confidence had improved immeasurably since he'd received an annual income from his family estate that year.

Most of the other dinner guests were already gathered when they arrived. Loo and I were both pleasantly surprised by their appearance. As always, Frederick was dressed impeccably and looked exceedingly handsome. His companion did so too; in fact he looked remarkably dashing. I nudged Loo and she giggled as they entered the crowded room and introduced themselves to our hosts. After that, they crossed over purposefully towards us. I have to say my expectation increased with each step as they approached; I had to nudge Loo again to stop her giggling. Of course, as always, she looked gorgeous too. It was said at that time she was one of the best-dressed ladies in society. She was the very image of the Empress Eugénie. Her beau (and later her husband) Garnet Wolseley was safely off soldiering in Canada. I remember though that their families were really not keen on the match at that point, and she certainly had a number of other admirers! So Kempe was in with a chance.

'Charles, may I introduce you to Miss Harriette Wynter, the daughter of the President of St John's, and her companion Miss Louisa Erskine,' Frederick said grandly. He was already the Steward of St John's at that time (like his father before him), which was how we'd originally met.

'E-E-Enchanted!' Mr Kempe responded. I noticed his

stammer immediately of course, although I took it as a charming affectation rather than a real impediment. He proceeded to kiss each of our hands in turn like a true gentleman. Loo curtseyed endearingly; she was always the more confident and spoke first to him with that lilting Irish voice of hers (which to my ears was really quite enchanting). She was quite a petite girl and very fair in complexion, with delicate features. I remember her auburn hair was piled luxuriantly over her head in a French style that evening. Although she was brought up in rural Ireland, she was very refined and well-educated, having an excellent command of French as well as a love of fine clothes and furnishings, tastes that even then were somewhat beyond a mere soldier's pay. I believe Charles was probably cautiously emboldened in his approach to her by suggestions Frederick had made. Later we enjoyed a number of riverside walks together. I've always thought they'd have made a fine match if Garnet hadn't claimed her first!

Harriette Anne Morrell
Black Hall, Oxford

CHAPTER SEVEN

THE ENVOYS

*Whose artist-spirit knew so well,
To appreciate and read the spell,
Hath not Old Place a genius? Tell!*

T. Herbert Warren, *Envoy*

The same day, Lindfield, Tuesday, May 26th

As soon as she'd left Old Place, Ellie went straight to Ryan's workshop at the far end of the grounds to confront him about the text messages. She found him stripped to the waist oiling his shotgun in the tool shed ready to go out shooting. When he saw her standing in the doorway he grinned and began provocatively to rub oil onto his ripped torso. Maybe in a deep corner of her brain she was tempted by his alpha male display, but she also had some scruples and in that same instant, she realised she still had more willpower than that. She looked away and asked him to put him to get dressed properly.

'What do you mean by all these texts Ryan?' she asked, still turned away from him. He could tell she was irritated but he was intrigued too by her visit and deliberately left his shirt off. He flicked the safety on the gun, put it down on his workbench and walked towards her.

'Sorry, but I just had to see you.'

'What's so bloody important? You know I'm busy,' she replied infuriated. She felt his breath on her neck and turned towards him. He was still shirtless. She was momentarily distracted by the sight of him standing there, flexing his pecs, arms thrust provocatively into the pockets of his jeans. He was far too handsome for his own good.

'It's Monica. She's on the rampage about the furniture, and now this BBC guy's interfering as well and she thinks you...'

'You've dragged me here to tell me Monica's angry with me?' she replied exasperated.

'She thinks something's going on. She's told me to get it together or the whole thing's off between us.'

'And would you care?'

Her eyes were blazing now. He went to put his arms on her hips but she brushed him away and stepped back.

'I don't know. I suppose so,' he said, seeing but ignoring her irritation. His face looked worried. She felt her resolve weakening. He didn't look at all convinced that he knew what he thought at all.

'Just suppose? Aren't you sure?'

'She says I need to sort things,' he replied and took another step towards her.

'Well you'd better speak to your gran, then?' she said sharply and turned as if to leave.

'I can't. She won't answer my calls. Please Ellie I need your help,' he whispered. She turned to face him again and he placed his arms around her hips again. This time she shoved him away more strongly.

'Look, just don't involve me in this, okay?' she said. She felt her hackles rising. *How dare he?* But then remembered she had other things to discuss with him too. But this clearly wasn't the time for that.

'Please Ellie.' He grabbed her and pulled her towards him and kissed her while clenching her tightly. She could feel him hard up against her hip. She slapped him and tried to pull away, but he was too strong.

'You brute,' she said. 'Get off me.' She was struggling now, but felt her resistance weakening by the second. Suddenly they were kissing. Then there was a noise behind them.

'Ryan, what on earth…?' Monica's shrill voice rang out across the shed. 'Ellie, what the hell do you think you're doing, you bitch?'

Ellie looked at her in shock and then without a further word ran out to her car and drove away as quickly as she could. She heard him calling after her. She was angry. Monica was angry. God how had she been so stupid? What a mess. But once she was safely inside the temple of her car she suddenly felt glad as well. His little machismo display had sorted out quite a lot for her. Emotionally she was boiling, but she was also crystal clear in her mind. She turned her radio onto full blast and therefore didn't hear the two shots ring out in the shed behind her.

By the time she got to Ovingdean, she'd decided exactly what she was going to do next…

After Harry left Old Place, Maggie pondered what to do. She'd guessed exactly where Ellie had rushed off too. She knew that Ellie had had all those texts from Ryan during the morning. Somehow he must have already found out about Harry's visit, she assumed from Monica. That made things complicated given past events, but she also wasn't at all sure how the filming idea would go down with either Ryan or Mrs Ross. She in particular was so fussy about the house and its contents.

Maggie liked Harry, and of course the fact he was potential sibling boyfriend material had a bearing too. She therefore hadn't really wanted to broach the full complexity of the Ross family issues with him. She didn't want to put him off. In any case, she had to go over to Poynting's later, the house where Mrs Ross had taken up residence, to deal with some paperwork that needed signing. She could take over two boxes of ornaments that they didn't want damaged too. They were too valuable to leave in the house while the movers were around. That might just give her the chance to try and get Mrs Ross's agreement.

She loaded her car up with the boxes and texted Ellie: 'Minx, you didn't say he was DDG!' she said, adding a 'wink' and kisses.

The reply that came back was just: 'driving, saw Ryan, mad as hell, speak to you later' and an angry face. She tried to ring her immediately but there was no reply. Ellie must have switched off her phone as soon as she'd texted.

Maggie noticed that she'd also missed an earlier text from Ryan asking to meet up. She texted him back to suggest that if he wanted, she could meet him in at one-thirty in the deli; it was a neutral place and safer than the house, she thought. Having done that, she dashed back to the house to prepare lunch. By one, her husband still wasn't back, so she left him a note to heat up what was in the microwave and then drove the mile or so to Poynting's. *This whole situation is going to require some careful diplomacy*, she thought.

The village looked really good that afternoon. She was so glad she hadn't moved away like Ellie, even though on many occasions she'd felt the same temptation to escape. But unlike Ellie, she'd never thought of herself as having much of an ambition; she wasn't a dreamer, she was much more practical, but even so living in such fine surroundings had certainly always given her a positive view of life. She'd also always lacked Ellie's decisiveness, and of course now she'd met and married her 'soul mate' she had something to settle her down at last – well, that's what she kept telling herself, in any case. On the way over to Poynting's she passed Harry coming out of the back of the pub with his bike but didn't acknowledge him. He really was quite good looking, she thought. Sis had done well. She was a tiny bit jealous. She was, after all, becoming increasingly aware of the vast difference between enjoying sentimental love affairs as a single woman and the need now to work hard at a marriage that would last for the rest of her life.

When she arrived at Poynting's, she was surprised to see Ryan's van there too. Monica Malling was standing next to the van, smoking. They'd always had a difficult relationship. If anything Ellie had been closer to her, although that had all ended in a falling-out over boys at some stage. Monica was wearing a tight pencil skirt, fishnets, a cropped see-through top and a big diamond RING on her ring finger. So it had finally happened, had it? Ryan had actually gotten his act together. She noticed how Monica looked so confident and well, womanly. *This could be awkward,* Maggie gulped. She pulled up, got out of the car and picked up one of the two boxes she was dropping off, partly for protection.

'Hi Monica, how you doing?' she asked as politely as she could as she passed, not wishing to refer to the ring straight out.

'None the better for seeing you,' replied Monica sarcastically. She threw down her cigarette and twisted it into the gravel before lighting another, making sure to flash the ring as she did so. Maggie had memories of someone doing that in a film she'd seen as a kid. It was pretty crass behaviour; she hated smoking.

'Wow, are congratulations in order Monica, then?' she asked sweetly, glancing at the ring she now couldn't avoid noticing.

'Some might think so,' Monica replied, her voice triumphant and somewhat acerbic. She continued to stare at Maggie with daggers drawn, flaunting and rubbing the ring victoriously with her fingers. She'd never liked Maggie but now she had the power at last, it felt good. She was going to get the respect of those Swift sisters yet. This one certainly needed taking down a peg now she was little Miss Village Sweetheart.

'Come on Ryan, I need to get to the cash and carry,' she yelled insistently in the direction of the house.

The front door was open and Maggie could see Ryan standing at the entrance, talking agitatedly to someone inside. She presumed it was Mrs Ross. She heard words which suggested a strained but still polite disagreement. He was dressed in his working clothes and unshaven. *He needs a haircut, but he's undeniably a hunk*, thought Maggie, as she climbed up onto the doorstep beside him. Thoughts of Brad Pitt invaded her mind briefly. She put them away into the too dangerous category. She wondered what had happened to make him propose to Monica at last.

'I need a word with you,' he whispered sharply.

'Didn't you see my text? And should I wish you congratulations too?' she replied as sweetly as she could.

'Yes but…'

'Well, you must be so happy!'

'I guess…'

'So I'll see you in half an hour, okay?'

He looked at her and nodded reluctantly and then it dawned on him that that wouldn't work.

'Sorry, I've got to take Monica over to the cash and carry.'

'Well later then, at Old Place?' she suggested chirpily. She was very conscious that Monica was probably watching her every move.

'Okay,' he said. 'I'll be an hour or so though.'

She noticed the strain on his face. She probably shouldn't be too hard on him, she realised he was stuck in the middle of a face-off between two strong-willed women, so to speak. She wondered if maybe she could really help? But at that moment, Serena Ross emerged exultantly from the hall, carrying a magazine and saw at once the delicious tension in their faces.

'Hello dear, how lovely it is to see you? Please come in, I won't be a moment,' she said and then added loudly enough for all of them to hear, 'Now here's someone else who likes nice things, Ryan.'

Ryan grimaced and looked at his grandmother in irritation, but she ignored him. Instead, the formidable Serena turned her head and addressed Monica who was still standing brazenly by the van.

'Monica, your mother left this publication when she was here last week. It's called "Hot Gossip" or something, full of tittle-tattle and nasty photographs. I'm sure she's got more use for it than me.'

And with that she launched the rolled-up magazine into the air in an unnecessary large arc towards the van. However, Monica, with the easy habit of a sportswoman, reached out her hand like a spring and caught the offending magazine in mid-air as if it were a tennis ball or something.

'Good catch,' shouted Ryan and laughed. 'She's got the measure of you, Gran,'

'Maybe for now,' said Mrs Ross, 'But somehow I doubt it will last long.'

Ryan and Monica got into the van and drove off hurriedly, while Mrs Ross led Maggie into the house.

'Are they really engaged at last?' Maggie asked.

'Apparently so, he asked her this very lunchtime.'

'How exciting!' Maggie replied. Serena didn't answer and there was an awkward pause for a second. 'Gosh, it's wonderful what you've done with the house already,' said Maggie, trying to find a safer line of conversation. 'Look, you've even put up that little Maltese painting that Ellie admires so much.'

But instead of accepting her praise, Serena turned to her and said abruptly, 'I'd give up the house and all the things in it for Ellie, you know. She could still get him,' she added deliberately as she walked past.

'But he's only just got engaged!' protested Maggie. *How could you even suggest that?* she thought.

'There's still time.'

'And Monica's such a perfect match for him,' Maggie replied slightly ironically under her breath. Although she didn't really mean it, she'd also guessed what Serena was up to and was dead set against it.

'He's an idiot. But no matter dear, Ellie would still make a far better match. And actually, even though they're now engaged, I know it won't last.'

'Why not?' asked Maggie innocently.

'I won't let it. Oh and he wants the house and all the things back, but that won't happen either, will it?'

Maggie was quite angered by her words. She saw how Serena was trying to manipulate things, but to involve Ellie as well was despicable. There was grit in her voice as she spoke her next sentence.

'What if he gets the lawyers on to you?'

'Oh I think I'd rather enjoy that, being dragged out

kicking and screaming. What a scene that would be! Let him come, burn me alive!' she laughed.

'I don't think you…' she started to reply but thought better of it. She had another subject to raise and it wouldn't help to get into an argument first. 'Look Mrs Ross, I'm afraid I've something else I have to ask you. It's a big favour, really.'

'You mean the filming, dear?'

'You know?' she replied surprised.

'Yes, of course I do.'

'Well, I know we should have discussed it first, but it could be excellent. It'd get great publicity for the auction.'

'Really, are you sure?'

'Absolutely.'

'And is that Ryan's opinion too?' she asked. Maggie looked at her: by now she'd assumed that was one of the things they'd been arguing about.

'Ryan?'

'Yes, Ryan, my grandson, the man it seems you and your sister love to hate?'

'Well, yes, we need to get him onside, too.'

'I suspect you mean I do?'

'Well, I suppose so, but I'll help if I can?'

'If only Ellie would let herself go a bit dear,' Serena sighed. 'Wear some make-up and nice clothes, show a bit of flesh.'

'Really Mrs Ross!'

'Well, he's only a man, isn't he? They all want the same thing.'

'How could you…'

'Are you really so shocked, dear? Or isn't that how you got the curate interested? I wonder how he noticed you otherwise; he's always so other-worldly.' She saw the shocked expression on Maggie's face and knew she'd had the desired effect with her words. 'I know I'm quite coarse when it comes to such things really. Practical I like to think. If only she would, my dear, everything would be so very much simpler for me,' she said, shaking her head to exaggerate her point.

Maggie was fuming but tried hard to keep her cool. But as she drove back to Old Place she realised there was more than a grain of truth in Serena's last statement. Having seen Monica dressed like that and Ryan so vulnerable, she found that her own emotions were strangely divided on the matter too…

Back at The Tyger, having showered after his cycle ride, Harry was lying on the bed with only a towel over him. He had just skimmed back over the introduction to his edition of *The Spoils of Poynton*. He was intrigued to find further references to Mrs Harriette Morrell, the lady in the photograph Maggie had shown him. The more he got into this research, the more connections he was making. He was now absolutely convinced that this was the right location to film.

> *There was a tradition that the original for Mrs Adela Gereth was Mrs Harriette Morrell. She was a passionate collector and lived in the seventeenth-century-house of Black Hall on St. Giles, Oxford. She was a good friend of Henry James and he would have seen her when he spent the summer in Oxford in 1894… However, there is another candidate in the shape of Henry James's old friend Viscountess Wolseley. She was a strong-minded Scottish lady; born Louisa Erskine… she was also an avid collector of antiques who helped James furnish several of his houses. Indeed some of her possessions were literally 'spolia' of war. Both Viscountess Wolseley and*

Mrs Morrell were friendly with a number of architects who come, roughly, into the category of 'arts and crafts' – George Frederick Bodley, Edward Prioleau Warren and… Charles Eamer Kempe.

'Pay dirt,' he whispered to himself. He texted Ellie to say how happy he was with the morning's visit, and got a strange reply.

'Maggie seemed pretty taken with you too, you two been plotting?'

But before he could think of a suitable response, he heard a knock at the door. Then Monica was staring round the open door. Hurriedly he pulled the towel further up over his chest.

'Will you be staying longer Harry, as I need to sort out some rooms for the end of the week?' she asked. He could feel her eyes on his body.

'Yes please, do you think I can have the room till the weekend?'

'Well, I've got a wedding party in on Saturday, so definitely till Thursday night, but we'll have to see about Friday, though,' she said. 'I'll see what I can arrange.'

'Thanks Monica, that's very kind.'

He saw for the first time the flash of the diamond on her finger.

'Gosh, Monica, has Ryan proposed?'

She grinned and showed him the ring properly.

'I guess you could call it one of those shotgun proposals, so to speak,' she replied.

'Well congratulations!' he replied. He was pretty sure it was weddings that were shotgun not engagements, but all the same…

'Well your friend Ellie gave me a bit of a hand too. In fact, between us we didn't leave him with much choice.'

'Really?' replied Harry puzzled.

'Of course, I had to give him a bit of a shove, my best shot so to speak, after Ellie gave him a helping hand you might say. Talking about that, were you wanting a clean towel?' she asked winking and looking down towards his groin.

When Ryan eventually turned up at Old Place, it was past three. Maggie was pretty well done with the inventory and packing and had sat down to enjoy a well-earned tea break. She still hadn't heard from Ellie though and was slightly worried about her. She offered Ryan a mug. He was still dressed in his work clothes, sweaty and unshaven, but not for the first time she noticed he had a kind of rough manliness to him. The way his shirt clung to the muscles of his chest was, well... quite distracting.

'Is Ellie here?' he asked.

'No, she's in Brighton.'

'Damn,' he said. 'You were at Poynting's, you've seen what Gran's gone and done?'

'Yes, I was a little surprised.'

'Does she take me for an idiot?' he replied crossly, answering a question that was in her eyes but had remained unasked. His eyes ran idly over the boxes that were stacked up in the kitchen. He was reassured at least that things were still moving along. 'I've given her bags of time. Do you think it's fair?'

Maggie didn't answer. She didn't know and didn't want to know the precise details of the dispute between grandmother and grandson, especially not now that Ryan was obviously engaged. She'd heard the gossip that the legal position was clear enough: according to the will, the house and its contents belonged to Ryan once Serena no longer occupied it. Despite Monica's objections, Ryan had seemingly allowed her to take what valuable objects she desired to the small house on the common. That seemed only fair given she'd collected them in the first place. So the dispute had to be about more than material things and household goods. After all, Mrs Ross was obstinate but not greedy; in fact the girls had found her quite generous. And although she did not have a strong legal claim to the 'spoils', she certainly had a moral claim, having spent most of her life building the collection.

But from her words earlier that afternoon, Maggie had realised that Serena Ross was not entirely blameless either; she would have no qualms whatsoever when it came to interfering with Ryan's choice of partner. That dispute had clearly been raised to another level. She was now worried that the filming project would become yet another pawn in their tedious battle, one that Mrs Ross could play as long as she wanted to prolong Ryan's waiting period. Maggie was also concerned that Ellie was being increasingly manipulated by the players in this family power struggle. Even more distressingly, she knew that Ellie still liked him quite a lot, and was now being encouraged in that thinking by Mrs Ross's own preferences in respect of Ryan. God, what a mess! Harry was her only hope.

Indeed, Ellie had only on Monday confessed to her that over the past few weeks, she'd found herself thinking more and more about Ryan, her racy daydreams about him often interrupting their tedious inventory of objets d'art. Yes, he was ruddy-faced and leather-legged, full of swagger and cheerful ladness, but he was also beautiful, she'd said, *those eyes and curls and that physique*.

Ellie had told her how she'd come across him in the garden working without his shirt and watched him from behind a yew hedge. It was almost more than she could bear. Maggie in turn had pleaded with Ellie to forget him and not to goad Monica further, which is why when she'd heard about this new guy Harry at the weekend she'd been so pleased. Having met him in the flesh she was now even more hopeful. Okay, so he wasn't exactly an Adonis, but he was smart and kind of cute. She'd concluded that morning, that she needed to do her own bit of matchmaking. Ryan with Monica, yes; Ellie with Ryan, definitely no; Harry with Ellie, perfect; he'd appeared on the scene just in time like the proverbial cavalry. With the news of the engagement, that need seemed less pressing but still she could tell Harry needed some help. She'd have to work on sis and get her in the right place as quickly as she could, maybe invitee Harry to make up a foursome with her hubby at the weekend?

'No, you've behaved perfectly reasonably Ryan. But she's getting on. And this isn't just about a few tables and chairs, is it? She needs time to adjust to the new situation,' she replied carefully and truthfully.

'Adjust! She's had months. I could set the lawyers on her tomorrow.'

'Yes, but you won't, will you?' she stated and then changed the subject. 'You've heard about the filming, I assume?' She looked at his face and saw it colouring. Given his negative reaction, she wasn't quite sure how to proceed.

'That'll be another of her fricking delaying tactics.'

'But it's a great idea for publicity for the sale.'

'For heaven's sake,' he said. 'You know I need that money like tomorrow.'

'But I thought you were going to sell off some land?'

'Well, I can't yet until the legal stuff is settled, can I?'

'Well, what if the BBC paid you for the delay?'

'Fat chance. Anyway, that's not the point,' he said.

'What is the point?' she asked.

He looked at her pleadingly. He'd never fancied her as much as Ellie but she wasn't bad looking either. He wondered if she might be more persuadable now she was married and probably bored.

'You know Monica and me, we've kind of been together for a while, and now I guess we're engaged too.'

I guess, she thought. That didn't sound too committed.

'That's brilliant and everyone thinks you're just perfect for each other. Have you set a date yet?' she asked trying hard to contain the irony in her voice. He frowned at her words.

'Not exactly. But she's already putting a lot of pressure on me. To get stuff sorted with my gran. I don't know how. She says I've only got her on approval till then, whatever that means?'

'More like false pretences! Anyway is the problem that she's angry with you, you're afraid of the commitment, or afraid of your gran?'

'Kind of all of them… But I was wondering?'

'What?'

'What about Ellie and me?'

Maggie looked at him astounded. Had she really heard that? Had Serena been working on him? Would he really dare? As far as she knew, his reputation was well-deserved, so she supposed he would.

'There is no Ellie and you.'

'What if…'

'You mean what about Monica?'

'Well, she flirts with men all the time. I reckon I can still see other girls?'

'No you can't Ryan, and certainly not Ellie!'

'Well, how about with you then?'

Maggie couldn't believe what she'd just heard. Had he really just tried to hit on her too?

'Didn't you hear me?'

'I mean, I could buy you dinner for all the work you've done here?'

'Sorry, Ryan, that's impossible. What would Monica think?'

'Seriously?' he asked.

'Yes seriously,' she replied exasperated. 'Look Monica's a wonderful girl. She's a real catch. Go and do what you need to do and sort things out with your gran.'

'I guess but…'

Before she could stop him he had his arms around her and was sobbing onto her shoulder. She gulped. This was a side to Ryan she had definitely not expected. Gingerly, she held him as a friend might do to try and calm him. His grip tightened. She tried to break away but he wouldn't let go. He was holding on to her much more firmly than was appropriate in their situation. Reluctantly, she allowed it rather than fight him off, trying not to get flurried. God, he felt so virile, she could see the attraction for Ellie. She breathed in deeply and smelt the musk of his aftershave and caught herself inadvertently rubbing her hand up and down the firm muscles of his back. She felt his golden hair flop across her neck and his cheek warm against hers. His hands had moved down to her waist.

Guiltily, she pushed him away. He looked at her, pleading with a little-boy-lost look. She shook her head partly in disbelief but partly to say firmly 'no'. Then he turned and left disconsolate. Hurriedly, she shut the door behind him and then sat down on a stool, flushed, then put her head in her hands and laughed. That was just too painful and much too dangerous. It was the first time since her marriage she'd ever held a man like that, and she wasn't proud of herself at all. But from his look, she knew he'd been winging it. Monica clearly had him twisted around her little finger.

'Damn the Rosses,' she shouted into an empty house. Now somehow it felt like she too was being dragged into their horrible family mess. And his strong embrace had felt far too good. Although she'd been married for two months she still wasn't sure about such things. She loved her husband dearly but it had all happened so quickly. She knew what she really loved about him was the certainty that he would always be there for her. But physically, she wasn't sure. And to be with one man for the rest of her life and never feel that thrill of being desired by another again? Clumsily maybe, but Ryan had awakened something she had been trying to deny for some time.

She hurried home to make her husband his favourite meal for dinner. They were due at bell-ringing that evening but she planned to offer him something even sweeter after that for desert.

Ryan had returned to the pub and shouted up the stairs for Monica just in time to save Harry from her potential advances. The expression on her face was a picture. When she'd left, Harry hurriedly dressed and locked his door. That was a narrow escape. He could soon hear them arguing downstairs but tried to put that out of his mind.

For the rest of the afternoon, he continued to work away at his plan for the survey on the assumption he'd get a green light from Mrs Ross. Although he hadn't yet heard from Ellie or Maggie he was hopeful. He thought he could get it all done pretty quickly with help – in fact, he could have the whole thing wrapped up for a pitch by the weekend. He made a few calls and speculatively booked the team in for Thursday and Friday. The trump card from his perspective was that both the interior and exterior would provide more than enough locations. There were also plenty of little places along the High Street that might do for street scenes. So it would all be very efficient. He walked up and down the road making a list of potential prospects then decided to call it a day. If he was due at the church at seven-thirty, he'd better think about dinner. Oh, and then there was the hair cut…four o'clock, he just had enough time. First though he popped into The Pond sweet shop next door to the barber's to stock up on his favourite mints.

The two girls serving behind the counter seemed very glad to see him. It was half-term and they'd been deluged with youngsters and their mums all day, but it'd suddenly gone quiet around three when they all went to pick up their elder siblings from the holiday club. He got chatting with one of the girls and thought to ask her about Old Place. However, she didn't know that much about it. But while he was being served another customer came in and asked the other assistant if she'd heard about Ryan. Harry's ears perked up. He was amazed what he heard. *So that's what the gunshots were all about.* And from the drift of their conversation, the story of Ryan's lunchtime 'shotgun conversion' was apparently already well known around the village. It was certainly eliciting great amusement from the girls behind the counter.

'Are you talking about Ryan Ross?' he asked innocently.

'Yes, he's just agreed to get hitched facing the barrel of a shotgun!'

'A shotgun?'

'The pub landlady didn't give him no option, sorted him good and proper. Let off both barrels so to speak and then threatened worse. She's a little crazy mind, been stalking him for a while.'

'She has?'

'Mind you she's not the first to go after him, he's been with most of the girls in the village at one time or another!' said the other girl.

'Yeah, he's too cute by half, thinks he's god's gift. They call him Flash. It's normally over in a couple of minutes they say,' replied the girl who'd served him.

'Well it nearly was 'flash and it's all over' at lunchtime,' the other girl laughed hysterically.

'Well, you'd know about that, wouldn't you?'

'Leave off, Chloe!'

'Mind you… with those muscles and that hair.'

Harry coughed, somewhat embarrassed by their girlie banter.

'He's a piece of work too, mind.'

'He is?'

'There was that girl of his they found in the pond last year an' all,' she said. 'Fell in drunk or something. Had to give her the kiss of life; she was as blue as a fish when they pulled her out…They reckon someone might have pushed her in but they never charged no one.'

'And don't forget that other one in the bell tower over at Pilstye a couple of weeks back! She was one of his flames too.'

God what was this?

He paid up. Now he was really worried about Ryan Ross; it seemed as if he was trailing the clouds of his own destruction in his wake. The barber's was shutting up soon so he'd have to be quick. He looked around and saw there was some commotion going on further up the High Street, a dispute over a parking space. As he stepped out to cross over to the barber's he was nearly run over by one of the two drivers accelerating quickly towards Haywards Heath. She was driving a white van with a landscape gardening sign painted on it. He recognised Monica at the wheel and Ryan beside her, but neither recognised him; she just hooted the horn in irritation.

What on earth's got into her? he thought. *She's driving like a homicidal lunatic.*

CHAPTER EIGHT

PHOTOGRAPHIC MEMORIES

Oh, 'tis love, 'tis love that makes the world go round.

Lewis Carroll, *Alice's Adventures in Wonderland.*

Poynting's, Lindfield, Wednesday, 27th May

Ellie got back from Ovingdean early Wednesday morning and went straight round to Maggie's house in Raphael Road. After Maggie had related (most of) the details of her meetings with the Ross family the previous day, Ellie realised she'd better smooth things over with Mrs Ross before Harry turned up at her door.

She was welcomed enthusiastically. After the usual pleasantries, Ellie got straight to the point.

'You know Ryan wants you to bring everything back to Old Place, don't you?'

'For you dear, I'd send it all back.'

'For me?'

'You're keen on him, aren't you?' Ellie blushed but was careful how she answered.

'I really don't know what would give you that idea. Anyway, it's irrelevant, he's engaged to Monica now.'

'She's trash. You can get him away from her anytime.'

'Well even if I could, why would I lift a finger against her?'

'Because you love him. Let yourself go, save him from himself.'

'Love him? You've got to be joking.'

'I know what I see.'

'Yes, but obviously not how I feel,' she replied and then bit her lip. Serena saw the expression on her face and interpreted it as a partial confession.

'I think I do.'

Ellie winced again. She paused and then decided to change the subject; it wouldn't help to say what she really felt about her grandson. 'Look Monica's putting a ton of pressure on him to get the things back. Don't you at least feel sorry for him?'

'He's a donkey,' she replied and then added thoughtfully. 'Do you think she'll break up with him if I don't?'

'I didn't say that.'

'But that's what you meant?'

'Not at all. She'll never break it off now. Why would she?'

'We'll see.' Ellie paused for a moment and then decided to launch into the real reason for her visit.

'Look Mrs Ross, about the filming…'

'Oh yes the filming. Well, anything for you girls, but you know what you've got to do.'

'It's just my friend Harry…'

'Yes, I'm seeing him later. Do you want me to be helpful to him?'

'If you could?'

'Well, I'll try my best.'

'And what do I tell Ryan, Mrs Ross?'

'My dear, I think you know in your heart exactly what you need to and what you want to tell Ryan.'

Ellie was left even more troubled by that conversation but at least Mrs Ross had been positive about the filming. It was her father's birthday that weekend and so on the way back from Poynting's, Ellie popped into the gift shop in the High Street to pick out a card and a present. Joe collected old cinema curios and she'd seen a limited edition replica poster of *Brighton Rock* that was just right for him. She knew she couldn't run to an original, they went for hundreds even thousands. After she'd selected his present she was absent-mindedly browsing some silver jewellery when she sensed someone come up behind her. She recognised the smell of his aftershave immediately but still her body started when she felt his two great hands form a bowl around her waist.

'Ryan get off!' she grimaced between her teeth as she turned round. She wanted to slap him again, but there were other people in the shop and she didn't want to make a scene.

'I'm glad I found you here,' he whispered in reply, resting his chest on her back. 'I haven't been able to sleep all night. My head is so mixed up. I hear you've just been to see her?'

'Well, yes, but how did you know that?' she asked, trying to move away. Ryan ignored her question and pulled her towards him, brushing his lips against her neck provocatively.

'What did she say? Is she returning the things?' he asked.

'Not exactly.' She elbowed him in the stomach and he moved back.

'Damn,' he said, raising his voice. 'Were you firm with her?' The other couple in the shop turned round to see what was going on. She shushed him to be quiet.

'Very, I told her you wanted everything returned immediately,' hissed Ellie between her teeth. She was blushing and noticed the glances from the other customers, but didn't dare move away. She indicated to him that they should move into the back section of the shop that was empty.

'And she didn't move?' he said when they got there.

'No, she wants you to ditch Monica first,' replied Ellie looking into the front of the shop nervously. The last thing she wanted was rumours spreading, the whole village knew about the engagement.

'But I can't now.'

'No, of course you can't, you dork.'

'You know, it might have been different if...' She felt him nuzzle up to her again, his hand around her waist. She could smell the intensity of that scent and felt queasy inside.

'Don't start that again Ryan, you know how I feel about that. You're engaged, you had your chance,' she murmured. He was really beginning to bug her now.

'But you mean we could start again? If I were free, I mean?' She rolled her eyes; she was going to have to be more direct.

'Look you idiot, I didn't say or mean that. You have obligations now and I won't be any part of breaking faith with those obligations or encourage anyone else to do so either. Do you understand?' she said firmly. 'Now just leave me alone will you?'

There was a silence for a few minutes. She'd moved away but he soon regained his close proximity to her, so close in fact that she could feel his breath again on the hairs on her neck. She pushed him more firmly away, this time with her elbow in his groin. He just grinned. He clearly still hadn't got the message.

'Do you like that jewellery, Ellie?'

'Yes Ryan, it's very fine work,' she lied. It was actually quite poor workmanship but of course he wouldn't recognise that in a million years. 'Now for the last time, leave me alone. I don't want to make a scene but I will if you don't leave right now.'

'Then let me buy it for you then, choose anything you want. All of it if you want.'

'You've got to be joking. I couldn't even accept so much as a pin cushion from you, let alone jewellery.'

'Please?'

'No way, Ryan. Now please just go away and sort yourself out.' She was on the edge of sobbing and tried to hide the fact with her handkerchief. She pushed him away again, more roughly this time when he tried to kiss her. The shopkeeper was looking over at them frowning. 'Ryan, just go!'

Finally, he got the message. As soon as he'd left, she took a minute to settle herself and then paid for her father's present and ran out of the shop back towards Old Place. The young assistant smiled to herself as she left; it wasn't the first time she'd witnessed such a scene with Flash. In fact, she rather fancied him herself. She certainly wouldn't have turned down that jewellery if he'd offered it to her.

Harry had just chained up his bike after a morning ride and was surprised to see Ellie running towards him at full pelt up the High Street. He was even more shocked when rather than run straight past, she ran directly into his arms and buried her face in his chest, hugging him for dear life and sobbing her heart out. For a minute he just stood there, somewhat alarmed, but with his arms tightly around her, waiting for her to breathe and speak. But she said nothing.

'What's the matter,' he asked at last. 'Did you argue with Mrs Ross?'

'No, worse,' she said breathlessly. 'Look, can we go somewhere private, Harry?'

Harry considered taking her up to his room but thought better of it and instead guided her round to the back of the pub. He knew of a more secluded section of the garden for residents only where there was a small rose arbour and a bench overlooking a fish pond. She sat on the bench beside him, holding him tightly round the shoulders, her head buried in his cycling vest while she cried. He could feel her jerk every so often as another sob emerged. During that long period of silence, interrupted only by the trickling of the fountain and cooing of collared doves, Harry stroked her hair as soothingly as he could. After five minutes, she seemed to calm and the jerking stopped. She raised her head to look at him. Her face was stained and blotched with mascara running around her eyes but at least she was smiling. Her hair looked heavenly in the sun. She stroked the stubble on his cheek.

'I'm sorry,' she said. 'I feel such a fool. Thank you for holding me. I needed someone to hug.'

'Of course,' he said, ignoring the 'someone'. 'You know your smile is something else.' That made her feel warm inside and she kissed him on the cheek.

'Thank you for being a friend.'

'Anytime.' Ellie cleared her throat and made her best effort to recover a businesslike demeanour.

'She'll let you film, you know, if you ask her nicely. Mrs Ross I mean.'

'That's great news, but I'm more worried about you right now. Tell me what's happened to upset you so much?'

'It's a long story,' she sobbed, but this time it was a happy sob and she hugged him tighter. He could already tell she wasn't going to tell him the full story, but somehow he also knew they'd just made a breakthrough. He didn't press her for an answer. He could guess it must have something to do with Ryan. He was just happy to be there for her. He walked her back to Old Place and left her in Maggie's capable care. He really wanted to stay but he was already late for his own appointment with Mrs Ross. Somehow he was going to need to speak man to man with Ryan Ross pretty soon.

During that appointment, Harry confirmed his suspicion that Serena Ross was not a woman to be trifled with.

'Ah Mr Jamieson, please come in,' she said effusively. Despite the fact that he was late, she was quite taken by the appearance of the fine-looking young man standing at her doorstep. *'Tall and unusually handsome with curling red-brown hair, a long sensual mouth and soft brown eyes,'* she later wrote in her diary.

'Maggie told me you'd be calling today and Ellie's been round pleading your case already,' she said disarmingly.

Harry was taken by her appearance, too. She was around sixty, nearly six foot tall and lean, although worn-faced from too much sun. Her clothes were vintage, made from the most vibrant and flamboyant materials, free-spirited in there vividness. They were certainly not what he'd expected from a woman of her age. He was surprised also by the brightness of her lipstick, the rouge on her deep-crested crimson cheeks and the ample colour applied round her agate-coloured eyes. Those facial adornments belonged to the face of a woman half her age, he thought. Indeed although her hair was touched with grey, it still blazed with copper, just as it probably had when it'd dazzled the young men of her youth. He recalled what Virginia Woolf had once said of one of her own flirtatious ancestors: *'I was so much overcome by her beauty that I really felt as if I'd suddenly got into the sea, and heard the mermaids fluting on their rocks.'*

He'd read what he could about Serena Ross overnight.

There was more than enough scandal about her to fill a book. Remarkably, her tolerant but insipid husband had never been that interested in her as a lover, perversely preferring subaltern affairs while pretending devotion inside the bedroom to the rest of society. During an outburst of sexual freedom in the eighties and nineties, she'd become infamous for her male liaisons, especially those that stimulated her mind or fanned her sense of true worth. Not all of those affairs were physical. 'Making love' was a term that still possessed innocence in those days. Just as she wasn't conventional, neither was she supine; she was certainly not someone to be pushed around or controlled. Rather she was often described as pushy even strident, quite ruthless in her own beliefs. Yes, she had many friends, but she'd also made more than her fair share of enemies too. Some of whom had been only too glad to spill the beans to a grateful press.

'Thank you Mrs Ross. I do apologise for being late and having to disturb you like this,' Harry replied.

'Nonsense, how many handsome young visitors do you think I get these days?' she replied sternly but with a mischievous smile. She spoke in a soft, sensuous, almost rapturous voice. He hardly dared to guess the answer to that question. He imagined she was still quite capable of stirring quite a few men's hearts. He could see little resemblance in her face to the brawny Ryan, except perhaps a jaunty crookedness to her nose.

Given his need to persuade one or eventually both of the Ross's to let him use the house, he was keen to get her onside first. Ellie's news about the filming that morning had been very welcome, because his initial fear was of someone likely to be quite fixed in her views. He knew he still had to sell the project to her himself, but he was hopeful that he could appeal to her obvious aesthetic passions. She showed him into the best sitting room stocked with fine Chippendale furniture. He'd already guessed its provenance. Each piece shimmered with a deep rosewood and mahogany glow. She noticed his admiring expression.

'Ah, so you like fine furniture, young man?'

'If it's as good this,' he said. He thought back to Adela Gereth's famous description of her collection in *Spoils*:

Well, there isn't one of these pieces I don't know and love – yes, as one remembers and cherishes the happiest moments of one's life. Blindfold, in the dark, with the brush of a finger, I could tell one from another. They're living things to me; they know me, they return the touch of my hand.

'You have great taste.'

'Well, thank you. Of course, when I'm gone they'll probably all end up in some depressing antique shop or worse repainted lilac by some awful interior designer. I'd rather deface or burn them myself than let them fall into the wrong hands. But that's my concern, Mr Jamieson. Let's get to the point. I hear you've a proposition to make?'

'Well yes Mrs Ross. I know I should have asked you first, but I was overwhelmed when I viewed Old Place yesterday.'

'Please call me Serena, young man. Yes, Ellie was a little naughty there. She should have told me beforehand. But so be it. I'm very glad you liked it.'

'I hope Ellie explained that I'm interested in using the property for a BBC film of the Henry James's novel, *The Spoils of Poynton*. We'd like to shoot there this summer.'

'She did indeed. Fortunately for you, I'm also an avid James reader, although unfamiliar with that particular work. What did someone once say about him?' she said, pretending to search her memory.

It is not deeds that he values as important, but thoughts, personality, goodness; the 'invisible man' of shot-silk human nature.

'Wow, what a great line!'

'Yes, well I've little else to amuse myself with these days but read and sew.'

'Well, Old Place would be perfect for the filming,' he said. 'It's got exactly the right period feel to it, and I should assure you straight away that our adaptation will be very faithful to the original.'

'Then I'm a little disappointed in you,' she said mischievously, 'seeing as James was never faithful to any particular human being or convention. In fact, he was a total social chameleon in my view, with some very strange tastes,' she laughed. Harry looked a little taken aback by this and wondered how to respond.

'Well, you're right he did have a lot of very different friends.'

'Let's call a spade a spade, shall we. He was sexually confused; in fact we'd probably call him gay these days wouldn't we?'

'Well, I'm not sure…'

'Don't get me wrong, young man. I know how sensitive you media types can be and I'm not disapproving, nothing wrong with that, just pointing out his lack of conventionality. Interestingly, somewhat at odds with Mr Kempe's conservative views, don't you think?'

'Possibly…'

'Mind you, there were also rumours about Kempe in his time.'

'There were?'

'He never married you see, so it's natural speculation. But I don't believe any of it, of course.'

'Of course not.'

'No. He had a great many lady friends. Just as my husband was an expert in art, I count myself an expert in men's affairs. I'm sure he was ardent but just shy. But anyway I shouldn't waste your time with women's gossip. Back to the house, it's such a shame of course that Mr Tower sold the best glass to those Black Country paint and varnish traders!'

'But there are still some very beautiful pieces…'

'Yes, but not his finest work. For that you don't have to go too far though. A lot of his best work is in Sussex. Have you been to Wakehurst or Cuckfield yet or indeed Danehill? There you can see some very important examples of his work. Danehill in particular is absolutely magnificent.'

'I haven't. But it sounds like a bike ride might be on the cards if the weather's fine later!'

'Yes you should do that, but I'm afraid I won't be joining you. My cycling days are over,' she added. 'I travel in comfort nowadays.' They both laughed. 'Now, I assume you know the basic history. Kempe bought Old Place shortly after his mother's death. It was quite a wreck. It had been used as a poor house for many years, but he spent an absolute fortune on it. He had the finest taste but he was still a bachelor at heart. Up till then he'd been living alone in Marylebone. So he depended a lot on his closer female friends to advise him on how to make it a home. By the way, there's some evidence he was looking for a wife even then!'

'Really, there is?'

'Yes, there's a funny letter somewhere in the archives from his friend Skef Dodgson, Lewis Carroll's brother. He recommended to Kempe that he use a marriage agency in Bedford. It's all quite amusing and all the more surprising given, as Dodgson says in the letter, there were so many women who'd be interested in him, including his younger sister apparently. I think he probably could have taken his pick, but he worked too hard, poor man, which happens sometimes. Then it was too late. So be warned if you're that way inclined.' She looked at him curiously. She couldn't really tell whether he was that way inclined or not, and normally she was a good judge of such things.

'I'll be sure to remember that!' he laughed.

'I doubt it,' she replied. 'Anyway, because Kempe had no heirs, the house passed with the business to Walter Tower, a distant cousin. He wasn't particularly popular with the rest of the workforce and was seen as something of an impostor. Kempe's lieutenants, especially his chief draughtsman, John Lisle, resented Tower stealing their glory. I knew Lisle's daughter, you know. A very learned and cultivated lady; she wrote an excellent book on Kempe's life. She had quite a few tales to tell about those days, of *base animals and humans*, so to speak. Some good gossip too.'

'I'd love to see that book.'

'Well, I'm sure I have a copy somewhere. And I'll see if I can look out that letter too. But let's get back to the point. How long will you need to use the house, do you think?'

'Well, the filming should take three to six weeks once we start, but we have to prep the location, so maybe three months in total. We'll obviously make sure it's absolutely back in the best of shape for sale and we'll compensate you for the delay.'

'I'm not worried about that, I don't need the money. In fact it quite suits me, keeps the wolves in the family at bay for a while.'

Harry looked a little disconcerted at this oblique reference to Ryan. But she sought to reassure him.

'Don't worry, I'll handle Ryan. If that's what you're thinking?'

'I was. But well that's brilliant. Of course there's quite a bit to do, a survey, etc., but I'm pretty sure that's a formality from what I've seen.

'...and you promise me you'll give full credit to Mr Kempe's work in the production.'

'Of course. In fact, I'd be surprised if the BBC didn't want to do a background documentary too.'

'Well, first-rate. That too would be long overdue. Then please go ahead with your survey and draw up the necessary documents. I'll put you in touch with my solicitor in due course.'

'Thank you so much, Mrs Ross, er Serena, that's really very good news.'

'Well, I'm going strictly on Ellie and Maggie's recommendations.'

'I won't let you down.'

'Now, let me turn to my next subject. So what do you think of Ellie. Very sweet, isn't she?'

'Well, I ...er,' he stammered.

'She understands what I'm all about. She'd make a fine match for my idiot grandson Ryan if only he'd get his finger out. I wonder if you could arrange for them to be extras, you know, create a little bit of off-stage romance. I've told her she needs to let herself go a bit, too. She will wear those dungarees and her hair's always such a mess. You can't confine natural beauty like that, can you? Now if she was properly made up and in period costume...'

'I...' he started to reply, seeing her calculation, but he was unable to stop her.

'And have you met Ryan yet?'

'Actually…'

'He's a good boy at heart, but remarkably stupid and easily led. Always going after this or that fashion, gadgets, cars, what have you? His speech is so full of slang nonsense, despite my best attempts to get him properly schooled. If he'd got his act together, he could have married any one of a dozen girls from the better families roundabouts.'

'Er…' *She was a piece of work,* he thought. *What a character!* He thought about mentioning his own romantic interest in Ellie at that point, but realised that would be a landmine.

'Instead, he's wasting his time on that awful trollop, Monica Malling. She's the epitome of verbal vulgarity, quite the philistine. Her mother's even worse. There isn't a jot of taste in her. And look how she dresses, skin-tight leather or skirt halfway up her thighs, bra on show for everyone to see. There's something odd about that family; too much in-breeding for my liking. And a history of—' She bit her tongue and stopped herself. 'Anyway while Ryan's chasing after Mistress Malling, he'll get nothing from me. Now Ellie would be different…she's someone I'd be glad to endow, as my grandfather did for me.'

'Well…' Harry paused, unsure quite how to deal with this embarrassing conversation. She could see that in his eyes.

'But there's no need to fret, Mr Jamieson. My life's not over yet. "Wednesday's child is full of woe," they say. Well that's not my experience. Think about what I've said, though. I might call on you for some help in return.'

'Er, of course,' Harry said. Mrs Ross rose and moved towards the door, expecting Harry to follow her. He realised the 'interview' was over.

'Well, goodbye, Mr Jamieson. I do hope I'll have the

pleasure of talking with you further. I'm afraid I have my bridge group arriving soon, so I'll have to kick you out,' she said. 'Remember what I said, though,' she added, dropping further stiches of a web she'd presumably proceed to weave over the next few days.

Harry left the house pleased but also deep in thought and somewhat disturbed. If the price of getting her agreement to the filming was to break off his pursuit of Ellie, that would be really tough. Not an eventuality he was at all minded to consider given their 'progress' that morning. There had to be another way. But as soon as he'd reached the main road, he heard raised voices behind him. It was the voice of a man and he seemed very angry about something. He also heard Mrs Ross's calmer but insistent trill firmly punctuating the spaces between his expletives. Harry waited under a chestnut tree for a few minutes, worried about what was going on inside. Then he heard the front door slam and heavy booted feet stamping across the gravel. A minute later, the flash of the now familiar white van screeched away from between the bushes, out on to the road in the direction of Haywards Heath. It forced another motorist to brake sharply.

'That must be Ryan again. I suppose I'd better have a word before this gets out of hand,' he said to himself, shaking his head.

Maggie had warned him again about Ryan's likely opposition the night before. In fact, she'd seemed quite agitated about what Ryan might do. She was alone as her husband had a young couple to see about their banns. Harry had noticed Ryan had texted her while they were drinking with the bell ringers. From her expression, he'd obviously been quite rude.

Maggie had told Harry that Ryan was dead set against

the filming, especially if it was going to delay the sale process. She said he'd even accused them of organising it all to spite him. She didn't tell him though about Ellie's earlier argument with him before the shooting incident.

In fact, the call had disturbed her so much that she'd made her apologies and headed back home early to her husband, leaving him to chat with the rest of the bell ringers. Naturally, they were full of the gruesome tale of that accident the girls in the sweet shop had mentioned, one that'd occurred in the bell tower of a neighbouring church the previous month. Nobody knew why, but a young girl (yet another of Ryan's previous conquests, apparently) had gone up the bell tower alone and got tangled up in the ropes. She was carried twenty-feet above the platform and had to be cut out by the fire brigade. She was still alive, just, but they were too late to save her from a serious back injury. Even bell-ringing was dangerous in Sussex! He'd only realised after Maggie had left that she'd clean forgotten to tell him the tale about the Kempe bells too…

Despite Ryan's opposition, he knew he had to press on with his pitch. He worked away for a couple of hours on the plans for the survey. He'd already booked the team to start on Thursday, and he wasn't going to give up after he'd found the perfect spot. But he also knew he needed to find a way to get to Ryan alone. He was sure he could find some way of getting him onside. Maybe Screna's suggestion of involving him in the process as an extra was a good idea; it was remarkable how starry-eyed people became when there was a film-crew around!

Just then there was a knock at his bedroom door. He opened it and a young boy was standing there with a neatly wrapped parcel.

'You Mr Jamieson?' he asked. Harry nodded. 'Mrs Ross asked me to bring this round to you.' Harry gave the boy a pound for his troubles, the boy's eyes almost falling out of his head. 'Thank you mister,' he said and ran off straight towards the nearest sweet shop.

Harry took the parcel and opened it carefully. It was the book by Lisle's daughter that Mrs Ross had spoken about. And inside were a couple of photocopied documents. The first was the letter from Skef Dodgson she'd referred to. It was written to Lisle and contained an account of a visit Kempe had made to the Dodgsons in their rented summer village in Bognor in 1872. The second letter was from Dodgson's sister Louisa but was in a much more difficult hand. It appeared they'd had a very interesting collection of visitors that day.

'Charlie, Charlie, welcome, it's so good to see you,' I cried. I was standing at the door of Wellington House, the little seaside villa we'd taken for the summer in The Steyne. Charlie Kempe's carriage had just stopped outside. I walked to the road and shook his hand as soon as he'd stepped down from the running board of the fly. Then, without a moment's further thought, threw my arms round his shoulders in a joyous bear hug.

'Gosh, it's years since we last saw each other, Charlie. Not since Oxford. Please come in,' I added. 'Our little coven is dying to meet you inside.'

'Thank you Skef,' he replied. 'It's so good to see you, too.'

I could tell, however, that I'd somewhat embarrassed him with my affectionate embrace; he was pushing me away gently as best he could. He looked tired from his long journey and seemed a little taken aback.

'Indeed, it's so good to get out of London for a change,' he added restoring his dignity. He passed the housekeeper his coat and cane and then entered into our long hallway, whilst the carriage driver dealt with his luggage.

'Ah, yes, what does the poet say? "To leave behind the noise and smoke of town, to breathe the sea air again,"' I added [Tennyson I think but I'm not certain]. I slapped him gently on the back again and then stood aside to look him up and down. 'Well I have to say, Charlie, you are the very picture of wellbeing and prosperity.'

'Thank you Skef and indeed you look very well, too; the sea air must be doing you good. Now, how's Wilf [my brother]? Will he be joining us this weekend? I haven't seen him since he was up at Christ Church.'

'No, Charlie, but he's doing very well and sends his best wishes. You know he married last year, of course. To a lovely girl called Alice Donkin. He's the land agent for Lord Boyne up in Ludlow. They're all doing very well, but are all far too dull for my liking. But look man, don't stand there, come on into the sitting room, let me introduce you to the coven, er… my sisters,' I said. 'I think you may well remember one or two of them. They certainly remember you!'

Wilf and I had been at Twyford prep school with Kempe. We were also later at Oxford at the same time although at different colleges. About that time, I'd got my first curacy at Chertsey. As we entered the sitting room, four of my sisters stood up in unison from their embroidery, all eager and anxious to greet our keenly anticipated bachelor visitor. I introduced him to Fanny first, whom he had not met before. She was the eldest, in her mid-forties, and, with Aunt Lucy's help, had ruled the rest of us with a rod of iron ever since our mother passed on.

'Fanny, this is Mr Charlie Kempe, my very dear friend

from Twyford and Oxford. We haven't seen each other for, oh, goodness knows how many years. He's become a very handsome fellow though, what?'

'Well we're absolutely delighted you could visit with us, Mr Kempe,' she replied, shaking his hand. 'I do know of and admire the work you're doing in the church. Of course, we also know your colleague Mr Bodley very well. He sings your praises on every occasion we see him.'

'And these charming ladies beside her are Louisa, Margaret and Henrietta, my younger sisters,' I added. 'I believe you may have met them once before, with my mother at Twyford?'

Charles nodded and bowed graciously to each one in turn. I still had a vague recollection of that summer's day when my three unruly sisters had visited us at the end of term with our mother. Tragically, shortly afterwards she'd passed away with brain-fever.

'Mr Kempe, please tell us about what you're working on at the moment,' asked Louisa; she was the fourth eldest of my seven sisters (if you believe it, six of whom were still at that time unmarried!). Louisa was always the most vocal and gregarious. She must have been eight or nine when she met Charles at Twyford and had also seen him once since at Christ Church. She'd told me before the visit that she was sure he wouldn't remember her, but I knew she'd always carefully followed news of him and I suspected held a bit of a fancy for him, too. Maggie and Hattie both smiled at him and then seeing Louisa's slightly captivated expression looked at each other knowledgeably, rolling their eyes as if to acknowledge her clear interest in our guest. I noticed and chuckled to myself. So I was right about that, then.

'Please ladies, let the poor man recover from his journey before you start bombarding him with any more questions!' I said. 'There will be plenty of time for that later.' Secretly I was pleased. I'd arranged that visit at Aunt Lucy's urging with the secondary purpose of introducing my worthy bachelor friend to our formidable gallery of sibling spinsters. 'Please Charlie, come through to the garden and take some refreshment with us. We have a number of guests with us today, some of whom you know. We should really all be enjoying this gorgeous summer's day en plein air rather than cooped up inside.'

We passed through the French doors of the little shaded sitting room on to a covered veranda at the back of the house. It overlooked a small but pretty garden with a distant aspect of the pier and the sea. Kempe commented that it reminded him of his boyhood: the scent of salt and the scraping sound of seagulls in the air. He soon seemed much more relaxed following his rather stiff appearance on arrival.

Our guests were seated on a wooden platform in the shadow of a rose-clad pergola. My elder brother (I am sure you will know him better as Lewis Carroll) was talking with our four guests — two gentleman and three ladies, the latter all dressed in beautiful summer lace.

'Ah, the Morrells; what a lovely surprise! How delightful that they could join us Skef,' Kempe exclaimed in delight. 'And isn't that your elder brother too, the writer? I wasn't expecting him to be here today?'

'Yes Charlie, my little surprise. Sorry, I should have mentioned this all to you earlier. We have the whole family visiting us here at one time or another over the next few weeks,' he laughed. 'I wasn't sure if you'd ever met my brother before? Perhaps when we were all at Oxford?'

'No, I'm pretty sure I've never had the opportunity to make his acquaintance, but of course I'm a huge admirer of his writing. It will really be an honour to meet him at last. And pray, who's that lady and gentleman sitting next to Mrs Morrell and Freddie?'

'Oh yes that's my second surprise. But I'd somehow assumed that you'd know them? That's Mr Edward Godwin, the architect, and his friend Mrs Ellen Terry Watts, the actress. They're friends of my brother's and staying in town for a few days with their young family before going on to see the pier at Hastings. We suggested they join us this afternoon, knowing your interest in architecture, as it were. I hope you don't mind?'

'Of course not. My, well yes, I know the gentleman's name of course and I'm very familiar with his work, but I'm not as yet acquainted with Mr Godwin. And as for Mrs Watts, clearly I should have recognised her at once. In fact how could I not have done?' he enthused. 'I once had the absolute pleasure of seeing her play Titania at the Theatre Royal in Bath. But that was years ago now; she was just a girl. I can see that she's blossomed into a yet more beautiful woman.'

'Yes, she's a peach and now a mother too,' I nodded in agreement. Of course we both knew but left unspoken the scandal that surrounded that couple. We walked over to the seated group, who were laughing and joking, taking afternoon tea around a wooden trestle table.

'Of course our charming tea party is slightly more refined than that dreadful Mad Hatter scene in my brother's little book,' I whispered jokingly as we approached. My brother heard us laughing, looked up from the volume he was reading and scowled. At that time, he was really at the height of his fame. He'd had his second work published about little Alice's adventures through the Looking Glass. Of course, it had been an instant success, a sell-out, with more than 8,000 copies ordered.

'Skef, who's this imposter?' he asked jokingly.

'My dear friends, may I introduce you to Mr Charles Kempe, the famed church decorator?' I announced. My brother laughed again but more cautiously. I suppose he realised he'd no longer be the centre of attention for a while. Sensing that Kempe had paused, I hurried to make the appropriate introductions on his behalf. I noticed and was intrigued to note that he blushed somewhat as he greeted the Morrells – indeed Mrs Morrell was a lady for whom I later learned he had a more than a passing admiration.

'Tell us then, please, Mr Kempe, what are you working on now?' asked Louisa again, impatient to get the formal introductions over. She was just thirty and the one keenest of my sisters to lose her spinster status.

'Well, let me see, we have so many projects on the go at the moment,' he began. 'Last year I had the honour to restore a fifteenth-century window at St Tyrnog near Denbigh: the crucifixion and seven sacraments. I've recently been incorporating elements of those designs into new windows for Barsham in Suffolk. Today, I've just come down from Harlington Parish Church in Middlesex. We're designing a crucifixion scene there with three windows in an unusual triptych; there, I've taken my inspiration from the magnificent glass at Nuremberg.'

He pulled out a sketchbook from his briefcase and turned to a vivid sketch drawn in watercolour. It was a glorious design of rich sap green and tawny ruby figures with gold fleur-de-lys and roses, and amber and white ostrich-feathered angels.

'Why, that's truly remarkable, Mr Kempe, really beautiful,' said Fanny.

'Thank you, Miss Dodgson, I'm indeed very pleased with the composition, although we're still struggling a little with the technical side of things,' he replied. 'The effect of stain on white glass is so very difficult to achieve with delicacy; the medieval masters still seem to have an advantage over us there. But I intend to persist with our chemical experiments and discover the secret!'

I could tell from his face that he was actually very proud of the cartoon, but he told me later that he'd had quite a frustrating week trying to make progress on the staining process necessary for the finer detail to the angels' feathers.

'Yes, yes, truly it's very pretty,' added Louisa. 'But please, what news have you brought us of London, Mr Kempe?' she asked, impatient again to direct the conversation. 'It's so dull here on the south coast. Did you see the Albert Memorial yet? And "Whistler's Mother" at the Academy? I'm told it's a dreadful hoot. And isn't it terrible about Mr Rossetti and the reception to his latest poetry. They say he's even made an attempt on his own life?'

'Calm down, Louisa, please. All in good time,' I said, somewhat irritated again at her over-eagerness. I was worried she might frighten Kempe off with her over-attentiveness. 'Please Charlie, take a seat, perhaps Louisa will offer you some tea at last!' I said, admonishing her.

'Yes, there's p-p-plenty of room!' laughed my brother. Charles at last took his seat in a large armchair at one end of the table. He was offered tea and cake and began to chat to Mrs Morrell and Freddie about his journey.

Later on that afternoon, I listened while my brother and Kempe began to talk seriously for the first time.

'Mr Kempe, I assume you must be familiar with photography in your line of work. You might be interested to know that I've some of my more portable equipment here this weekend. I've set up a small studio in the back parlour if you'd do me the honour of sitting for me later?' my brother asked. 'Mrs Terry Watts, Mrs Morrell and Frederica have already very graciously consented to do so already.'

'Indeed, I'm only a little familiar with it, but I'd love to learn more, Mr Dodgson. And I'd be very happy to sit for you, of course.'

After the photographic session, Kempe took quite a great interest in the chemical apparatus in the studio that had been temporarily installed. But he also seemed to have something else on his mind. He took my brother aside and asked him a question he'd been dying to ask.

'So, Mr Dodgson, I couldn't help noticing that like me you have a speech hesitation?'

'Yes, indeed, but it's improving. It's mostly now around the letter 'p' – in words such as impossible, patience, power. But still, failures that have rather deferred the hope I'd formed of helping in church again, I'm afraid. For if I break down in reading to only one or two, I should be all the worse, I fear, in the presence of a congregation.'

'And do you see anyone about it?' asked Kempe.

'Mr Henry Rivers at Tunbridge. I've found him a very great help,' replied my brother.

'Then I might seek out that gentleman, because I have a very similar impediment.'

'You should indeed; for £20 he can do a great deal of good.'

Kempe looked very satisfied with that information, but now my brother was emboldened.

'May I in turn ask you a question, Mr Kempe?'

'Of course.'

'Have you never thought of marriage?'

'I can't say I've ever yet had the temptation,' he laughed.

'I just wondered whether your speech hesitation bothered you in that respect. I'm sure with your fame you must have plenty of admirers?'

'I can't really say so, although it's not helped. Is it then so with you?'

'Well, no, not really. The simple truth is that I'm far too busy with my university work. And as yet, truthfully, the right woman has never really crossed my path. Anyway, you can that see we're certainly in no shortage of feminine company in this family!' he laughed. 'But what about yourself, Mr Kempe? Wilf is shortly to tie the knot. I'm pretty sure Skef will be captured before too long too. Will you not be tempted like my brother and follow Wilf down that treacherous path?'

'It's the same story; pressure of work. We've been besieged with new orders. Moreover, I've just set up a small glass studio in Camden. It's been hard work trying to get the technical side right. I don't think I'd make much of a husband with all that on my mind!'

'But all the same Mr Kempe, you are both a very handsome and I'm sure desirable man, there's no doubt of that. There must be many eligible ladies who'd be only too delighted to make a settled life with you. Take my sister Louisa, for instance!' he chuckled. Kempe blushed.

'Please do,' I muttered under my breath but out of earshot. I'm afraid I could no longer contain myself; I'd been listening in on their conversation with increasing amusement.

'You poor suffering bachelors!' I interjected. 'To that point, I've heard of a matrimonial agency in Bedford that has many eligible ladies on its books, who I'm sure would be only too happy to make a fitting match for both of you. Although in your case, Charlie, I'd suggest that there are plenty of willing volunteers closer at hand!' He looked at Louisa playing croquet with my sisters. Kempe blushed and quickly changed the subject.

'So, is this what they call wet-plate photography, Mr Dodgson? I know there's a new technique in development, one that I've heard of, but for the moment I can't recall its name?'

'Yes, this is wet-collodion, Mr Kempe, or at least my own version of it. The latest format you refer to is dry-plate but it is still very experimental. Wet-collodion is still my preferred method, but as you can see, it's not very portable. My studio in Oxford is much better set up for that. There are a lot of chemicals involved and they are not at all easy to apply.'

'I would be very interested to see the whole process, though,' added Kempe. 'I'm struggling with many technical issues myself in the glass-staining process. Maybe there's something I could learn from your knowledge of photographic chemicals?'

After dinner that evening, Mrs Terry Watts delighted us with a rendition from the part of Portia in 'The Merchant of Venice', a play that she was rehearsing. After she'd finished, we men retired to the study to smoke and partake of a very fine bottle of Madeira wine. Our conversation soon turned to my brother's recent literary successes and then once again to his interest in photography.

'Charlie, you know that you were asking my brother earlier about wet-collodion photography. Well I've had an idea. Do you by any chance still enjoy boating?' I asked.

'Well, of course, but it's not something I've really had the good fortune to pursue since I was a boy. I still have a fancy for it, yes.'

'Well, then, why don't we all take a boat over to Yarmouth tomorrow? We could get the early train and hire a skiff, or if you'd prefer, we can catch the steamer over. There's a lady I know of, a Mrs Cameron, who lives near Freshwater. I've heard she's doing some very interesting work with the wet-collodion technique.'

My brother interrupted somewhat churlishly at that point. 'My dear Skef, I'm afraid that I'm all too familiar with

Mrs Cameron's work. I'd hesitate to describe it as interesting. Indeed I'm not taken at all with her photographs. Although some are quite picturesque, others are taken purposely out of focus, even hideously so. Overall, I cannot say that they are triumphs of art at all.'

'All the same, Charles, I'm sure she would be very glad to show us her work and the trip over would be so delightful. The countryside there is very fine I hear. We can stay over at Plumbley's Hotel, maybe take a peep at old Tennyson's place later in the day?'

'But…' my brother started to protest again.

However, before he could finish, we were joined by Mrs Watts and Louisa. It was time for her and Mr Goodwin to take their leave of us and return to their hotel.

'Mrs Watts, I've seen the beautiful pictures that Mrs Cameron took of you a few years ago. Have you ever been to Dimbola Lodge? Would you and Mr Goodwin be agreeable to join us on a trip to Freshwater Bay tomorrow?' I asked. They both coughed and Mrs Terry Watts blushed.

'Er… I don't think that's such a good idea Mr Dodgson,' said Goodwin. He looked around the room. There were concerned faces. 'Of course, I'd be delighted to join you, but I suspect Ellen would rather we stay here with your sisters and our children.'

'Indeed, Mr Dodgson, unfortunately my husband may well be staying in Freshwater at the moment,' she added, unruffled.

I realised at once with horror my terrible faux pas. At that time Mr Goodwin and Mrs Terry Watts were lovers, although she was still George Watts's bride. And Watts would probably be staying with the Prinseps near Tennyson. What an idiot I'd been. Fortunately, Kempe came to my rescue.

'What a wonderful idea, come on Mr Dodgson. Three men in a boat, what fun that would be!' he said to my brother.

'Well I suppose so,' my brother agreed somewhat unhappily. He hadn't revealed, at that point, any of the true reasons for his own reluctance to accept my proposal.

'Don't forget me, I'm coming too,' piped my sister Louisa.

The Revd Skeffington Hume Dodgson,
Vicar of Vowchurch,
Herefordshire

CHAPTER NINE

IMAGO AMORIS – FILIA

River Spirit: 'Sleep'st thou, brother?'
Mountain Spirit: 'Brother nay – on my hills the moonbeams play.'

Walter Scott, *Lay of the Last Minstrel Canto First*

Later that day in Lindfield.

Harry looked at his watch. Ellie had the auctioneers in that afternoon so didn't want him around. He'd arranged to meet up with her that evening for dinner, but that meant he still had the whole of Wednesday afternoon to fill. In fact, to complicate things further, he'd actually had a second invitation that morning. Monica had suggested he might like to join her and her friends for a bite to eat after her dance class. He guessed that was likely to wind up Ryan even more though, and he'd probably better not exacerbate that situation further, tempting as the invitation was.

It was a nice afternoon, so he thought he might go for a long ride. But on his way to collect his bike, he bumped into Monica round the back of the pub. She'd been in the storerooms and looked rather shocked to see him standing there as she emerged. She was cursing about something. He could smell there was some sort of flammable material on her hands, turps or varnish or something. When she saw him, she shut the door hurriedly and relocked the padlock before he could stare inside.

'You're back early?' she asked, trying to divert his attention.

'I had a great meeting with Mrs Ross,' he said, 'so I thought I might go for a ride.'

'You got her permission, then I take it?' she asked bluntly.

'Well yes, she seems quite pleased with the idea,' he replied. Monica seemed somewhat put out by this but quickly recovered her cool.

'Are you joining us then tonight?' she asked. 'The girls will be so disappointed if you don't.'

'I'm not sure yet,' he lied. 'I've got to get on with my planning for the survey.' Monica could tell from his voice that he wouldn't be along that evening. She'd have to change her plan then.

'By the way, did the old witch show you the "spoils"?' she asked.

'You mean the furniture, yes…'

'She has no right…' she replied, shaking her head, but stopped to look at his expression for clues to which side he was on.

'But I thought you said you didn't like that old stuff?' Harry asked. 'Not to your taste?'

'Oh, they're alright,' she replied, 'even if some of that dark furniture's hideous. A bit of stripper, a good sanding and it'd stain down nicely enough. But as I said, it's the principle. Fair's fair.'

'Yes of course,' he replied circumspectly. His facial expression gave away all she needed to know.

'Well might see you later than?'

He nodded and smiled. Mrs Ross's words were still ringing in his ears. He wondered if Monica was really quite the philistine that Mrs Ross made her out to be. In fact her idea of 'style' seemed quite modern to Harry, apart from the infamous 'winter garden'. Still, he could understand why Mrs Ross would have preferred Ellie as a wife for her grandson. Her 'spoils' would be safe in Ellie's hands, whereas with Monica…? Sanded down and repainted as shabby chic? Still, he suspected Mrs Ross wasn't going to let that happen either!

For her part, Monica's immediate thoughts were simply that she would now need to find another way of getting Mr Jamieson into a compromising position that she could later take advantage of. For now the pole-dancers were a no-go. But she still had plenty of ideas.

Harry looked at his OS map. It was a hot day, cooling with a light wind but still clear of rain. He worked out that he could head up to Danehill, then on to the National Trust property at Wakehurst, where the guide indicated there was a particularly fine example of Kempe's work – a triptych of St Mary and St John standing either side of the Cross. It was described in a blog he'd read as being '*a bravura silver-stained fantasy-like medieval city roof scape of cloud-capped towers, streaming pennants, bartizans, pantiles and buttressed walls*'. After that, he'd circle round Ardingly Reservoir to Balcombe and then head over to Cuckfield church. He asked her what she thought of his route.

'Perfect,' she said. 'But mind you don't bumping into those fracking protestors on the way…' A new plan had already come into her mind. Even Goths had friends. She just about had time to arrange things.

The Peace Camp, Balcombe Woods, Thursday, May 28th

Thursday morning. It was cold and damp in the camp. His head was thumping. All around him, Harry could smell a choking mixture of wood smoke and joss sticks. There was something stirring in the tent beside him, turning over slowly in its sleeping bag. He felt an arm plonk unconsciously on his head and then stroke his hair. Although he was trying to focus, something very deep and very powerful had largely erased his memory of the night before. Dogs were barking outside, a woman's voice chanting, quietly insistent, the sounds of food being prepared. He reached for but couldn't find his glasses. The rump of the body in the next sleeping bag had shifted position into the pit of his stomach. He looked at his watch: seven-thirty in the morning.

'Shit!'

The body next to him started at his cry and a face turned towards him.

'God!'

'What time is it?' a female voice asked.

'Sshh, it's still far too early,' was the sleepy reply from her friend. Before he knew it, his face was full of a tongue, like a dog slathering. He sat up. It really was a dog and a real hound of a dog at that. He hated dogs.

'Where am I?'

'Where do you want to be, darling?' said the woman next to him, who'd now sat up.

'God, I'm so sorry, I don't…I didn't…'

'Sshh.'

His memory had begun to return. The bike ride, the peace camp, intrigued he'd stopped for a while to chat with the protestors and then? Had he drunk something, had he taken something? Music? He couldn't remember. Drugs?

His head hurt. He was naked apart from his underwear inside the sleeping bag. Who'd undressed him? He had no recollection. He felt around and found his clothes in a pile by his head. They felt damp as if they'd been out in the rain; the inside of the tent was covered in condensation. What were these women's names?

'Jade,' she said, as if she knew from his expression what was on his mind. Yes Jade. That was it. Oh my god, Jade? 'And Claudia,' added the other voice.

'Sorry…'

'Look, stop apologising…'

'And be happy,' said her friend. 'It's not as if anyone knows you're here. And we're not telling.'

It was nine by the time he'd sneaked back into his room at The Tyger. The sky was clear and it looked like it would turn into a fine day, with the wispiest of clouds in the sky. He was just in time to shave and shower and change before the survey gang arrived. He roughed up the bedclothes so that Monica wouldn't think he hadn't slept there that night. But the bigger question was: how on earth was he going to explain his absence the previous evening to Ellie?

The women at the peace camp he'd met were the determined remnants of a larger group that'd successfully protested against the fracking surveys being carried out by an international oil company the previous summer. They'd somewhat split the local community: some wholeheartedly supported their determination to stop the local countryside being despoiled; others were annoyed by the attention-seekers and less-salubrious elements they'd attracted to the previously quiet village. Most were just worried about the impact on local house prices and wished the issue would just go away.

Before Harry had left the protesters' camp, he'd tried to establish at least that 'nothing had happened'. After a good deal of teasing he thought he'd got their assurance. Jade was a photographer camping out there with her girlfriend Claudia for a month. Claudia was an artist too, usually working in glass: green-eyed, thick eye-browed, neck like a tower, abundance of rosy crimped hair, a real Pre-Raph. But although their denial of anything untoward was a relief, it didn't change the fact that he'd stood up Ellie. That was an entirely different thing? Could he have made a bigger mistake? *Thursday's child has far to go*, he muttered. How on earth was he going to explain his way out of that?

'You idiot,' he cursed.

Monica couldn't have agreed more. The photos her friend had taken and sent over to her phone were excellent. She checked his room and things for any more evidence of his night's exploits. Now she nearly had what she needed, he wouldn't be troubling her when the time came.

Fortunately or not, before he'd really had the chance to perfect his story, Harry bumped into Ellie in the corner shop as she was buying groceries. In fact she was so mad when she saw him that for a second she thought about just ignoring him and walking out.

'Ellie,' he said. 'I...' but she didn't let him finish his sentence.

'What on earth happened to you, last night?' she demanded. She was clearly very upset. 'You just disappeared off the face of the earth. I called and called and then I had to go round to The Tyger and everything. I didn't know what to do. Of course, Monica was simply lapping it up. She said you'd been out for a bike ride earlier, but then when we checked, you weren't in your room and your bike wasn't there either?'

It was true. He had three unanswered calls and several texts on his phone. What's more now Monica knew as well. He realised he was in a lot of trouble.

'I'm really sorry, I did go for a ride, then I ran into some interesting people over in Balcombe Woods. We got chatting and had a few drinks and I kind of lost track of time. I should have let you know but my mobile ran out of charge and I didn't know your number. I got back very late. I was completely out of order,' he said, patching together a story as best he could from what he could recall. But even he wasn't convinced.

'Well, I was really worried about you. I even wondered if you'd had a run-in with Ryan. Whether I should call the police or something? And now you're telling me you were off with the fairies in the woods?'

'Nothing so exciting, I'm afraid.'

'You're as bad as the rest of them. I thought you at least had some sense about you?'

'Please Ellie; can I have a second chance? Make amends?'

'A second chance? You really expect me just to continue on like nothing happened?'

'Please?' He paused while she waited and then reluctantly she nodded. He reached out to hug her. She placed her head on his shoulder and started weeping again. The stress was really getting to her.

'Well don't ever, ever do that to me again. I was really frightened,' she said quietly.

'I won't. I feel dreadful,' he said then paused. 'I'll make it up to you, I promise.'

'I'm not sure I should even give you the chance.' She paused but he detected the warmth in the movement of her hands.

'So who were these people you met, then?'

'Fracking protestors, you know from the peace camp.'

'I thought they went home a while back?'

'No, there are still a few hanging on, just in case. I thought you'd be impressed with my new green credentials?'

'I'll give you green, you moron!'

He'd just about skated past that then and so changed the subject rapidly.

'Does he do that sort of thing then... Ryan?' he asked referring to her earlier comment.

'What?'

'Have run-ins with people?'

'There've been rumours, disappearances.'

'Really?'

'Of course not, I'm joking. But at one point last night I wasn't so sure.'

'Look, I'm just so sorry.'

'Well anyway, for the time being you're grounded.'

'Yes, I get that feeling. Will I be allowed out later?'

'I can't tell yet.'

'Okay.'

'I heard from Maggie your team are coming in today. I'm not sure I shouldn't tell them to take a hike.'

'Please don't Ellie. Look I'll make it up to you, I promise. How about lunch?'

'I can't. I'm afraid I'm going to be in Ditchling most of the day.'

'Again, but what about the survey?'

'I'm sure you and Maggie can cope.'

'How about a drink this evening, then?'

'You won't stand me up again?'

'No way!'

'Well maybe. I'll see how I feel later.'

About the same time back at the house, Maggie had a visitor, too.

'Ryan, what on earth are you doing here again?'

'I need to talk.'

'Well, I'm busy.' She wasn't at all happy about him turning up at her house like that. What if her husband had been there? She would have had to make up some horrible white lie to explain his presence.

'It's Monica, she just won't let go of stuff.'

'And that's my worry?' she asked caustically.

'She says if I don't do something about my gran she'll dump me.' He tried to laugh but failed. She realised he was upset. But she was damned if she was going to get dragged into this as well. She had enough to do already and she was three days overdue. She was going to have to buy one of those testing kits later.

'Well, you know how to solve that, don't you?'

'Look, could you do something for me?'

'Ryan, I'm really busy.'

'Could you just speak with my gran again, she might listen to you?'

'For heaven's sake!'

Of course Monica had heard all about the little scene in the gift shop the day before. The girl had been sure to let her know about that, even if her motivation had been one of spite. She was building up a good picture of what had been going on. After visiting the camp to collect what she needed from her friend, she'd followed Ryan to Maggie's house and listened in surreptitiously through an open window. Her plans were rapidly developing. She gave him a few minutes to get back to his workshop and then burst in on him.

'What you been up to this morning?' she asked half-accusingly, trying to knock him off balance.

'Nothing Mone, I've been thinking about stuff, that's all.'

'You thinking about stuff, what stuff?'

'Well how to get my gran to return the spoils, like you said.'

'Don't worry about that. I've got that sorted. I'll do the thinking round here from now on,' she said. 'You just keep your grubby fingers off the Swift sisters and do as you're told. No more little assignations. Understood?'

'Yes Mone, of course.'

Harry and the recce team worked hard throughout Thursday. By mid-afternoon it was warm and sunny. Harry's late-night adventure was catching up with him and he felt very tired and sleepy. But they still had to check out the logistics of getting heavy equipment in and out of the site, parking, facilities for the talent, electrical and power supply, ambient lighting and sound. Fortunately, the crew had done it all a thousand times. They were finding no insuperable problems. While they worked on the technical stuff, Harry organised for video footage to be taken of potential locations for each scene in the script. Even after the survey and the producers initial okay, there would still be a lot to do: contracting, insurance and permissions, as well as letters to residents warning them of disruption and all the rest. But he was hopeful, and by the evening he felt they had a good plan. He was confident that with another push on Friday, they'd be ready for the pitch to the Location Manager the following Monday.

Maggie in turn was quite fascinated by all the video kit and equipment.

'As I told you yesterday, I'm a bit of a photographer

myself,' she said, as she prepared to walk home to prepare lunch.

'Really, I'd love to see?' he replied.

That afternoon, she returned with a few of her pictures from her portfolio. 'Some of them are a bit out of focus, I'm afraid. I'm experimenting with a new technique!'

Harry picked up one shot that was clearly of Ellie, looking over her shoulder, her eyes downcast and pensive, her face unsmiling. But there was a proud determination to her expression.

'I love this. In fact, they're all very good. They remind me of something? I love the silvery effect you've captured on Ellie's face. Like moonshine on her cheeks with such brilliant depth to the shadows.'

'Thank you, I've been trying to emulate Julia Margaret Cameron with this series. I'm doing a project with the kids at school. We've made a primitive box camera, but I don't really have the right equipment.' She showed him some of the other photos she'd taken of the children dressed up in period costume.

'Julia Cameron? Do you know, for once I think I might have something you might be interested in!' he replied. He pulled the two photocopies out of his folder that had been in the book Mrs Ross had sent round. 'This is a journal entry by Louisa Dodgson, the younger sister of Kempe's friend Skef Dodgson and Charles Dodgson aka Lewis Carroll. I think she had a bit of a thing about Kempe, reading between the lines. It's very revealing.'

Freshwater Bay, Isle of Wight, August 1872

We travelled to Freshwater Bay yesterday morning. The weather dawned fine, although by the time we were ready to leave Bognor the sea was beginning to cut up rough. So my brother dismissed the idea of sailing and instead we took the London, Brighton and South Coast Railway via Barnham to Portsmouth Harbour where we caught the steamer across to Ryde. The Duke of Edinburgh is a beautiful paddle steamer, narrow-beamed and schooner-rigged. It's been adapted to local waters and has very powerful engines which allow it to make the crossing in under seventeen minutes. It has a lovely deck promenade and superb saloons; all fitted out luxuriously with mirrors and crimson velvet seats. During the crossing, we were tracked by its rival, the smaller wooden-hulled Shanklin. We laughed to see it rolling in our wake, lacking the stability of our larger vessel. Mr Kempe was very knowledgeable and amusing about such things, and I tried my best to keep up with the conversation. He said that he was certainly glad we were not riding on that inferior machine!

From Ryde we hired a fast trap to take us the ten miles or so through Newport and then over to Freshwater Bay. When we finally arrived at the marvellous Dimbola Lodge it was already mid-afternoon and we were quite tired and thirsty. The interesting-looking house faces towards the sea but at some distance. It has been made up from two separate gabled cottages joined by a castellated central tower. Skef had wired ahead and therefore we hoped that we'd be expected (Mrs Cameron had previously invited him to visit her this week, but we still approached the front door with some apprehension). My elder brother was grumbling at the very idea of the visit, but he at least, was completely taken aback by the next turn of events. Specifically the particular person who greeted us as the stained-glass front door opened.

'Alice!' he exclaimed in shock, 'Is it really you?'

'Yes Mr Dodgson,' the young woman replied. 'It certainly is me, at least I think so, and at least I know who I WAS when I got up this morning!'

At first, the rest of us were quite puzzled by her strange words.

We looked at my brother's perplexed face; it was truly a picture of amazement. The two clearly knew each other, but who was she? Indeed, the more I looked, the more her face seemed familiar: she had an inscrutable, somewhat haunting expression; defiant eyes staring out from beneath broad eyebrows. Even then it did not occur to me who she must be. It was after all some years since we'd last met and then she'd only been a young child. The striking-looking woman before us was certainly no child. She was wearing a lovely but simple white lace-trimmed gown, almost as if she was dressed like a medieval queen. And she was soon joined by a beautiful white-haired old man wearing a royal purple dressing gown. He introduced himself at once as Mrs Cameron's husband, Mr Charles Hay, and apologised to us that she was presently indisposed, but said she'd be down to greet us shortly. The 'strange' young girl spoke again, this time to me, but even then I still had no firm clue as to her identity, although from her words she obviously knew who I was.

'What a pleasure it is to see you again,' Miss Dodgson. We were so excited when we received your brother's telegram this morning and I'm very glad that he persuaded you to come along, too. But as for that wire, let there be no talk of staying in a hotel. Mrs Cameron has instructed that you are to stay in the lodge next door. My sisters are all here too; they're waiting inside for you. We're staying in Whitecliffe House over the road. We've had such fun posing for Mrs Cameron these last few days. It's been exhausting but such a lark. But forgive me going on, you must be tired. Please come in; we should get you something to drink straightaway after your long journey.' And with a smile she presented us with four bottles of ginger beer, each with a little tag round the neck saying: 'Drink Me'.

Then it finally dawned on me. This woman was, of course, the famous Alice Liddell, my elder brother's girlish muse. How delighted I was by that discovery and so was Mr Kempe. We obediently followed the unlikely regal pair into the small central hall of the house and then round into the drawing room.

The reception rooms of Dimbola Lodge all had a peculiarly Eastern feel to them, created by quantities of intricate carvings painted with whitewash and draped with exotic fabrics. It was a curious mix – fashionable Morris wallpaper mixed with the furnishing of a maharajah's palace. Moreover, the open spaces had been newly augmented by a variety of theatrical scenery and photographic equipment laid out in a series of 'sets'. Alice and her two sisters had apparently been working with Mrs Cameron on a new collection of photographs of Shakespearean scenes. In the latest, Mrs Cameron's husband was playing the role of King Lear and the Liddell sisters his three daughters: Goneril, Regan and, of course, Alice as Cordelia.

My eldest brother still seemed quite stunned and strangely silent with all this, but we ignored him and continued in animated conversation. After taking tea we were shown into the lodge that adjoins the main house via a communicating door.

At last, Mrs Cameron appeared, flowing into the lodge's drawing room wearing her trademark red Ceylonese Chuddah shawl and flamboyant violet robes (fringed with dust). Up to that point, she'd been busy preparing the bedrooms for us with the help of her maid Mary. Unlike her famed sisters at Little Holland House, she is by her own admission no particular beauty, but she makes up for that deficit hugely with her extraordinary antique style. I noticed that her face was dirty and smeared and her hands were stained black (I later learned this was caused by the chemicals of her trade). I'd heard before that she was a most tender-hearted and generous woman, if a little unconventional. She is clearly fanatical about her photography too, a hobby that started when she was presented with a camera by her daughter ten years ago.

* * *

'You're most welcome, my friends. When strangers take this house I keep the door between us locked; with friends never,' she gushed, and invited us upstairs to see our rooms. After settling in, we heard the gong and went down to the dining room where a simple but inviting spread had been laid out for us.

We were joined for high tea by Mrs Cameron's niece, Julia, and several other family members who were staying nearby at the time. After taking tea, we all went into the studio where we reviewed the first prints from the previous day's photographic session.

Mr Kempe was fascinated to learn how they had all been printed on to finely grained paper coated with egg white, using light-sensitive nitrate of silver fixed with 'hypo' (the common name for sodium thiosulphate, I understand). We watched while Mrs Cameron carefully posed Alice into a series of new scenes. Her camera seemed quite an unsophisticated affair, consisting of a large exposure box which had a slot to take the glass plate negatives. These had been pre-soaked with the chemical called 'collodion' before being dipped into the silver nitrate in her dark room in preparation for the 'exposure'. The box camera stood on a tripod that was fixed to the ground. Having arranged the light, she beguiled her patient sitter into standing stock-still, unable to bat even an eyelid, as she removed the lens cap and began to make the short exposure.

The new portrait was almost full length, her subject elegantly coiffed and dressed in a defiantly adult style, leaning pensively on her hand looking directly at the camera. The pose reminded me of my brother's earlier and now famous photograph of her as the young Alice; the timeless Alice. I knew my brother had taken a similar serious 'adult' picture of her two years previously. But I could see on his face that to him this new photograph was almost a betrayal. The Alice of his imagination was unmistakeably grown up, but she was still in his mind his possession alone. Mrs Cameron's image was of a fecund twenty-year old woman; although paying homage to her five-year old self, it was a very grown-up homage. My brother continued to brood and scowl during the whole process. He seemed unimpressed, even displeased, and gave no doubt that he was keen to get away. Unable to find anyone to accompany him, he suddenly announced that he was setting off alone to walk up to the lighthouse that looked out over The Needles. I was glad when he was gone and we could all relax a little more.

After she'd finished the exposure, Mrs Cameron dashed off with Mr Kempe in tow to her little 'chicken house' where she poured her witch's brew of developing chemicals over the plates. The rest of us took tea while we waited and talked of recent visitors to the Bay and the wedding of Louisa Prinsep the previous spring.

It was then that Skef told me a curious story of the reason he thought my brother was in such a stormy mood that day. It was a story I'd never heard before and it somewhat amazed me. He told me how ten years earlier, as a young mathematician and photographer just down from Christ Church, my brother had visited Freshwater Bay once before. He'd come to photograph the landscape and visit his hero, Tennyson. Skef said that at that early stage he was full of impatient confidence, but rather touchy and easily offended. He could be flirtatious, insinuating, even demanding of his sitters; he was a young man used to charming ladies into doing whatever he wanted, apparently. In fact, he was so unused to being opposed that when one certain young lady on that occasion refused his invitation to sit, his indignation apparently knew no bounds.

Her name was Anny Thackeray, the novelist's daughter. Skef showed me these lines she wrote about their first meeting:

He blinked his eyes at the sight – a white figure standing, visionary, mystical, in the very centre of a bed of tall lillies, in a soft bloom of evening light.

And these were my brother's words written, apparently, in response:

> *He saw her once, and in the glance*
> *A moment's glance of meeting eyes,*
> *His heart stood still in sudden trance*
> *He trembled with a sweet surprise…*

Charles Dodgson, *The Three Sunsets*

I'm not sure my brother has ever really recovered from that amatory experience, but it makes me see him in a new light too!

Anyway, last evening we dined in style. The total size of our party was over a dozen, including the Prinseps who live nearby. I was fortunate to sit between Mr Kempe and Mrs Cameron, but Mrs Cameron's husband was undoubtedly the star of the evening. He is a most interesting personality, once described by Tennyson as having a beard 'stained by moonlight'.

Before we finally retired to bed, Mrs Cameron served us strong cups of Ceylon tea as we sat talking around the fire. The drawing room was decorated with blue and white Morris wallpaper and inlaid mother-of-pearl furniture and floored with rush matting. The men took brandy with water while we ladies sipped our tea wearing picturesque Indian shawls in the flicker of oil lamps and the flames from the hearth. Later we all went out on the terrace in the moonlight. I attempted to engage Mr Kempe in further conversation as best I could, but he was still distracted by the photographic process. In fact, Mr Kempe, Mrs Cameron and I stayed up until two this morning soaking the plates of her new photographs in freezing cold water.

* * *

I was therefore still very tired when I drew back the curtains to my little gabled attic room this morning and opened the window to let in the glory of Freshwater Bay. The caramel sun was blazing cheerfully through the window; the sea sparkling in the distance and the green hill of the Down top looked splendidly inviting in the morning mist. I was very happy.

After dressing, I went downstairs to join the others. We all had a good appetite and gorged ourselves on bacon and eggs and jam and fresh-baked bread bought from Orchard's general store. During the morning, we paid a visit to The Briary, a little further up Bedbury Lane, where Mr Kempe's old Oxford pal Val Prinsep is staying with his father. He was great fun. We found their other guest to be George Watts the painter, Mrs Terry Watts's husband. So she was right not to come to Dimbola with us, then!

After lunch, Mrs Cameron suggested that we pay a visit to Mr Tennyson's nearby house at Farringford, passing through the special gate that she'd had built for them between the two properties. Again my elder brother made his excuses, going off instead to explore Freshwater Bay on his own.

However, Tennyson was not there when we arrived. Instead, we were given tea by Emily, his lovely wife, in the great oriel drawing room, which was full of green and gold and the sound of birds and the distant sea. The shelves were filled with books and busts, and paintings of friends' faces filled the passages. I loved the house. Everywhere, there was a general glow of crimson. The round table in the drawing room was set generously with a white cloth and dishes filled with fruit and crystal glasses and decanters. Emily Tennyson is almost an invalid and spends most of her time there on the sofa, attending to her embroidery.

After refreshments, we were shown to the garden house where we at last found the great man, working, wrapped in his great black cloak, spouting poetry in his burry Lincolnshire accent as he looked out over the estate. Mr Kempe particularly enjoyed meeting him. He made a point of admiring the murals painted on glass he found there, depicting dragons and sea creatures and storms – writhing monsters of different sizes and shapes swirling about as in the deep. As we walked outside towards the cliffs, we could see white-breasted gulls flying sideways against the wind. Further off still we could hear the scream of shingle on the beach – "listening now to the tide in its broad-flung shipwrecking roar, now to the scream of a madden'd beach dragg'd down by a wave", a field-lark twiddling solitarily but most beautifully overhead.

All in all, it has been a perfect and memorable weekend. As we returned with Mr Kempe to the station to catch his train back up to London this evening, he spoke to me of the learning he'd gained from Mrs Cameron that weekend. I hope that his experimentation with staining techniques may in future be influenced by what he has seen of the complex chemical processes involved in photography.

My brother teases me already that he has failed in his amatory alliance-making this weekend, but we will see. For now I am quite content to call Mr Kempe a friend. My eldest brother's views on the weekend I will not record!

Louisa Fletcher Dodgson,
The Chestnuts,
Guildford.

CHAPTER TEN

IMAGO AMORIS – STORGE

Love rules the court, the camp, the grove,
And men below, and saints above

Walter Scott, *Lay of the Last Minstrel: Canto Third*

Lindfield, later that day, Thursday, May 28th

That evening, Ellie turned up exactly on time as agreed with Harry at the White Lion. She'd calmed down considerably having had a successful meeting with her client in Ditchling and was feeling quite mellow about things. At least the whole issue between Ryan and Harry had been effectively resolved for her. She was looking forward to spending some more time with him. But as the clock ticked on she became increasingly displeased.

'I've been smiling to myself thinking about you,' she said ironically, when he arrived out of breath fifteen minutes late. He'd clearly been running.

'Really?' he asked incredulously. He'd expected an ear-bashing. But that was almost the most positive she'd ever been with him.

'Yes, I've been thinking what a crazy idiot you are?'

'Crazy?'

'Yeah, standing me up last night like that and now late for your second and probably last chance?'

'Okay I'm sorry; I had a few things to sort out.'

'Didn't I make it clear you're in the last chance saloon?'

'Look I may be crazy, *but I would do anything for love…*' he began to sing. Despite trying to look stern, she had to laugh.

'God please stop it,' she shrieked. 'And don't think I'm letting you off that easily,' she added sternly again, but squeezing his hand as he sat beside her.

Neither of them was particularly hungry so after a couple of drinks, Ellie agreed to Harry's suggestion to see a new film called *The Theory of Everything* that was being screened that night at the King Edward Hall. He'd never been to a film with someone who insisted on commenting amusingly on it the whole way through the action. Like raising her eyebrows at him when Jane Hawking said 'Your glasses are always dirty.' By the end, Harry was marvelling at this new chilled side to Ellie, she seemed to have acquired an almost cosmically reflective mood all of a sudden. He wondered what on earth had happened.

'But I too have a slight problem with celestial dictators,' he murmured to himself.

Later, when they left the screening, the first stars were emerging. Harry suggested they get some air before going for a take-away and she agreed readily, taking his hand in hers. They walked fairly aimlessly around the village for a while, chatting about this and that. Of course, Harry was full of the progress they'd made on the film survey during the day. Ellie was more interested in whether he'd bumped into either Monica or Ryan. It was getting much cooler and she began to shiver a bit in the evening breeze. He put his arm round her, to which she didn't object, in fact she rather liked it. As they walked she pointed out the constellations to him and named the brighter stars. He started to hum and then sing the first line of "Starry, starry night", but before he could murder it any further she put her finger to his lips and then kissed him.

'Sshh. You're quite a cool guy really,' she said, 'despite your dubious upbringing. But I have to object to your complete inability to remember the right words to one of my favourite songs.'

'And you brush up pretty well yourself, despite the carbolic oozing continually from your working-class roots,' he replied for good measure. She laughed. He was beginning to get the measure of her. She liked this more confident Harry. She liked him a lot.

They'd reached an interesting prefab he'd spotted the day before tucked away in a little lane called Alma Road. He asked what it was and she explained it was the range for the Miniature Rifle Club. Curious, he followed her to the side entrance. They stared in through the cobwebbed windows, using their mobiles to shine torchlight into the void. Harry was somewhat amazed by what he saw in the dim light: the range was twenty-five yards or so long, with walls lined with thick steel panels. She explained how the original had been built a century earlier to improve shooting skills after the war. Harry admitted he'd never actually fired a gun. Well, outside of a fairground shooting gallery, that was.

'I used to be a pretty good shot with an air-rifle at school,' she said. 'I could whip most of the boys.' But at that moment, something scrabbled over their feet. It was a rat. She screamed, fortunately it disappeared quickly into the undergrowth. He picked her up in his arms and carried her back to the path.

'But you're not so brave now,' he whispered.

'Put me down you jerk,' she protested. He pretended to drop her and held her upside-down. She giggled and struggled to get free. He lowered her gently to her feet but she continued to hold on to him. Instinctively she kissed him again. Yes this Harry was much improved. He returned her kiss and then a thought came into his head.

'Before we found out about Monica's little accidental discharge, Maggie thought Ryan was out shooting vermin at Old Place yesterday. But surely he'd need a licence for shooting crows and stuff so close to the village?'

'Nope, you can shoot anywhere all year round with the landowner's permission, except game birds of course. And I guess his gran's the landowner. But of course he'd still need a licence for the gun.'

'I see, and he'd have one, would he?'

'Knowing Ryan… I'm not so sure.'

'I thought so.'

'Why do you ask?'

'Just looking for some negotiation leverage with him, that's all.'

'Don't go there, it won't help.'

'Sure?'

'Sure. Have you fixed a meeting with him yet?'

'Yes, I'm going for a drink with him tomorrow night.'

'Watch him then,' she said. He looked her directly in the eyes.

'Did he hurt you by the way yesterday?'

'How do you mean?'

'When you came running up the road?'

'How did you know about that?'

'Well it was pretty obvious something had happened.'

'No but just be careful, that's all. He might seem like a hapless oaf, but he's got a vicious temper.'

'It sounds like you did have a bit of a run-in with him?'

'Kind of, but nothing I can't handle. He's afraid of me really. Just be careful though and keep an eye on Maggie for me too. I'm a bit worried about her. She's been acting strangely this week. I don't want him bothering her.'

As they walked off towards the take-away to get their supper, two figures emerged from the shed beside the range. Both were dishevelled and only half-dressed.

'That was close,' the girl from the gift shop laughed. 'What was that about, what did she mean by your temper?'

'Don't worry your pretty little head about that, my lovely. Just some business I've got to sort. She's just stuck up that one,' said Ryan. She kissed him and ran her hands proprietarily down the V of his manly chest. They'd told her it was always better in the open air with Ryan Ross. And she could now confirm that.

CHAPTER ELEVEN

IMAGO AMORIS – EROS

In peace, Love tunes the shepherd's reed;
In war, he counts the warrior's steed

Walter Scott, *Lay of the Last Minstrel: Canto Third*

On Friday morning, the weather was dull and overcast and the forecast was for storms. Maggie had now told Ellie the details of her conversation with Ryan the previous day. As a result Ellie had thought further about his latest request for help and decided to go over early to see Mrs Ross again.

In a way, by rejecting Ryan, given what Mrs Ross had hinted, Ellie realised that she'd be acting against her own financial interests, of course. But such an endowment didn't sit at all with her socialist principles, in any case. And surely she wasn't that calculating, was she? And then there was Harry. Despite standing her up, he was still growing on her, although she'd been careful not to go too far that previous evening given his poor behaviour. She still didn't really buy his explanation about the frackers, which made her a bit distrustful of him. After some late-night wrestling with her conscience she'd made up her mind, however, what she was going to do about the Rosses. She certainly wasn't going to be the one being manipulated any longer. She was going to take things into her own hands.

Mrs Ross poured her tea and they sat down in two armchairs by the fire. Ellie's errand was simple; she spat it out before her senior had any chance to direct the conversation.

'Ryan wants you to sell the place as soon as possible and auction the furnishings. He says you can keep the best stuff like he promised,' she said firmly.

'Quite a demand, dear?' replied Mrs Ross.

'He's serious.'

'He'll send the lawyers round?'

'He might.'

'Or even better, the boys!' Mrs Ross joked lightly.

'How little you know him,' muttered Ellie and then realised her mistake. 'I'm sorry, I didn't mean…'

'You're right, I don't know him nearly as well as you!' added Mrs Ross triumphantly.

'I didn't…'

'For you, you know, I'd do it.'

'You keep saying that, but why in the world for me?'

'Because, like I said, you're obviously so keen on him.'

'But you know I hate him.'

'I doubt that. Will he break off with Monica if I refuse?' asked Mrs Ross changing the subject.

'Never,' replied Ellie.

'You have that from him?'

'Yes.'

'So you've seen him again then, at least? What will you do if I comply?'

'Anything.'

'That's easy to say,' Mrs Ross replied. 'Get her away from him, that's all I ask.'

'How in the world do you think I'm going to do that?'

'You know how.'

After she'd left Mrs Ross's house, Ellie texted Ryan and asked him to meet her at Maggie's house in Raphael Road mid-morning. She had no idea what she was going to say to him but thought at least it was better to pick a neutral spot this time. She didn't want him turning up at Old Place with Harry and the survey gang there. When he arrived, she had her painting things out on the kitchen table and for the first time in a long time was trying to do some work for her upcoming exhibition. He arrived promptly and was dressed smartly. She got out the tea things and biscuits but he didn't wait.

'So did you or Maggie speak to her again?' he asked.

'I did. But we had a bit of a bust-up.'

'And?'

'She won't move.'

'Damn,' he said. 'I've had it with this.'

'I still think we can persuade her in time.'

'I don't have time. I've been patient like you told me to be. How hard did you push her?' he asked.

'Quite hard. Look Ryan, sorry I know it's wretched. Have you quarrelled with Monica about it again?'

'She's going spare.'

'Oh dear, is the engagement off already, then?' she asked somewhat spitefully. He ignored that tone in her voice and continued. She bit her tongue; she really hadn't meant to say that.

'No, but I've got to bring this to a head somehow.'

'I don't understand what she wants; she never wanted the furniture before?'

'Things are different now. Do I really have to get the solicitor involved?'

'No just be patient a little longer. Does Monica still hate me then?'

'Let's just say, she's very insistent.' He paused before saying the next sentence. 'I still wonder what would have happened if I'd tried harder with you after that wedding…'

He looked at her again and went to kiss her. She ducked his embrace easily enough, but in doing so knocked the plate of biscuits off the floor so it smashed. At that moment they heard a knock. The front door was open and a woman marched in. It was Monica's mother. She saw the biscuits and broken plate on the floor.

'Mrs Malling, how nice to see you,' said Ellie surprised. 'How can I help you?'

'I came to drop your sister's wedding present round, the one that I've just finally finished, but now I see I've interrupted something. I thought you were packing up Old Place? What's going on?'

'Mrs Malling, please don't speak to Ellie like that, she's only trying to help with my gran,' said Ryan.

'Help my foot. After what Monica told me, I guessed I'd catch you two together sometime!' she declared, seeing the proximity of their bodies. 'Well I haven't come to plead with you if that's what you think, young man.'

'Mrs Malling, I—' said, Ryan, half-acknowledging the compromising situation.

'Come with me,' she said, dragging Ryan out of the hall by the ear. 'And you madam can keep your thieving hands off him, do you hear?'

Ellie didn't know whether to laugh or cry; even Monica's pushy mother was in on the act now. However, her next words were probably not best chosen: 'Like I was the guilty party in all this, you mean?'

The recce crew left Lindfield mid-afternoon. Although he hadn't been home since Monday, Harry had decided to stay overnight again as he was going to Village Day with Ellie on Saturday. She was having supper with her sister and the curate that evening, so he'd made a tentative arrangement to meet Ryan later. He knew that it was going to be a difficult discussion. But he was pleased with his work to date – *'Friday's child works hard for a living,'* he thought.

When Maggie had discussed the filming with him during a coffee break that morning, she'd asked if Harry could also get the kids in her class involved.

'It'd be great to do a history project with them,' she'd said. 'Maybe even use them for extras?'

He thought that was a great idea. Maggie had told him Ellie was going to be tied up during the day with the auctioneers, but mentioned to him that there was choir practice that evening in the church. She'd hinted that Ellie might well come along as well and that she was keen to see him. He decided to have an early supper at The Tyger and then make his way up to the church before seeing Ryan later. He realised it would be the fourth time in a week he'd entered a church building; if he wasn't careful he might even have to take this religious stuff a little more seriously!

When he arrived at the church, it was in fact Maggie whom he met first. She said that Ellie still had a couple of errands to do but might still join them later. It sounded like they'd had a good chat at supper; Maggie said her sister had seemed in a very positive mood, almost gushing. She didn't tell him about the baby, however, as she wanted to tell Joe, her father first.

As there were still fifteen minutes to go before practice started, Maggie suggested taking a whirlwind tour of the church. She pointed out the various connections to Charles Kempe. She showed him the brass plate that commemorated the installation of the bells below the bell tower: C. E. Kempe was recorded as a churchwarden for 1887 alongside his arch-rival George Masters. Masters had apparently had his name added to the plate even though he'd opposed the bell appeal, much to Kempe's distaste. He'd written a furious letter to the *Mid-Sussex Times* about it.

Next she showed him the famous rood screen, the subject of further disputes. In the south chancel, there was also a beautifully carved roll of honour to the fallen of the Great War made by Kempe's firm, and in the south chapel a window depicting the Virgin flanked by St George and St Michael.

Harry laughed. 'So there's actually more by Kempe in the church than meets the eye,' he said.

'Yes, if you know where to look!' Maggie replied.

She took up position with the music group and Harry sat back into a pew to listen. He closed his eyes and allowed the music to slowly take him to another place. Maggie's voice was very fine; she was clearly the star and sang with great confidence. However, he was disappointed that Ellie had still not shown up.

'I expect she's busy, you've thrown the whole place into a bit of a tiswas with your filming proposal!' Maggie offered as she was packing up. 'You know there are one or two villagers who don't like the idea, don't you?'

'Yes, I'm meeting Ryan next!' he joked. 'But I hadn't heard of any opposition from the other villagers?'

'Well there are always some who don't like change. The church is having the same problems with some of its renovation proposals,' she explained. 'It's a nightmare. But I wouldn't worry. If you can get Mrs Ross and Ryan onside then you won't have too much trouble with the rest. Ellie is doing her best.'

'Any tips?'

'Well, he's a landscape gardener, isn't he?' she smiled and winked. He saw her meaning immediately.

'Got it! Thanks, Maggie.'

'Good luck, send Ryan my best wishes and I hope to see you alive tomorrow at Village Day. Remind Ellie to come and see us in our photo booth. I've got the kids set up to take some old-time shots of folk, dressing up and everything. It should be great fun.'

'Okay, I definitely will! 'But wait, the bells,' he said. 'You said you'd tell me about the bells.'

She smiled and they quickly climbed the steep stairs up to the bell tower, then made a second ascent to see the bell cage itself. She pointed out the tenor and three treble bells marked with Kempe's logo and the inscription *'Felici Anno Lmo Regni Victoriae AD MDCCCLXXXVII Lavs Deo'* that had been added to the four older treble bells dating from the sixteenth century.

'Here you are then,' she said, passing him another photocopy. My turn this time! It's by Tommy Heasman, one of Kempe's designers.'

A few years ago, I spent a weekend with John Lisle and his new wife Florrie in Rottingdean. It was the summer of 1900. On the Saturday, we visited the Pavilion at Brighton and then took the electric railway to Ovingdean Gap. I remember we walked up to the little church to look at Mr Kempe's windows. They looked like they'd been there for years.

After that we strolled back across Beacon Hill towards Rottingdean where we were staying at the White Horse. The old coaching inn had been converted by then into an impressive three-story building with a great portico facing towards to the sea. We were tired after our walk and so after a wholesome supper, retired early to bed.

The next day after breakfast, we took a pleasant stroll round the village and went to morning service. Lady Burne-Jones was there, but I couldn't help contrasting the inferior yallery-greenery of her late husband's windows with the majesty of Mr Kempe's the day before. Later, before luncheon, we wandered down on to the shingle beach. Mr Scribbets' horse-drawn omnibus, that would take us to the station later that afternoon, had arrived with its meagre load of day-trippers from Brighton: a family with three young children and an elderly couple. A delivery boy with a bicycle was loading up his first round for the day. Down on the beach, the dishwater-grey sea lapped sullenly against the glinting shingle.

It was a quaint and peaceful scene. There was a line of pastel-striped bathing machines halfway up the beach, waiting hopefully for their first customers. A few boats were lashed to iron rings anchored into the shingle. To the east, the stained chalk cliffs stretched out towards Saltdean; to the west the newly installed lines of Dr Volk's railway were visible where the tide had receded. In the far distance we could just see Brighton, and in-between the new railway pier. We spent the rest of the morning until luncheon on the beach. Just as we were about to return to the White Horse, we heard the tenor bell of St Margaret's ring dolefully for a funeral, prompting a new thought to enter into John's mind.

'The more I think about it, Mr Kempe was very much hurt by that affair with the bells in Lindfield, you know, Tommy,' said John pensively.

'Yes, it was a rum old thing, that,' I replied.

'I don't think I know the story?' asked Florrie. She'd linked her arm more closely around John's for warmth. Although the day was bright, the wind was quite strong and biting and there was a light sea drizzle which chilled our faces. Despite the weather, the family we'd been watching had made a small picnic lunch on the beach. Their three children were running happily amok, poking for crabs amongst the seaweed in the rock pools left by the retreating tide, whooping and enjoying the fresh air. I could tell in her eyes that Florrie very much wanted a family like that one day.

'It was all going on about fifteen years ago, around the time I started at Nottingham Place,' said John. 'I was fifteen or sixteen, still studying drawing at Lambeth. Bill Tate, who was already Mr Kempe's architect, introduced me to him one day at my mother's request. They both worshipped at St Agnes's in Kennington. She was always on at me to do something more 'worthy' than figure-drawing and had hit upon church decoration as the solution. Bill suggested to her that Mr Kempe might be able to offer me a place, and indeed, although he'd nothing immediately available, he was very helpful in suggesting how I might continue my studies. A year or so later, when I did join the firm, I remember one of the lads asking him something about the church in Lindfield. We'd all heard the story of 'the bells'. He went red in the face, but didn't say anything. Afterwards, Bill asked us lads never to discuss the subject again in Mr Kempe's presence!'

'Tell me, then!' said Florrie a little more impatiently.

'I think Tommy can probably tell you better than me. After all, he was there when it happened,' he teased.

'Well Tommy?' she asked.

'Yes, well as far as I remember it went like this,' I said. 'I was still a boy living in Lindfield then. I must have been eleven or twelve about the time it all started. I was in the habit of going to the old house with my brothers to deliver the groceries. That was before I got apprenticed to the grocer, mind you. Later the old grump sacked me for drawing on the sugar bags! Mr Kempe's mother had died around ten years earlier and he bought Old Place soon after that. He spent a decade and forty thousand, they say, doing it up under Bill Tate's direction.

Anyway, around the time it was near finished, Mr Kempe organised a big event in his grounds to raise money for the church. It was all hands to the pump in the village. 'An Elizabethan Festa' he called it. He and his friends all dressed up in real Tudor costume. I remember plainly how he was walking around with Nora, his deerhound, that day, proud as punch. He loved that bitch and her daughter Sistona. Together they were a real familiar sight in the village.

Bill Tate had built a whole Tudor marketplace in the grounds. There were sideshows and games and an exhibition of Mr Kempe's embroideries and textiles. The Garden House was fitted out with tapestries and his collection of old Prayer Books and there was a new altarpiece on show for the church. Me and my brothers were roped in to help out with the tea garden he'd set up: 'Ye Olde Pelican and Wheatsheaf' he called it. His good friend Mrs Morrell helped him organise it all, with her daughters. Her girls put on a demonstration tennis match – all the local dignitaries were there. It was a great event. Hundreds of people, the whole village, turned out and everyone made an effort to look the part. I must still have the notice bill somewhere – it was a couple of years before the Queen's Jubilee.'

'But what about the bells?' asked Florrie again. She was getting quite frustrated by then I reckon.

'Well, yes. That bell business was a year or so after that. It started with the pews, though. Mr Kempe was churchwarden and wanted to get rid of them all as they were falling apart. He was very High Church and the Parish Council were wary and didn't like his suggestions. Mr Kempe wanted to put in bench-seats and chairs; the Council wanted to keep the old arrangement. It all got quite bitter with public meetings and letters to the newspapers an' all, but Mr Kempe appealed to the Bishop and somehow got his way.'

'The bells?'

'Yes, well, that was the next thing. The church already had five of 'em, some of which went back 'undreds of years, but they were in a dreadful state, all cracked and out of tune. Mr Kempe offered to replace them for the Jubilee with a brand new set at his own expense. The Council refused but agreed that they'd keep the old tenor bell for funerals and special occasions and a fund would be raised for a new treble peal. Mr Kempe relented and had John Taylor's of Loughborough build the set and they were put in place and everyone was happy. But then they had another argument about the inscription above the bell cage or something and then another about the brass plaque to commemorate it all.'

'That's it?'

'Yes, I reckon so.'

Ernest 'Tommy' Heasman

CHAPTER TWELVE

IMAGO AMORIS – AGAPE

Love rules the court, the camp, the grove,
And men below, and saints above;
For love is heaven, and heaven is love.

Walter Scott, *Lay of the Last Minstrel: Canto Third*

The same day, Lindfield, Friday, May 29th

Harry wandered down to the White Lion where he'd arranged to meet Ryan around nine. He was nervous. Ryan was a big man and Ellie's warnings were still ringing in his ears. He knew, if he wasn't careful, that his intellectual manner, even his accent, would probably wind-up the self-employed landscape gardener, even if he was a privately educated one. Like Monica, Ryan was one of those types in life he found difficult to deal with: brawny and brash and probably a bit of a bully. But he'd also found that bullies were usually the first to back down if met with unexpected opposition. He was banking on his careful planning plus a couple of other cards he had up his sleeve to see him through, if he could at least get a hearing.

He found Ryan out in the garden, already half-cut and decidedly groggy. It wasn't an encouraging start. He was sitting alone near the bandstand drinking cider. Harry joined him and after a few initial scowls and grumbles they began to get down to business.

'Look Mr Ross, I know you want to get Old Place sold, but I'd really appreciate it if you could help us out with the filming. It's an ideal location; we'd only need the house for a few months, till the autumn. It'd also be great publicity when you come to sell it.'

'Maybe, but I need my share of the cash from the sale for my business. The sooner the better as far as I'm concerned.'

'But there'd be plenty of work on the project: staging, scaffolding, garden work etc., maybe even a bit of accommodation and catering for the crew. We could do with some local knowledge, someone to coordinate the local trades. We pay well.' Ryan's ears perked up at the mention of work and money. Harry could see him beginning to make his own calculations.'

'You spinning me a line?' asked Ryan.

'Not at all, it's the BBC after all.' Harry could see him thinking further about it and left him to ponder his offer for a while.

'But it still doesn't help my cash flow. What's more, we've got a lot of work on already.'

'I'm sure we could work something out, a down payment or something.'

Ryan hesitated, he was obviously thinking hard about the proposition. Harry could see he was tempted. He also knew it wouldn't stop him selling off the Wilderness if he wanted to. That must be worth a pretty penny. Of course, he was a bit out of line in making such an offer. He'd need to talk first with the location manager, but he was sure he could swing that.

'Well, I might consider it, I suppose, if we could fit it around other work, that is.'

Ryan's eyes had widened and Harry knew he almost had him; just one more hook.

'And there'll probably be a couple of parts for extras, too. I'm sure they could use a handsome guy like you.'

'Now you are joshing me.'

'No, I'm serious. You've definitely got the looks.' He clinked Ryan's glass and said, 'So you up for it?'

'Look, I said I'd think it over, no promises,' Ryan replied.

'Great, well let me buy you another drink then.'

'No, Mr Jamieson, it's my shout,' he said. 'And call me Ryan.'

As Ryan headed towards the bar door, Harry smiled inwardly. Maggie's suggestion had been a master stroke. Ryan soon returned with two more glasses of Sussex cider and they drank steadily until closing time. Despite their manifold differences, they found they had a common interest in gaming. The conversation moved on to action movies and then Ryan quickly started on the attributes of certain movie actresses. Harry felt himself getting somewhat tipsy and a little out of his depth, but he was suddenly getting on fine with his new friend. Every so often, Ryan asked him again about the proposal, to check if the proposition was real, but Harry knew he really had him hooked.

'So what about Monica, Mr Jamieson? I reckon she could kick that girl from *Tomb Raider*'s ass. You got a part for her?'

'She's gorgeous, Ryan. Very striking. And she seems like a pretty sharp businesswoman too. I'm sure there'd be something for her.'

'Good, because she's not going to be too keen on the idea otherwise. We've been having a few wobbles just recent, like.'

'But you got engaged this week, didn't you?'

'Yeah, but I'm a bit under the cosh on that too.'

'She certainly seems like a woman who knows what she wants!'

'Yeah, that's the problem!' he laughed. 'She absolutely knows what she wants. Still, I expect she's worth it.'

'I'm sure she is.'

'And what about you Harry, a little bird told me you were keen on Ellie?'

'Yes, I kinda like her.'

'She plays it cool that one. Great body though.'

'Quite!' Harry replied embarrassed and they chinked glasses. He hoped he wasn't going to have to get into a debate about the relative attributes of either lady. Maybe it was time to call it a night while he was still ahead.

'Well, I'd better get off to bed, Ryan, it's been great this evening,' Harry said as the barman began to call last orders. 'I really appreciate your thinking about this and thanks for the drink.'

'Oh we aren't done yet Harry; the village club's open after hours!' he said winking at Harry. 'And it's cheaper than this place, to boot.'

Harry groaned inside; it'd been a long week and he really fancied getting his head down, but having got this far with Ryan he didn't want to ruin it. He followed Ryan unsteadily down the High Street to the village hall. There they took a back staircase up to 'the Club'. Inside it was full; there was a small licensed bar and folk of all ages playing darts and dominoes. They ordered a couple of shots. Fortunately, Ryan's other mates were there, so when Harry finally made his excuses half an hour later, Ryan seemed happy to leave him be. Harry left, but as he passed the pond, he noticed two people dressed as smugglers mucking about in a canoe, trying to get over to the island in the middle. He shouted over to them asking what they were up to.

'Digging for hidden treasure on the island,' they said and then burst into laughter.

'This is a strange place,' he whispered in reply.

When he finally got back to The Tyger, Monica was closing up downstairs.

'How'd ya get on with Ryan?' she asked, somewhat defensively.

'Like a house on fire,' he replied. 'I think I've got a solution to his money issues and he seems to be on board!' Monica looked surprised. She stared at him doubtfully for a second, but seeing that he was serious, continued her interrogation.

'Well, that sounds good, but I don't know how you pulled that one off,' she replied, dying to know more.

'Let's say he won't be out of pocket,' he added. She was intrigued; she had no idea how someone like Harry could have worked his magic on Ryan – although it was true that his wallet was usually a fruitful approach.

'Tell me more?'

'Oh, I'll let him tell you. He thinks you'd make a good extra, too.' Now he had her on the go as well. She looked at him with new respect. Maybe she'd underestimated him. She quite fancied being an extra as well.

'There'd be parts for extras?'

He nodded slyly. He was enjoying this. Fascinated, she offered him a brandy or hot chocolate but he refused both. He desperately needed his sleep. She was pouting and preening in the bar mirror but before she could offer more, he went straight back to his room, undressed quickly and snuggled under the feather duvet on his bed. He felt good.

He'd played a blinder. Overall he was delighted with how the week had gone. It was great when plans came together like that. Although he was disappointed not to have seen Ellie, he'd had a very successful evening and now had a day off with her to look forward to. Yes, he'd need to prepare the pitch Sunday night, but in the meantime he was going to enjoy the weekend. As it was late, he decided not to phone Ellie, but instead sent her a text and almost immediately got a nice one back. After a few minutes, he was deep in sleep.

However, about one in the morning, he was woken up by the sound of an argument along the corridor. He could hear Ryan's raised voice and Monica shouting back at him. Suddenly, there was a crash as if something had been thrown at a wall. A second later he heard a door slam and heavy boots stomping along the corridor before hurrying down the stairs. After that outburst, all was quiet for a while.

Then he heard sobbing from outside in the corridor. He wondered what to do, but felt it best not to interfere. But a few minutes later he heard a tentative knock at his door and then the click of the handle being tried against the lock. He got up quickly and went across to the door. He opened it carefully and saw Monica's face staring back at him. She was obviously in some distress and her face showed a large red welt and a cut across her cheeks. He opened the door fully and let her in. She was weeping uncontrollably.

'What on earth's happened?' he asked her, holding her against his shoulder to steady her body.

'It's Ryan, he's gone crazy!' she replied. Her pupils were dilated; she was either genuinely scared or a very good actress.

'But I thought...' While he was speaking she sneaked a look up at him and smiled. Yes she had him in the palm of her hand.

'No, it's not about not the filming, it's his gran,' she replied before he could finish his sentence. 'She's gone and sold the house already, to a developer or summat. For much less than he thinks its worth. And she intends to see that he's doesn't get a penny either.'

'I don't understand? He was as happy as Larry when I left him an hour ago at the Club?'

'One of his mates caught up with him, shortly after you left I guess. He's an estate agent in the Heath; he was full of it. When Ryan heard, he stormed out and went straight over to his gran's place, but she wouldn't answer the bell, just shouted down from an upstairs window. Then he came here in a right old mood. He was effing and blinding like a trooper. He's gone crazy, on the rampage. Even says I had summat to do with it, but of course I never...'

'God—' He was beginning to think about the consequences for the filming, but stopped himself, realising it was probably not the thing uppermost on Monica's mind.

'Now he's gone off to find that Ellie of yours. He's got it into his head that she'd to blame. I'm worried what he might do to her. He's in such a foul mood. Please, Mr Jamieson, I don't dare call the coppers. Would you try to find him, try to talk some sense back into him? He might listen to a man?'

'Of course,' Harry replied, at the same time wondering how on earth he was going to accomplish that new feat of diplomacy. How had things turned sour so quickly?

Ryan had left The Tyger in an absolute fury. He felt the whole world was against him and he'd had far too much to drink to think rationally. He bellowed loudly in the street, swearing at the top of his voice. Those interfering women, they were all in it together, and now that bloke from the BBC. He'd been conned, but he wasn't sure by whom. He'd sort Ellie out at least. He headed towards Raphael Road but then had another idea. The first sensible thought he'd had in an hour. Why should he be the victim? He'd take the process into his own hands. He knew where the deeds were kept, and without those…

He stormed up to Old Place and let himself in through a side entrance. The door through to the kitchen was bolted but he knew that the lock was loose and after a few minutes he'd worked it free. He entered the kitchen and went straight to the electrical board to disable the alarm; he was surprised to find that it hadn't even been set. He swore again. Things were getting lax.

He made his way up the old servants' stairs and into the back bedroom. It was dark but he didn't turn on any lights in case the neighbours became suspicious. He fumbled about on the wooden panelling until he found the latch to the hidden cupboard he wanted. He opened it up. Inside was an old gun safe. He flicked on the light on his phone so he could see and then twisted the combination locks until the safe was open. Good, the old bat hadn't changed the code. That was a lucky break. However, a minute later he was cursing again. He opened the box where he knew the deeds were kept, but there was nothing. She must have taken them to the lawyers already. He wondered what to do next, but at that moment the side door to the room opened and he saw Ellie standing there in her nightdress, ghostly pale, holding a torch.

'Ryan, what on earth are you doing here?' she asked, shocked to see him but relieved at least that it wasn't a burglar. That's exactly what she'd feared when she'd been woken by the noise of him fiddling with the safe. She had an iron poker from the fire ready in her hand.

'I might ask…?' he began to reply, but thought better of taking that tack. Of course, he'd completely forgotten that she was staying there while the packing was being done. But maybe there was another way to get back at her. Opportunistically, he reconsidered his plan and turned to face her.

'Come here,' he said beckoning for her to come closer. 'I'm free again and Lord you know I want you.'

She backed away cautiously. She knew his form, and indeed she knew that from his voice it was partly the drink talking. The previous morning, he'd been dragged away from Maggie's by Monica's mother, frustrated that she wouldn't back him against his grandmother, and now he was back? What had gone on? She wasn't happy at all at his unexpected reappearance so late at night. She heard anger, even danger in his voice.

'Ryan, it's late,' she said nervously. 'What are you doing, you scared me, and you could have been anyone?'

He thought quickly for an excuse for his presence.

'I needed to talk. About what happened this morning?'

'At this time of night?' she asked.

'It's Monica's mother,' he replied.

'What did she want with you?'

'She asked me point blank if I was sleeping with you.' Ellie hesitated for a moment. That was unexpected. She hardly dare ask the next question for fear of hearing the answer.

'And what did you say?' she asked quietly.

'I said it was none of her business,' he said boldly and took a couple of paces towards her.

'Oh Ryan, now what have you done?' she said shocked, and backed against the wall.

'Don't you see I'm free now?' he said, moving right up to her. What was she to do? She couldn't move without it looking like she was afraid and she was hardly going to win a struggle with him. She thought about using the poker for a second but decided it would be a bad idea. He might turn violent.

But before she could make up her mind, he took her in his strong arms and embraced her without another word, lifting her up against the wall. Ellie could smell the booze on this breath. She thought back immediately to the previous occasion she'd been in that situation with him. This was a lot scarier. The trouble was there was some part of her, some little buzz in her heart, which did still want him. She found all her nice thoughts about Harry disappearing into momentary lust for this splendid Adonis. But she still had her head on straight didn't she?

At first she resisted, but he was insistent. He kissed her. Breathlessly she turned her head away. But he just moved her head back and kissed her again. She could feel his hand on her thigh. Within a few seconds she found she'd returned his embrace, pulling her hands through his hair. Strangely, she remembered Mrs Ross's last words to her. Maybe she was right? Something inside her head had clicked and she decided that this time she would really let herself go, especially if Monica was off the scene. She'd been the other woman for too many years and at least he was single, sort of. She felt the heat and urgency of his passion; something that she had tried to fight against earlier that week almost now neurotically compulsive. She could feel him too, physically, muscled and vigorous against her. As they kissed she became more and more excited. She wanted him and began to reach instinctively for what she craved. But as he kissed her further and more roughly, she became aware again that his breath stank of drink. She began to have doubts; this was all going too fast. Shouldn't she tell him to stop and come back in the morning? Then they could talk about this, not rush in. Belatedly she tried to push him away, gasping for breath.

Sensing new resistance, he began to grip her more determinedly. He was holding her so tightly she could hardly move. He had one hand inside her nightdress and she could feel the inexorable progress of his hand across her body. She began to feel sick inside. She knew he'd been rough with other girls before. She was really beginning to worry. How was she going to get away from him? What was he doing there at that time of night in any case? He was clearly completely drunk. She tried to push him away again but he forced himself back on her and pushed her backwards towards the bed.

'Get off Ryan, what on earth are you doing?' she cried, now trying desperately to push him away. She felt herself being forced back through the doorway on to the bed. Now she was really worried.

'Come on Ell, I know that you want me. Don't pretend. Just relax...' His hand was....

She screamed and then bit his lip and he reeled away in pain for a second. He wiped the blood off his face and grabbed her arms pinning them down roughly on the bed. He tugged with his own bloody teeth at the shoulder strap of her nightdress until he'd pulled it down towards her waist. She was yelling her head off now and continued to fight back and resist the best she could but he was too strong. She felt him, his hand inside her underwear. Now, she was really scared. She started screaming at him to stop, but then felt his free hand move back over her mouth. With his movement he'd released her arm, allowing her to twist free from his grip. She squirmed off the bed and ran screaming towards the open door of the bedroom.

At that moment Monica and Harry appeared breathless at the top of the stairs. They'd found the outside door open and followed the sounds of shouting up the stairs. They both stared at her in shock. Ellie looked back at them realising her predicament had suddenly gotten a whole lot worse. She realised what this must look like. She decided in an instant she didn't want Ryan in that sort of trouble. He was drunk; he clearly didn't know what he was doing. The last thing she wanted was the police involved and some rape case.

'It's okay, he's just had a bit too much to drink,' she said. They looked at her incredulously, seeing the blood on her lips.

But Ryan certainly wasn't thinking rationally at that point. He'd recovered his balance and run after her towards the door, only to hear voices, too, then the sight of those two people in the shadow of the servants' stairs. It was Monica and that interfering BBC guy? Damn, what was he going to do now?

He tried to push past Monica, but her thick outline didn't waver and blocked his exit. Harry too was too quick for him and blocked the way to the main staircase. He was trapped. By now, Monica had picked up the poker from the floor where Ellie had dropped it and was advancing towards him.

'You bastard, Ryan,' she said. 'What have you gone and done to that girl?'

She swung for him and missed. Ryan pushed past Harry but in the dark and his confusion ended up going too far in the wrong direction and up the main stairs to the second floor. Monica was too clever and quick for him. She ran after him up the servant's stairs, again cutting off his descent. Now trapped from either way down, he backed up towards the stairs that led to the belvedere. He realised she was now wielding a large pair of scissors as well.

'Let me past,' he said. 'Someone will get hurt. I can't be doing with more trouble from you lot.'

'No way,' yelled Harry. 'Not until you tell us what you've done to her.'

'Nothing,' screamed Ellie from below. 'It's a mistake, I'm fine.'

Ryan looked round the landing. He was trapped like an animal. Maybe he could get across to the fire escape, he thought, but then realised that was a stupid idea and it was probably locked anyway. He wouldn't have time to release the key. He found himself backing up the stairs to the belvedere as the others approached. The door was still unbolted and he felt it open and the cold air fall on his back as he reversed up. Monica was still following him, swearing and lashing out with the poker and blades. God, he could see on her face that she was really angry. He tried to grab the scissors, but she was too quick and dug them into his thigh.

'Ow,' he yelled out in pain. 'That hurt!'

'It was meant to.'

'Look Mone, it's all a misunderstanding, just don't do anything stupid,' he said. 'Let me past.'

But she continued to move towards him. He was backing on to the platform now; maybe if he got her up there too, he could grab her, squeeze past her and escape? But then there was Harry to deal with too. He reckoned he could take him; it was Monica he was worried about. She was behaving like a psycho, wielding those blades with venom he just couldn't believe. She clouted him with the poker. He backed up another step but at that moment the platform gave way and he fell backwards...

OYEZ! OYEZ!! OYEZ!!!

July 28th, 1885

OLD PLACE LINDFIELD HAYWARD'S HEATH

All Lovers of Music,
All Students in Antiquities,
All Skilled in the Art of Needlework,
All who seek Refection or Trifles,
All who would see the England of the Forefathers,
are summoned at TWO of the Clock,
TO HEAR Glees & Madrigals by the renowned Singers from Oxford, The Band of the Sussex Regiment of Rifles,
TO WITNESS a Grand Match of Tennis,
An Exhibition of Tapisteries & Needlework, Ancient and Modern,
'Alice ye Mysterie,' enacted by Mummers,
And many Lords & Ladies of Olde time.
TO CLOSE AT SEVEN OF THE CLOCK.
House, & all Out-door Amusements open to those who pay 5/- each

CHAPTER THIRTEEN

VILLAGE DAY

Please gather at Hickmans Lane Playing Fields at 12.15pm

King Edward Hall website

The Tyger, Lindfield, Saturday, May 30th

Without bothering to knock, Monica brought an early-morning cup of tea into Harry's darkened room. She opened the curtains gently. He was still snoozing lightly but recognising her presence sat up and pulled the duvet up round his waist to cover himself up. That was the second time she'd come into his room like that. She sat down on the side of the bed, her arm coming to rest awkwardly against his thigh.

It had rained further overnight and he could see the leaves on the trees glistening in the sun outside his window. He glanced at his watch, not even seven; he was surprised that she was up so early given their evening adventures. He was exhausted. Ellie had been afraid to stay on in the house by herself, so Monica had tended to the wounded Ryan while he'd taken Ellie back to Maggie's. Later he'd returned to Old Place to help her get Ryan back to the pub. It was two before they'd finally got to sleep. He hadn't slept at all well wondering about what had really been going on in that room.

'Thank you for coming with me last night, Harry. I've no idea what I'd have done without you,' she purred. He couldn't help noticing that the shirt she wore barely covered her torso, let alone her legs. Like the leaves outside, the golden hairs on her tanned thighs were also glistening in the sun.

'No problem, how's the patient?' he asked croakily, already wondering where this latest intrusion on his privacy was leading. He drank a sip of the hot tea she offered to clear his throat.

'Sleeping it off downstairs; his legs bad and his head's going to be sore, mind you. I clipped him proper with that poker! He won't bother us for a while.'

'He was lucky!' he laughed nervously. She was brazenly looking him up and down under the duvet. He could feel her arm firmly now against his thigh. It dawned on him there might be a motive for this early morning visit.

'If you hadn't helped me grab him, I've no idea what would have happened,' she said gratefully.

'Yep, it's certainly a long way down. So what are you going to do now?' He pulled his legs away from her arm, but she just used the opportunity to shift further on to the bed.

'Oh, I'll leave him to cool off for a few hours, and then we'll talk I guess. Meanwhile…' she began to pull abstractly at the duvet, loosening it where it was tucked underneath him.

'I'm sure he'll be fully repentant,' Harry gulped. 'He's got a good heart really.'

'Yes, I guess I just need to work on him a bit more,' she said suggestively. He felt her hand slip inexorably under the duvet until it was touching his thigh.

'Sure?' he rasped. He was feeling excited, this was not a

situation he'd ever been in before. He could see in her eyes that she was sizing up whether to take this further.

'I reckon so. Maybe work on him like this a bit?' He felt her hand gently stroking his thigh up and down. He pushed it away and laughed uneasily. He wondered what Tom would be doing in this situation.

'What was going on between him and Ellie?' Harry choked, changing the subject. He'd been wondering about that too. In fact he'd wondered about it all night. He couldn't believe Ellie was a willing participant in their liaison. He felt Monica's hand move up against his thigh again. He daren't move. They were now in a place of total ambiguity. What was he to do? Push her away or just lie back and enjoy whatever was to come?

'Nice legs,' she said, ignoring his question.

He glanced at his watch again. 'Is that really the time?' he asked rather pathetically.

'Oh we've got plenty of time,' she said and twisted round, so that she was resting on her elbow by his side. She slipped her whole leg under the duvet to rest alongside his as well. He felt her toes curl around his foot. 'You're nice and warm under here.'

'I'm meeting up with Ellie later,' he said, trying to drop a large hint.

'Oh yeah?' she asked. 'Well about Ellie. Ryan was certainly drunk, but I reckon she probably led him on,' she said matter-of-factly. 'Unfortunately for her, although she might be smart, she's no match for Lindfield's star dancer,' she added. 'Not with my legs.' Harry laughed uncertainly again and felt her move closer, slotting one leg under his and the other over it so that she could squeeze him with her thighs. 'Mind you, I think you might be in with a chance there, Harry, if you play your cards right. Do you know how to play your cards right, Harry?' He felt her free hand move on to his chest and begin to twist playfully at the hairs at the base of his spine.

'I think I do.'

'Well I could show you a move or two, if you want me to,' she added. She bent over to kiss him and he felt her hand move down over his abdomen. Surely that was enough, they'd reached the point of no return? Harry made up his mind that this wasn't going to happen. At last having the courage of his convictions, he ducked and slid away from her grasp. But she wasn't giving up that easily, and sat up and went to pull off her shirt in the way women do when they want you to notice them. He turned away trying not to look.

'Don't worry, I won't tell. This one's on the house,' she said and pushed him back on the bed. At that point he'd had enough. It had gone beyond a game. He pushed her away, jumped right out of the bed and pulled a towel around his naked torso.

'Look Monica, you're a mighty fine woman, and Ryan's an incredibly lucky guy, but I don't think this is really appropriate right now.'

'Really?'

'Really.'

'I can't believe you don't want to at least…'

'Please don't tempt me any further. You're gorgeous but…'

'Okay I get it,' she said reluctantly. 'Not good enough for you? But I must say it's a first for me.' She got off the bed and stood next to him naked apart from her briefs and kissed him on the forehead, while she stroked his chest.

'It's not that. I said you're gorgeous, but I really want to make it work with Ellie that's all.'

'Sure?'

'Quite sure.'

She figured she probably had enough footage in any case. Blackmail was a bit of a last resort but she knew that the video system she'd installed in that room would come in useful one day. Just in case.

'Okay as you want. Anyway, as I guessed this might happen, I still ought to thank you properly, so I've brought you breakfast in bed as well,' she said, pinching him on the backside before pulling her shirt back on.

After she'd gone, Harry took a deep breath and tried to calm down. His heart was racing. Had he really done that, refused an open invitation from someone as gorgeous as that? God, if Tom knew about it, he'd die laughing.

He finished up his tea and breakfast as quickly as he could, then showered, packed and pulled on his cycling kit. After his disturbed night and near escape, he needed some fresh air in a hurry. He found his bike around the back of the pub and freewheeled lazily down the High Street admiring the fresh green leaves emerging on the pollards. By the time he got down to the post office he was chuckling to himself. *Didn't those sorts of things, only happen in films?* He was kind of pleased with himself really. He'd done the right thing after all, even if he could never tell Ellie. It was chilly and the roads were wet, but he could tell it was going to be a great day.

As he approached the duck pond, he saw there'd been some sort of an early-morning 'occupation'. Two of the anti-fracking protestors had erected a model drilling platform on the island in the pond. They were camped out cooking breakfast surrounded by 'Frack off' posters. On closer inspection he realised it was none other than his two new 'friends', Jade and Claudia. They looked rather wet and forlorn but cheered up when they saw him. They waved across at him but he declined to wave back. He already had complications enough that day. The thought crossed his mind that they might turn up later at the village show. That could be embarrassing and disruptive; he'd better have his excuses ready for that as well!

He decided to take a longer route and cycled out towards the village of Walstead. From there he took the Lewes Road through Scaynes Hill to North Chailey. The countryside was alive with new growth, tall drifts of cow parsley, mayflower in the hedges and the chestnuts fresh with green leaves. From Chailey he headed north up towards the Ashdown Forest past the Bluebell Railway and Sheffield Park to Danehill. There he took a break and popped into the church to see the incredible glass that Kempe had made in Bodley's church, before returning across country to Lindfield. All in all, it was a ride of just under fifteen miles. When he got back the wedding party Monica had mentioned earlier that week was getting ready in the pub garden. He showered quickly, paid his bill and checked out with the girl (another Malling scion) who helped out on reception on Saturdays. He'd come back for his bag later, hoping to avoid any more unfortunate encounters with Mata Hari.

'How about some tea, Mone?'

'Get your own tea, you're firmly in the dog house, you oaf.'

'But my leg?'

'Screw your leg. If you hadn't been trying to get your leg over Ellie Swift it wouldn't be a problem would it?'

'Ah come on, that's not fair, you know why I went there. It was all a misunderstanding.'

'You think I'm going to buy that given what I saw with my own eyes?'

'No really,' he said and grimaced as the pain spiked again. 'Anyway where've you been, I was calling for you just now?'

'Serving Mr Jamieson.'

'What?'

'His breakfast in bed, I mean.'

'You've never? You wouldn't?'

'Why not, you're not much use are you and at least he knows how to treat a girl proper. Nice legs too.'

Harry had arranged to meet Ellie at the deli for coffee around eleven-thirty. He had more than an hour to kill until then. He was still trembling a bit from thinking about his early-morning escape; he also had to work out how to settle exactly what had been going on the previous night. Ellie was in such distress that he hadn't wanted to press the point at the time. To settle his nerves, he decided to finally get that haircut he'd been promising himself. On the way down to the barber's he was accosted by a bunch of young pirates on their way to join their carnival float in Hickman's Field. An old Harveys horse-drawn dray was making its way up towards the start point, too. It looked kind of cool as it passed the pond.

After an excellent haircut, provided by a very friendly lady, he bought a paper and sat down for coffee and cake in the deli. From there they would be able to watch the parade in comfort as it wound its way down the High Street towards the Common. When Ellie arrived right on time, she looked a little tired, too. But apart from that, she was a revelation. She was wearing a pretty summer dress and, rather surprisingly, she was even wearing lipstick and had tied her hair with two pretty tortoiseshell combs. *Okay, so at last she'd made an effort,* he thought. He wondered guilty whether he should tell her about Monica's invasion of his bedroom, but decided against it. In the event their only real topic of conversation was the events of the night before, Ryan's lucky escape and speculation over the truth about the house sale. She was at pains to explain to him straight away that she'd found Ryan in the Dial Room after thinking she heard a burglar and then everything had gotten very nasty. Ryan could hardly stand he was so drunk, she said.

Harry accepted her explanation at face value even though it hadn't quite looked like that at the time. She was in such a chirpy mood, gossiping about various people she spotted in the gathering crowd outside that he soon forgot any thoughts to the contrary or dwelled on the events of earlier that morning.

The parade was a little late starting, but the crowds cheered enthusiastically as it went past. The theme was Caribbean; they'd got together a steel band and reggae dancers and plenty of willing young pirates. Once it had passed, Harry and Ellie joined the end of the parade with the other bystanders. When the lengthening procession reached the Common, the crowd gathered around the floats while they were judged. After that the event started in earnest beginning with the 'Firing the Anvil', a tradition whereby the local blacksmith detonated gunpowder plugs in two anvils to ward off evil spirits. It made the little children and old ladies in the crowd jump with glee.

The event was soon in full flow. The weather had cheered up and although there was a cool wind, it was sunny, with broken cloud. The Common was thronging with people: fairground stalls, a children's pet show, a tombola, bric-a-brac, cake stands, tea tents, and the tug-of-war competition to come. Harry and Ellie walked round happily, looking at this and that, perusing the stalls and still talking intently about the events of the night before and the improving prospects for his filming. At the miniature rifle stall, Harry challenged Ellie to show off her shooting prowess, but was still surprised when she got a perfect score.

'I told you I'm a dead shot,' she said laughing. 'Monica would be proud of me.'

'I'm guessing that neither she nor Ryan are going to be shooting much for a while,' replied Harry.

'Oh I don't know,' giggled Ellie. 'Maybe a few blanks.'

'Ha ha, that's funny,' he said. 'You should take that up for a living.'

'Well I'm a Saturday child, you know loving and giving,' she replied.

In the horticultural section, they came across a special exhibit dedicated to Frances Wolseley, the gardener Maggie had mentioned. They were interested to find out that she'd retired from her farm near Glynde first to Scaynes Hill and then to a cottage in the local village of Ardingly. Amongst the artefacts was a passage from her biography – a letter she'd written to her good friend Mary Campion, describing both her friendship with Kempe and how he'd first encouraged her interest in gardening.

May 1907

Dear Mary,

Thank you for your recent letter and for your kind thoughts about Mr Kempe's passing. I'm sorry I had to leave you in France so suddenly, but I'm sure you understood that I felt I needed to get back for his funeral. Generally, it was a well-organised affair and naturally very sad, but I believe we sent him off properly. I got the chance to talk with John Lisle, his deputy, who has taken it all badly, and Cox his valet, and of course Rose 'the smutty housemaid' as you once called her! There were such a lot of people there, I couldn't list them all. Many you'd know, but there were also so many strangers. The common thread was that he was admired (and I think loved) by all and sundry.

It's odd how his untimely death has caused me to ask questions of myself again. You know I did hold Mr Kempe in special affection – a kind of '*filia*', as he would have called it. Sadly, it could never have become more than that between us, never an affair of the heart; although he had a kindness and nobility that are rare in men, and we enjoyed so many common interests. But we were, unfortunately, separated by a generation. I believe I may now be already too old for marriage, too set in my ways to be enclosed within love's coils, but in any case I'm satisfied with that fate. I have much interesting work still to do and projects to pursue. Work that I trust we two can continue to pursue in companionate partnership for years to come. But in another time and another place, my dear, I think I could also have been quite happy planning gardens together with Mr Kempe for the rest of my life…

I know you are distantly related to him. You once told me that his cousin, Mr Thomas Read Kemp, was your great-grandfather. I wanted therefore to record for you a little about the first time I became acquainted with him. It was back in the summer of 1890. My mother, being the inquisitive person she is, had made an exchange of correspondence with him through the architect George Bodley and at once arranged to visit him at Old Place in Lindfield. I well remember us being met by Mr Kempe at Haywards Heath Station in his wagonette drawn by two sturdy little cobs.

We'd never been in that part of Sussex before, and at that time the country consisted mainly of fields and hedgerows.

That is until one reached the open common of Lindfield. The village street, terminating with the tall spire of the church, was much as it is today: houses of every description, timbered and plastered; stately William and Mary ones, intermingled with smaller and yet older buildings. As we swung round the last corner past the church we came in full view of the Challoners' old home, which Kempe had purchased and converted, and greatly to the delight of my mother, the carriage halted outside and we were able to look within.

Mr Kempe had left the old manor house practically untouched; it formed part of his servants' wing. Beyond it, however, was a beautiful wrought-iron gateway that led to his new quarters built in cherry brick. There, within a long panelled room, we found a refectory table, spread with great care to resemble a sixteenth-century banquet. We all sat on one side of it, and the servants handed the dishes across the table, just like a banquet in one of those Italian paintings.

As for Mr Kempe himself, I found him a most handsome man, of medium height and rather slender. His finely shaped head and pointed beard made him look like he belonged in one of those sixteenth-century paintings, too. In his sitting rooms, he'd laid out fine eastern rugs, hanging down from each end of the tables. Small recessed windows here and there were devoted to his stained glass. The whole place had the impression of age and dignity even though it had only recently been constructed. After luncheon, Mr Kempe, followed everywhere by his faithful deerhound Nora, led us to the south garden where the great new parlour was to be built. We passed through the formal garden, where brilliantly coloured flowers led the eye along vistas to his tall sundial. It was truly an inspiring sight, one which has stayed with me ever since.

But Old Place was still only in the making then; and that

very day we had the great pleasure of assisting at a ceremony whereby the foundation stone of the final wing was laid. I was asked to smooth the mortar and tap the foundation stone, saying 'Floreat Domus', after which a new coin was placed under the stone. Mr Kempe made a short speech, explaining the meaning and assuring us that, as it had been begun by good workmen, the new wing must flourish. There was certainly a spirit of comradeship between the master and his men; they obviously looked to him for those delicate touches that only an educated mind can impart. We then all joined in singing 'God Save the Queen'.

Since then, my mother and I have visited Old Place quite frequently over the years, the distance being not so great from Glynde. Despite his stern exterior, Mr Kempe always had a rascal's sense of humour and frequently made merry at my mother's expense (which I am certain she never fully understood). Our 'caravan', with lady's maids and coachmen and horses, gave him much amusement. As I've said, the gardens at Old Place were very fine and neatly laid out in a way that truly embellished the setting. I believe he had a real genius for garden design, a view shared by the likes of Mrs Jekyll. How often is it that Fate places us amongst people whose characters, pursuits and tastes we do not know? And how we then hesitate how best to melt that barrier of icy reserve and shyness behind which we English remain frozen? In my experience, there is at least one subject of conversation that usually calls for a response – and that is gardening!

I can still hear my mother's words in my ears: 'Young women must learn to love some solid hobby.' Well Mr Kempe, like Mr William Robinson at Gravetye, was always very kind in sharing his knowledge of those arts with me. During our visits, Mr Kempe and I would often talk for hours on the subject of gardening – we'd sit on his fine-turned chairs positioned on Turkey carpets in the rose garden. He'd read while I would attend to my drawing or embroidery, with Nora lying at our feet. Although his appearance was always most fastidious, his intercourse could often be quite mischievous. I remember one conversation in particular greatly influenced my own thinking in respect of the practicalities of gardening for women. As I recall it, it went something like this:

'Why is it do you think, that employers still hesitate to employ lady head gardeners?' I asked him. I confess, and you'll appreciate this, I was at the time admiring a rather strapping young man tending to the rose beds in front of us.

'I suppose it's mostly a simple matter of strength and capability,' he replied. '"For men must work and women must weep," they say.'

'You scoundrel!' I replied. 'I agree with you about heavy work, but that doesn't apply to the design and running of a garden. I believe there are many gardens where if a change is to be made, the owners might benefit from substituting a lady in the place of a man as head gardener.'

'Quite so, my dear, but what about the bother of working outside in all kinds of difficult conditions and weathers? What father would wish that upon his daughter? The digging, the delving, the rains and the wind, early rising, menial jobs, the struggle to compete with the strength of a working man?'

'Well, the thought of working in a stuffy London typewriting office and long, dark evenings in cheap lodgings would be far more repulsive to me.'

'Then, of course, there are the difficulties of male labourers working under a female head gardener. Can a lady possibly exert authority and influence over a working man, such as my friend over there?'

'I'm certain that she can, if she is the right kind of woman. But under all circumstances it is necessary to deal tactfully with the men who do the manual work. And by that, I don't mean to cast the faintest aspersion against the honesty of male gardeners.'

'Indeed! Then I hope you will without hesitation, dismiss the first drunken under-gardener you meet. Then the others will respect you, and not try to take advantage of you because you are a woman!' he laughed.

Anyway Mary, I should not go on any longer. You know that my view is that the lady gardener is still at heart a gentlewoman. What we may lack in physical strength we endeavour to compensate by other equally important, yet softer, womanly qualities: by lending intelligence, good taste and refinement to the art. I admit that Mr Kempe's words had struck a chord, reminding me of my attempts the previous week to direct Delver, our corduroy-clad, slow-moving Sussex gardener: 'All that there booklarnin' don't do not one any good. I knows what I knows, but reading don't teach 'un,' was his usual sultry reply to my urgings!

Anyway, thank you again for your letter and for your continued companionship. I really enjoyed the time we spent in Italy together. Wasn't it amusing seeing old Pannie again! I wonder if she still has all those brass ornaments to use as ammunition in the event of war. I'll try and get over to see you again at Danny Park as soon as I can.

Yours ever affectionately
Frances Wolseley
Farm House
Glynde.

CHAPTER FOURTEEN

LOVE'S LABOUR'S WON

1500-1515 Welly Wanging
1520-1535 Adults and Kids Wheel Barrow Races
1530-1555 Raffle
1600-1610 Final Tug of War (adults)

King Edward Hall website

Harry and Ellie bought lunch at the roast hog stall which they washed down with a pint of local cider. Ellie was really getting into the fair; she was realising she'd missed village life and seemed to know every other person they bumped into. Even though it was a bit too self-satisfied compared to the edgier Brighton, she still had a soft spot for Lindfield. And it was great how everyone was just trying their hardest to collect money for local good causes, wasn't it? As they ate lunch, Harry and Ellie watched a dance demonstration from the Zumba club as well as an exhibition by the local fire jugglers. Harry was especially taken with one of them.

'Stop it Harry, I went to school with her,' admonished Ellie when she caught him staring at her expert hoop-work. But before he could protest, they unexpectedly bumped into Monica. She'd just changed for her dancing demonstration with the local burlesque club. *This could be embarrassing*, thought Harry.

'Monica, how are you?' said Ellie somewhat apologetically and with a note of genuine concern.

'I could have done without seeing you here,' Monica replied rudely. Ellie realised that her question wasn't welcome. She was wondering if there was going to be a further misunderstanding about what had happened.

'I hope you don't think…'

'Leave it out,' she said. 'I'll think what I need to think.' She looked at Harry and pouted at him. Immediately he had a dread about what was coming next.

'How are you Harry? Did you enjoy the rest of your breakfast in bed?' she said, deliberately licking her lips. She glanced over at Ellie to make sure she was listening. 'Is your boy going in for the tug-of-war?' she asked. Ellie frowned. 'I mean, he'd be a hit in those tight cycling shorts of his,' Monica laughed. She really was a piece of work thought Ellie.

'Is Ryan up yet?' Harry asked hurriedly, hoping she wouldn't make any further reference, tangential or not to their little morning misunderstanding.

'Yeah, he's fine. He'll be up here later I expect. You can't keep him away from cheap cider and a good tug-of-war,' she said. 'But it'll be a while yet before I've forgiven him,' she said winking. 'Do you like it?' she asked Harry pointing at her outfit.

'You look great,' he said, trying to think of something sensible but non-incriminating to say. But from Ellie's stare he immediately regretted his words. Monica saw the look and hammed it up further.

'You should come along to our classes sometime Ellie. I can show you some moves to get lover-boy here going. I know he's a fan,' she said and then walked off, wiggling her backside, very pleased with the impact she'd had.

'Harry, what did she mean?' asked Ellie sternly. She had a very low opinion of such forms of dancing.

'She's just a tease,' he said. 'Ignore it.'

But she wasn't sure what to think and gave him a gentle thump. 'You can buy me a cream tea later for that,' she said, unsure whether to punish him further. The more she knew him the more she really didn't at all. 'Come on let's go and find Maggie,' she said somewhat irritated.

Eventually they tracked down the photography exhibit they'd been looking for. It was in a corner of the cricket pavilion. Maggie was there with members of her school class and her proud husband. They'd been working hard. They'd set up two different tableaux for souvenir shots, charging three pounds a time for a portrait and five pounds for a group shot. The first set was a centennial tribute to those from the village who'd died in the Great War and the second commemorated the two-hundredth birthday of Julia Margaret Cameron, based on the children's project Maggie had mentioned. Her husband seemed to be in charge and he invited Harry to join Ellie and Maggie in re-enacting the King Lear scene that Julia Margaret Cameron had originally created back in 1873.

'But we need one more 'sister',' he said.

'I'll do it,' said a voice he vaguely recognised. Harry turned round and started when he realised Jade and Claudia were also in the pavilion with them. Jade was inspecting semi-professionally a variation of a box camera that Maggie had borrowed. Fortunately it didn't require wet collodion, though, and used modern film. Harry's stomach turned inside. How much more trouble was he going to get into with women that day?

'We'd be happy to share him, you know,' whispered Jade to Ellie while they were getting dressed up ready for the shot, nudging her suggestively. 'He's rather scrummy!'

'Do you know him?' she asked confused. But Jade just laughed. 'Only in the Shakespearean sense.'

'Harry, who are those women?' she asked later when he'd returned from having his make-up applied by Claudia. He was dressed as Lear in a rich purple robe with a crown and shocking white beard.

'They're two of the anti-frackers I met in the camp at Balcombe, I think,' he replied, scowling at them to maintain complicity with another one of his rapidly mounting guilty secrets.

'Well then you're moving rapidly back towards the doghouse,' Ellie chided.

Later, in the tea tent, while Harry was off buying their cream tea in penance, Ellie came across Mrs Ross playing cards with members of her bridge club at one of the tables.

'Come and sit with me, my dear. You've been working so hard all week,' she said, in an unusually sensitive way. She was surrounded by friends and obviously proud to show off her pretty and intelligent little helper.

'Er…have you seen Ryan yet?' Ellie asked awkwardly. 'I haven't heard anything from him this morning. Since his fall, I mean.'

'Oh I'm sure he's *fine*, my dear, a donkey like him is made of stern stuff,' replied Mrs Ross. 'You know this poor girl worships the ground he walks on,' she added for good measure to her friends. 'My grandson's such a blockhead for passing her over.'

Ellie flushed and tried to change the subject.

'I heard you've sold the house already?' she asked.

'Really, well not that I know of. Sounds like a silly village rumour to me, my dear. Come on, join our game.'

'But Monica said…?'

'Monica? Now would you really believe anything she'd say?' Mrs Ross replied. Ellie considered that answer. Would Monica really have set the whole thing about the estate agent up? She wouldn't put it past her at all. That put the last evening's events in a wholly different light.

'But it's hard to know sometimes which game you're playing,' replied Ellie quietly, still doubtful and now somewhat confused.

'Bridge of course, and I have a trick or two left up my sleeve,' she laughed. Ellie laughed along at her joke but declined to join them.

'Well, we're just about done now up at the house, Mrs Ross. Everything's ready for the packers on Monday. I'll just give it the once-over tomorrow.'

'This girl's a star,' she said to her friends. 'She's worked so hard and discovered lots of interesting things I'd completely forgotten about.'

'It's certainly been an interesting project,' she replied.

'Well, are you all packed?' Mrs Ross asked. Ellie looked confused. Hadn't she just said that? Maybe Serena was getting forgetful.

'How do you mean? Yes the house is all packed.'

'No, no, I didn't mean the house. I meant are you packed? We're all going abroad to celebrate after it's cleared. I thought to Florence maybe?'

'Er…but I can't, Mrs Ross. I'm very busy at the moment!'

'Nonsense, I'm sure you can take a few days off. Ryan will probably want to join us as well.'

'He will? Are you sure?'

'Of course, if you say so?'

'But I don't understand, Monica surely won't allow that?'

'Monica? I told you she's history. Anyway, after last

night's performance, it's clearer than ever that he's sick with love for you. If only you hadn't tried to conceal that from me for so long.'

'No, er, no. You don't understand. I haven't concealed anything.'

'Well, didn't he rush off to find you last night after he heard that silly story that I'd sold the place?'

'How did you know that?'

'That's what Mrs Malling told me this morning. She also told me that she found you two together yesterday and then rang me again this morning to tell me about his fall. She said Monica was minded to issue him an ultimatum. I quite understand your modesty but you can put it away now.'

'Mrs Ross, I really don't think you understand.'

'But you understand he'd do anything to marry you.'

'He's never told you that?'

'No, but better than that, he's told you. I can see it on your face.'

'Mrs Ross, I've literally only seen him a couple of times recently.' Ellie realised that was a bit of a white lie, but she didn't have to tell her more, did she?

'You exaggerate the difficulties. He's yours for the taking.'

'How do you mean? That's just not true.'

'I've settled everything. I'll send all the things back tomorrow.'

'Everything?'

'Even the smallest trifle. So don't fail me now. He's free again. It's all yours for the taking.'

Of course it was at exactly that point that Harry had to rejoin her with their tea tray. Ellie stared at him in horror. She certainly didn't want him hearing all that nonsense. For a moment she didn't know what to do at all. Mrs Ross had just offered her a clear, calculated and crushing bribe. How could she play such a card so cruelly in front of her friends and, more importantly, in front of Harry? Ellie turned bright red, acutely aware there were a dozen eyes now turned on her, eagerly awaiting her answer. She felt her veins fill with poisonous thoughts and temptations.

'Look I'll see you tomorrow, Mrs Ross. I have to go and have tea with Harry now.'

'Find Ryan straight away, you fool. Find him now and drag him off with you before Monica turns his head again,' Mrs Ross shouted after her. But it was to no avail. Ellie's mind was absolutely made up. But her ears were bright red, hearing the cackling self-righteous laughter behind her.

As soon as they'd had their tea they left. They didn't wait for the adult tug-of-war. In fact Ellie had had quite enough of tug-of-wars that week. They'd eaten their cream tea mostly in silence despite Harry's valiant attempts to cheer her up. He tried to assure her that he thought nothing of the episode with Mrs Ross (he reasoned they were kind of even now on that score). She was still mortified, however, and angry at the way she'd been treated like a plaything in front of all those people. Now she remembered what she also hated about the claustrophobia of village life – being looked down on by the likes of Mrs Ross and her pompous friends. She pitied Maggie having to put up with that sort of behaviour all the time from the more self-righteous parishioners, although of course there were also still some very kind souls in the village.

They collected Harry's bike and bags from the pub, fortunately without running into Monica again, and headed back towards the coast. It was around five and the weather was looking distinctly stormy when the train drew into Brighton station. They'd arranged to meet up with Maggie and her husband at Harry's flat for supper that evening. It was a good mile and a half to walk there though, so Harry put Ellie in a taxi and arranged to meet her at the other end. At least she'd calmed down a bit by the time she eventually got to the flat. She was glad to be back on home territory.

But she soon realised that this was a different kind of home territory. There was none of the homeliness of the little place in Ovingdean that she shared with her father. No cats, no flowers, no untidy collection of movie artefacts overflowing from cupboards. It was her first time in the flat and she was immediately reminded by the smart furnishings and abundance of expensive 'toys' that it was a very rich boy's pad. To make it worse, Harry had to confess almost immediately that he was no cook and as she inspected the cupboards she realised there was virtually no food in the house apart from frozen microwave meals, cereal, milk and an abundance of booze. Harry suggested they call out for a takeaway, but Ellie would have nothing of it. She grabbed a couple of shopping bags and found a local store that was still open. At least she could rustle up something edible for them all.

Actually, in Tom and Harry's view, it was more than edible. In fact it was probably the best Italian food that had ever been cooked in their sparkling kitchen. They'd even discovered what the fan thing below the microwave oven was for. And fortunately, Maggie had thought to bring over some baked tarts from the Village fair for dessert. Tom had invited Sally over as well, so they were six for dinner. Of course, most of the conversation concerned the events in Lindfield over the past week. There was plenty to talk about. Maggie's husband in particular was keen to catch up on all the news. By the look of it, Tom and Sal probably, though, had other things on their mind.

After their meal, they gathered on the balcony to watch a storm approaching across Shoreham Bay. The lights of the boats out at sea were rocking uncertainly in the gathering waves. A little bit further to the west were the bright lights of Brighton Pier and the great wheel, which wasn't active, due to the high winds that were expected. In the other direction, beyond the Marina, they could hear the waves crashing in spectacular flurries against the sea wall.

'It's going to be a big one,' said Harry, marvelling at the power of nature and holding Ellie closely around the waist. She seemed to have mellowed completely; there was no resistance at all from her now. Even his gaffe about the dreadful green politicians that ran Brighton was met with supine laughter. Maggie was watching them closely, and secretly she was very pleased. This had been a great idea. Even her husband was behaving himself and not going on too much about boring parish stuff. She knew she would eventually grow to like her new life, but she had to try very hard sometimes. She thought it was worth the struggle, but she did envy Ellie all the same. For that reason, it was good to just be another young couple for once

'It *was* such a beautiful day,' replied Ellie, pulling Harry closer. He kissed her full on the lips for the first time. She tasted delicious, she smelled delicious, and he was almost in seventh heaven. Had he really found someone who liked him for more than his job and his accent for once? For her part, although she still had her doubts, she was content that evening to be wrapped in the arms of this cute and straight forward boy. Despite her initial prejudices, he really hadn't put a foot wrong, apart from Wednesday night that was, and a couple of awkward occasions that afternoon – she'd tried him again on the true story of Balcombe Woods after meeting Jade and Claudia and his version had become even less convincing, but she was no longer that bothered.

She glanced over to Maggie who winked at her. Ellie watched how her husband held her; he really did love her and was contentedly and affectionately stroking her hair. Of course, Ellie knew Maggie still harboured doubts about whether she'd married too early before she'd even seen anything of the world; and now she was already expecting their first baby. Inside, through the smoked glass, she could see Tom and Sal making out on the sofa. Sal wouldn't be worried about considerations like biological clocks. Tom had his fancy stereo system turned up full volume with something classical and very loud. Mussorgsky, she thought. What a peculiarly Jane Austen-like end to the day it was. All the twists and turns neatly knotted and wrapped up.

But at that very moment the two of them simultaneously received a text each on their mobiles: one from Ryan to Ellie and one from Monica to Harry. Ellie and Harry both glanced down at their respective phone screens. They looked at each other knowingly and then laughed out loud.

'He's really done it,' exclaimed Ellie. *They're married, at a registry office for heaven's sake, like a pair of low atheists!*

'Ryan and Monica have tied the knot!' shouted Harry to Tom, Sally, Maggie and her husband.

'Then we should break out the champagne!' Tom added, not actually knowing who the two people were. But Harry looked back at Ellie. There was something wrong. Strangely it seemed as though she was quite upset by the news. He put his arm around her again.

'You can do a lot better than Ryan. Trust me.'

Ellie turned to him, 'I know, I'm rather glad actually. It's just the shock of it, that's all.'

They returned inside.

'So Harry, this Charlie Kempe of yours you were talking about at dinner, have you figured out who his mysterious lady friend of his was yet?' asked Tom. It was the only bit of the story he'd found at all interesting.

'Well, there are quite a few possibilities,' Harry replied. 'In his late thirties, he was keen on Louisa Dodgson, Lewis Carroll's sister, and a decade earlier a lady called Loo Erskine. But I fancy the main candidate was probably a good friend of hers called Harriette Morrell, his best friend Frederick's wife! What do you think Ellie?'

Ellie looked doubtful but didn't immediately comment.

'Really? So a bit of late-life adultery,' asked Tom, his ears picking up. 'The old devil.'

'No, before she was married, you idiot.'

'Actually I tend to favour Lady Loo's daughter Frances Wolseley, the gardener,' said Ellie, after a further moment's thought. 'They were definitely soul mates and she never married. Although she did say she once came very close to a proposal but her parents didn't approve. However, as you pointed out last week, there was also Georgie Burne-Jones or Macdonald as she was known when Kempe first met her. She led the mourners at his funeral.'

'Sounds like this guy was a bit of a ladies' man,' said Tom. 'Maybe he just enjoyed himself and played the field. Works for me!' he said, Sal threw a cushion at him and pulled a face. 'Just teasing,' he joked. 'Sal, you of course are my one and only.'

'Yeah, right,' said Sally. 'Until the next 'one and only' comes along.'

'I'm sorry but I think you're all wrong. There's another

possibility, you know,' said Maggie. They all looked at her questioningly. 'Harry I've brought the last of those letters I told you about. This one is particularly poignant…'

37 Nottingham Place,
London,
May 1907

Dearest Mama,

Since I last wrote much has happened. I have to tell you now of the saddest of news. My poor dear master is no more confined to this earth. He passed away in this very house on the 29th of last month and now I am sure he's sitting with our Lord in Heaven. Mercifully, his death was swift. You know he was such a fine man and always such a kind and considerate master, if you know my meaning.

You remember me writing that he'd caught that silly chest cold in the spring. Well, it hung around him all last month and then developed into congestion of the lung. When John [Lisle] returned from his last working trip, he found him labouring for breath in the studio. Mr Kempe refused the doctor at first, or even a nurse, and would only take medicine and food from John or me. He wouldn't see no one else, but then after only a few days he took a sudden turn for the worse. He died before even a priest could be called. John, Cox and I were the only livin' souls at his side at the last. None of his fancy London friends were there; I don't think he wanted any of them to see him like that.

Of course, he'd put everything in place beforehand. That was typical of him. There was a service and communion at St Mary in Munster Square, right solemn and correct. Then that same evening we all went down to his country house at Lindfield. We caught the Brighton Pullman from Victoria. The train were a wonderful sight with its brown and white carriages, but I was too sad to appreciate it much and I didn't like the smoke.

From the station, we took a horse-drawn carriage over to Old Place. As I've told you before, it's a right fine house, hundreds of years old, but he's built it up into something quite splendid, with entertaining rooms and furniture and lovely gardens. John and Florrie were there already with the Rev. Fisher – he's our curate in Kennington. They'd travelled down in the Bentley with his coffin and laid it to rest in a little oratory he'd built in the East Wing. They offered me a room in the attic for the night but I didn't fancy being in that place with him lying there, so Florrie invited me back to their hotel to sleep on the day bed. I confess I didn't sleep much, though, that night. What with the owls and cats fighting and John's snoring from the bedroom. I was sick with worrying what would become of us all. Mr Kempe was everything. But at least it was good to be there together with his friends.

The next day, Alfred and George, his painters, came over to pay their last respects with a few of the other draughtsmen. Mr Tower, his cousin, was there too, with his wife Marion. They say he's inherited everything in the will. A bad piece of work that is. I don't know what Mr Kempe was thinking, not even a memento for his friends.

Anyway, that's another tale. We walked over to Haywards Heath with the bier and caught the train right down to Brighton. There the coffin was placed on a hearse with glass sides, black and tasteful. The horses had black velvet collars and plumes over their ears. It was all well staged, just as Mr Kempe would have wanted. We followed with forty other carriages and motor cars hired to take the mourners from the London train. I've never heard of such a procession excepting for our dear old Queen. We drove down the Old Steine, past the Pavilion and the Pier before running along the coast road. It was blowing quite strongly in from the sea by then.

As we made our way towards Ovingdean, we were soon back in nature, passing one swell of turf after another, great grey waves breaking ferociously across the cliffs. It was quite scary, the shingle sounded awful, like scraping boots as the waves went in and out. But the sky was clear and blue, full of tiny silver clouds like one of his windows, sinking into bright light that you couldn't dare look at where the sun spangled on the water.

When we got to Ovingdean Gap we turned inland but found the road into the village narrow and muddy. Our progress was very slow. It's a commonplace in those parts that Sussex girls have long legs 'cos they stretch them pulling them out of the mud. I can see why! The entire village lined the road respectfully outside their little flint cottages. I've never seen so many dressed in black. It was like a flock of crows had landed. Of course I'd never been there before, but it was right solemn, everything silent except the trotting of the horses hoofs. The old house where he was born is situated just across from the church. All in all, it's a pretty place, far too pretty for such a sad scene.

When we got to the churchyard, all his fancy London architect friends were there dressed in mourning suits, and all of their red-eyed women in their wool and crêpe. For a man who never married and was shy with the ladies, he had an awful lot of admirers. That Lady Burne-Jones was there in the front row, dressed in black silk with a hint of purple in its trimmings. Now she's a really tiny woman, but so sweet and patient, like a saint. She's nearly seventy now, but still has amazing eyes. But truthfully, her face is terrible worn. I guess we must all pay for the wine we've drunk.

Her nephew was there, too, Rudyard Kipling, all grey

and pinched. 'Old Giglamps' his kids call him apparently, on account of his reading glasses, although I'd probably prefer 'bushy brows' myself. He has mighty fine eyebrows and a 'tache. Mr Cox sometimes reads to us from his Just So stories. They were smugglers in those parts in olden times, and John gave me a poem of Mr Kipling's about it.

> *Five and twenty ponies,*
> *Trotting through the dark –*
> *Brandy for the Parson, 'Baccy for the Clerk.*
> *Them that asks no questions isn't told a lie –*
> *Watch the wall my darling while the Gentlemen go by!*

Rudyard Kipling, *A Smuggler's Song*

So who else was there? Well that old warhorse, Mrs Morrell, and her daughter Freddie (now Mrs Peel) and 'Lady' Ottoline. That one's got airs and graces – says she's descended from the Duke of Wellington – mind you, I hear she's not too proud to shack up with all her artist friends in her posh house in Bedford Square. Her husband's a scoundrel with the ladies, too, they say. I asked John if Mrs Morrell was the 'one', but he wasn't telling. She was a frequent visitor to Nottingham Place and tipped well, always a half-crown for us housemaids. Mind you, she has fancy tastes too.

Oh yes, and that Honourable Frances Wolseley. She's the society lady who prefers gardening to keeping a big house would you credit – lives in some farm cottage or other. She spoke with us, mind, and said she's just come back from a tour of the Palazzos and Duomos. She asked me if I'd like to come and see her 'farm' some time. I liked her. She weren't so posh as not to talk to the likes of us. She's never married, mind you.

John said she wasn't the one either, but I wonder. She was just his type. Fortunately, she came without her impossible mother, Lady Loo, who thinks she's an empress. They all hate each other, by all accounts, some argument gone on for years.

We did expect we might see that Mr Henry James, the American writer, who lives in Rye. He didn't turn up though; too busy with writing his books I dare say. But there were his old school friends, Lewis Carroll's brothers, Skef and Wilf Dodgson, and their sister Louisa. She's a nice lady, another spinster. From what I heard she was once quite keen on him.

Outside the church, there was a whole crowd of folks from London I didn't know. Most of Mr Kempe's workers from London and Sussex were there, plus all the artists and architects from Nottingham Place: Tom Woolf, Dickie Dyer, Tommy Heasman, and Bill Tate. Then all the craftsmen from Millbrook and their bright young lads with their caps doffed, and a few others from firms he worked with. There must have been over a hundred, all told.

The service was well done; a few spoke and we had his favourite hymns. The Rev. Fisher said a sermon and John read one of the lessons. I cried of course, but I weren't alone with the wailing. The church is pretty inside, lovely glass that Mr Kempe made special and a beautiful ceiling he'd painted. It's dedicated to St Wulfran, whoever that is. There's a memorial to Mr Kempe's father over the entrance door and to his mother's kin 'the Eamers'. After the service, we all crowded into the graveyard. The sun was shining bright and you could hear the birds singing their pretty songs, skylarks and such.

They said 'no flowers' but Lady Burne-Jones laid a small wreath on the grave, just as she did a decade earlier for her husband they say. Lady Pearson sent a large cross of scarlet geraniums – no class that one. It was a bit of a crush in the churchyard but respectful still; the family tomb is just across from the main door up against the south wall. Mr Kempe's workmen had lined the path under the cedar tree, but unfortunately folk had to trample over the graves and such to get close. It was like a vast congregation of black spreading out over the churchyard. I laid a posy of heartsease myself on account of how he was my true love always, as you know, whatever anyone says to the contrary. I still have the cards and little poems he used to send me. "Love ever only strives." If only...

> Your loving daughter,
> Rose

CHAPTER FIFTEEN

LOVE'S LABOUR'S LOST

But love, first learned in a lady's eyes...

William Shakespeare

Lewes Crescent, Kemp Town, Brighton, Sunday, May 31st

Maggie's husband had a service the next morning, so they'd dropped Ellie back at her father's house just after midnight before returning to Lindfield. However, Ellie drove back to Lewes Crescent the next morning, good and early, bearing freshly brewed barista coffee, croissants and muffins. The boys were still in bed when she arrived (including Sally, as it turned out). She soon had things organised for breakfast and a good spread on the kitchen table.

Harry shaved and showered. He was due to have lunch with Ellie, Maggie and her husband and the girls' father in Lindfield. He'd picked up there was going to be some sort of an announcement, but Ellie was staying silent about that. Tom was not so fussy about his attire and sauntered around the flat in his underpants, unshaven and unapologetic for the mess the place was in. Sally was equally unkempt, wearing only a borrowed shirt. It was like something out of *Notting Hill*. Ellie was not impressed though, and gave her a look along the lines of *'Tell me you haven't?'* She got a *'Tell me why*

I shouldn't have?' in reply. Ellie spotted that her make-up was still smeared from their nocturnal activities.

Rather than drive and not be able to drink, Harry and Ellie planned to catch the train back to Haywards Heath and then walk to Lindfield where they were having lunch. Joe was staying over with Maggie and her husband. The weather was bad and over breakfast Tom tried to discourage them, suggesting alternative Sunday diversions, like sitting in a pub by the seafront. Harry suspected he was trying to avoid spending the whole day alone with his new conquest; he had a habit of moving on pretty quickly. Outside, it was spoiling for another storm, all the signs of a late spring gale in the air. However, Harry wasn't going to be diverted now that he and Ellie seemed to at last be an item. He was determined to make the trip come what may.

Ryan had sent Ellie a text that morning, apologising intensely for his behaviour on Friday night. He'd added that he wanted her to choose something from the house, the gem of the collection. It was the least he could do. Although she'd had scruples about accepting gifts from him before, this seemed different, and anyway, it was effectively the same promise that his grandmother had already made to her.

In fact, even before that text, Ellie had already made up her mind which trophy she planned to ask for: the sweet little painting of a Maltese harbour by Luigi Galea in a jewel-encrusted frame. She'd removed it for safe keeping to Mrs Ross's house with the other treasures. In its own right, it wasn't that valuable, but it was a handsome thing and would go with the décor of her room in Ovingdean. The packers were due in on Monday. She'd have just enough time to finish things off at Old Place, collect the object from Poynting's and get back to Ovingdean that evening. She could just imagine the picture hanging in pride of place on the walls of her room and in her mind was already picturing her triumphant return with her prize.

So they sallied forth around ten by taxi. The weather was truly foul, with driving rain. They dashed into the station entrance with just enough time to buy tickets. But as the train trundled away from the coast, the storm began to subside. They passed through Clayton tunnel. After that, the dark clouds over the brooding Downs gave way to breaks of lace-blossom sunshine between Hassocks and Burgess Hill. Ellie was both excited and nervous. The previous days' encounters had left her in a state of some anxiety. However, she was eager to complete the last phase of the task she'd been set. She was with someone whom she liked and her mood was lifted by the thought of lunch with her family. Still, however, her mood swung erratically between triumph and doom, or at least the expectation of each.

The doom related to the fact that she imagined there might be a further row that morning between Ryan and Mrs Ross, following the late-night news. She feared her mission would in some way be thwarted. In her heart, therefore, she was urging the train ever faster past each familiar landmark, but it moved sullenly. Harry in contrast was in a much lighter mood. There was still an air of wild rain in the air, but no more than a rainbow or two would have demanded. Ellie's pot of gold seemed ever more tangible. And he felt ever closer to the big breakthrough with her too.

But with the opening of the train door in Haywards Heath all that daydreaming ended. An immediate shock of reality hit them, although not one that either of them could immediately recognise or name, merely a scent to the air that was bitter but unfamiliar. They could hear the distant sounds of sirens and see the arc of flashing blue lights against nearby buildings.

'What's up?' Harry asked the ticket collector by the turnstiles. He looked at Harry as if he was from Mars. They were alarmed immediately by his words.

'There's been a terrible fire over Lindfield way,' he said. Smoke, yes, that's what they could smell. It must be big. The air was full of the stench of it. They could see a black plume rising in the distance, sucked up by the wind into a broadening mass on the horizon.

'Oh my God,' said Ellie. What if it's…?' But her words were drowned by Harry's shouts as he called for them to get into a waiting taxi.

'Lindfield High Street,' he said.

'I'll have to go the back way round, on account of the fire,' said the driver. 'They've closed off Black Hill up to the post office,' he added.

'Where's the fire?' Ellie asked, now even more anxious.

'I don't know exactly, one of those big houses by the Common, I reckon. Fearsome blaze, they've been fighting it all morning. The house is all but gone I hear. There are five or six engines there still.'

'God, then it must be Poynting's for certain,' she said looking bewildered and frightened.

'Don't jump to conclusions,' said Harry. 'Driver, can you drop us round by the post office?'

When they got there, they saw that huge crowds had gathered to watch. They ran down towards the pond, but a police cordon prevented further progress. The officers were holding back all sightseers, fearful of the continued danger to the public. Smoke drifted in thick black waves across the Common. Crowds of black crows sat watching from the telegraph wires.

'Which house is it?' Harry asked one of the policewomen.

'Poynting's,' she said. 'It's a write-off.'

'Oh God. I knew it. Was anyone inside?' asked Ellie.

'The old lady and her grandson, apparently. They dragged them out on stretchers, sent them off in ambulances on account of smoke inhalation. Don't look too good for them, though.'

'Oh God,' said Ellie again. 'And what about all the furniture?' she added. 'What's happened to that?' The policewoman looked at her somewhat disdainfully.

'Well miss, that's all gone as well, I guess. They wouldn't be able to save much. There was a fire in the shed. They had a load of inflammable stuff stored in there apparently, contraband fags and stuff. God knows what else. But there was a mighty explosion, and something like gunshots. Apparently her grandson had a shotgun with him when they found him. I heard it myself while I was making breakfast for my kids. The whole place went up in minutes; the wind spread the flames so quickly. By the time the fire brigade got there, it was probably already too late. It was like an inferno.'

'I've got to get through and save them,' Ellie said, trying to push past. 'There are priceless valuables in there.'

'I can't let you do that, miss,' the policewoman replied, restraining her. 'You'd better get her away, young man. Let the professionals do their job up there.'

Ellie knew already in what direct way she was likely to have been affected. She went limp in his arms. She felt herself give up all hope. And had they lost Ryan and Mrs Ross as well? Everywhere there was smoke. She put her face in her hands.

'I'll go back.'

'Stop it,' admonished Maggie who had joined them, hearing her words. 'It's the people that matter Ellie, not some stupid paintings. We'd better find Monica, she must be absolutely distraught.'

'Yes, you're right,' said Ellie. 'Sorry. We should go to The Tyger.'

When they reached The Tyger a few minutes later, they found Monica sitting at one of the tables, calmly drinking vodka and lime. Her mother was with her talking anxiously on her phone. After she'd finished, she put the phone down, whispered to Monica and then looked over at Harry and shook her head.

'Monica, what can we say?' asked Harry, seeing the worried look on her mother's face and perplexed by Monica's apparent calmness.

'So it ain't just Monica no more,' she replied. 'You best be calling me Widow Ross from now on,' she said quietly but almost victoriously. He looked down at her hands. She was holding a DVD in a plastic case. The label said 'Harry's Game'. He could also see the stain of varnish, still black and sticky on her fingers, where it had congealed around her ring, fresh but no longer flammable.

'She always said she'd rather be burnt alive, than give away the stuff.'